Totally Bound Publishing books by Sharon Kimbra Walsh:

For the Love of a Marine
A Fallen Hero

I0607483

A FALLEN HERO

SHARON KIMBRA
WALSH

A Fallen Hero
ISBN # 978-1-78651-855-2
©Copyright Sharon Kimbra Walsh 2016
Cover Art by Posh Gosh ©Copyright February 2016
Interior text design by Claire Siemaszkiewicz
Totally Bound Publishing

A FALLEN HERO

Dedication

To my dad and my husband.
Thank you for all your encouragement and support.

Chapter One

'Love is like war.
Easy to start,
Difficult to end,
And impossible to forget'
Anon

Katie Anderson stood at the kitchen sink, frothy bubbles from the washing up water in the bowl clinging to her slow-moving hands as she absentmindedly washed a cup. Her mind churned with anxious thoughts as she stared out of the kitchen window at the panoramic view. There, in a large garden with its brightly colored summer flowers in landscaped beds, was Joe Anderson, her husband of two weeks, lying on a blanket playing with a young baby—hers and Joe's three-month-old daughter Josie.

She watched unhappily, as Joe laughed at some antic of their baby. A feeling of loneliness twisted inside her, bringing tears to her eyes, and a sudden powerful surge of memories swept into her mind. It was something she had been experiencing a great deal of lately—and something that she always found herself struggling to cope with.

She glanced down at the water, splashing the cooling liquid angrily with her hand, hating to revisit the past but unable to prevent herself from doing so. Glancing up and back out to the garden, the motion of her hands stilled as she remembered.

On Joe's last deployment to Afghanistan, during a search and rescue mission for hostages taken by the Taliban, an ambush had occurred in which a number of his men had been killed, and Joe — along with two other members of his squad — taken prisoner. He remained missing for nearly a year until suddenly and without warning he had arrived home, a changed man from the one that Katie had both known and loved.

During the long months without him, Katie's belief that he was still alive and that he would eventually come home to her and Josie remained strong and indisputable. His survival had been nothing short of a miracle until she came to realize — in a short space of time — that the gentle, loving side of her big, US Marine husband was gone, and what remained was a shell, hiding — she suspected — a secret of nightmarish proportions.

As the days passed, Katie began to realize that Joe's capture had been something more than traumatic. On a number of occasions, she had attempted to talk to him about what had happened, but he had responded — uncharacteristically — with fury, turning into somebody she did not recognize. These episodes — when they occurred — stunned and shocked her because one of the things that she had always loved about her husband was his strength and calmness under duress.

Before his capture, she had rarely seen him angry or agitated, and during their short, intense relationship, she had grown to love his compassion and understanding. Now—and she hated to admit it to herself—the bouts of fury frightened her.

Nightmares repeatedly disturbed her husband's sleep. Tossing and turning, he often moaned piteously, the noise increasing in intensity until eventually he jerked awake, drenched in sweat, the muscles of his body rigid with tension. When she attempted to comfort him, he shrugged her off, rejecting any offer of support and silently rose from the bed to disappear downstairs. On the one occasion that she had run after him—concern at his agitated state getting the better of her—again, he had impatiently dismissed her concerns out of hand.

He spent his waking hours restlessly pacing throughout the house and had taken up a fitness regime that was both rigorous and harsh, jogging up to ten miles every day and working out three times daily in a gym built in the basement.

Bumping into him following one punishing session, Katie had seen that he was dripping with sweat and exhausted, his face crimson with the effort he had obviously put into his exercise. She had voiced her worries but he had shrugged off her words with an almost cold indifference and turned away from her.

The rare times that they were together, Katie felt as though he treated her as if she were a stranger instead of his wife. He had proposed to her within two weeks of his arrival back home but his words—'*Our baby needs her father's name*'—couched in cool, emotionless tones, instead of thrilling her, chilled her to the bone and he no longer told her how much he loved her.

On the few occasions that they had made love—the first move often having been made by Katie—passion still flared between them. However, there was nothing left of the tenderness or consideration which he had once shown her.

Joe's physical injuries had healed quickly and he now sported a lean and well-muscled physique. However, despite his healthy physical appearance, Katie could not help but notice a distant, haunted look in his eyes.

Occasionally she had seen him abruptly stop what he was doing and stare off into the distance with the *thousand yards stare*, a phrase coined to describe the blank, unfocused gaze of a shell-shocked or battle-weary soldier.

Katie couldn't begin to guess—much less fully understand—what might be going on inside his mind and why he had become so unfamiliar. On one final occasion, when Katie had approached him since he was alone to ask, Joe had held up a hand in a warning gesture and with a now-familiar anger and usual avoidance of the subject had answered that he had nothing to say and even if he had, he didn't want to discuss it.

Although she did not profess to be a psychologist or psychiatrist, through her career as an army combat trauma medic, a CTM, Katie had heard numerous sad stories of combat veterans who had been exposed daily to the stressors and trauma of war suffering from post-traumatic stress disorder—PTSD. As part of her training, she had participated in a short course on that very subject and now she suspected that Joe suffered from the very same condition, triggered by his experiences in Afghanistan.

Maggie and Jack—Joe's parents—had approached her privately to voice their own concerns about their son but at Katie's tearful response had not brought up the subject again.

Despite Joe's cold manner, his physical efforts to keep his distance from her and the other changes in his personality, Katie still loved him — more than ever — and her wedding day had been the happiest of her life. She was less sure that Joe still loved her, however, and this suspicion — when she allowed herself to dwell on it — caused her a great deal of emotional turmoil.

Joe might have fallen out of love with her, but she was left in no doubt that he absolutely adored his daughter. She never knew that a man could become so involved with his child. He obligingly changed what he called *'nasty'* diapers, fed Josie when required and always managed to get the little girl to produce the obligatory burp whenever requested. He never complained at having to get up with her in the middle of the night and he played with her constantly, smiling, laughing, and baby talking like any normal father.

Katie sighed, glancing down at the diamond and white gold wedding ring on her finger.

She loved Joe — wanted and needed him — but intuition, well-honed over the years by her military experience, had alerted her to the inescapable fact that something was wrong. She knew that until her husband faced whatever demons might be haunting him, found some way of talking about his experiences and venting his hurt and anger then their marriage — their very life together — was at risk.

Staring once more out of the window, Katie saw Joe walking back up the garden toward the house, Josie in his arms. As preoccupied with her thoughts as she was, she couldn't prevent herself from admiring his body clad in faded, torn jeans that clung to his muscular legs and a black T-shirt that outlined well-developed muscles in his abdomen and chest. Her stomach muscles clenched with a mixture of emotions when she noticed the wide smile on his face, the way his strong arms gently held their baby, and she wished—with a powerful yearning—that he would hold her again and kiss her with that smiling mouth.

Perhaps things would change tonight because, for the first time since he had arrived home, she and Joe were going out. It was to a Marine ball at one of the local hotels and Katie was as excited about it as she was nervous. It could be that some dancing and relaxation would help break the impenetrable mental barrier that Joe appeared to have erected around himself.

Katie forced her gaze away from her husband and up to the wall clock. It was 1800 hours and Josie's feeding time, so, moving to the fridge, she opened its door and removed a ready-made bottle of milk, which she placed in a saucepan half-full of water to warm up. Right now, she had her baby to feed, bathe and put to bed.

Joe entered the French windows and walked through the lounge, all the while cooing and smiling at his daughter. After crossing the hallway, he slowly entered the kitchen and immediately felt his eyes drawn to Katie as though she were a magnet.

He admired the way her tight jeans clung to her hips, bottom and long legs like a second skin and loved the way her white T-shirt outlined her feminine-muscled upper body. Continuing to stare at her, he felt a familiar ache of sexual arousal begin in his lower stomach and travel downward to coil in his groin, almost causing him to groan aloud.

He desperately wanted to make love to his wife— needed to. But Joe had no idea why he didn't follow through with those feelings—why he couldn't give her what she wanted anymore — a need he often saw in her eyes when he caught her staring at him.

He had no problem with the physical act of having sex with her but his inability and what he classed as his failure to show her any of the love or tenderness that had always been a part of their lovemaking was almost torture. He had sworn to himself that no matter the temptation, he would not make love to her because — in his eyes — that would be tantamount to using her for his own primitive satisfaction.

Joe often remembered their days in Afghanistan — how they had loved each other, hadn't been able to keep their hands off each other and were not afraid of showing their feelings — and he felt a desperate sense of loss and confusion. He was fully aware that over the last few months his mind had somehow erected a barrier, forcing normal emotions deep down inside and leaving behind an almost callous indifference. The only demonstrative feeling he felt safe with was the love that he could show his baby daughter.

Joe suspected that Katie knew there was a problem. He understood that his unfeeling attitude was hurting her deeply as well as his parents but he could not bring himself to tell either his wife or mother and father the details of what had happened to him in Afghanistan.

He was unable to face the memories himself and a rational part of his subconscious frequently screamed for help and support but he'd never actively sought help before and he was not about to seek it now. He resolved to himself that he would sort out the issues personally — and sometime soon — before he destroyed his marriage and Katie's love for him.

He had a vague sense of unease, however, that the solution might be worse than he could imagine.

There was another matter that was causing Joe a great deal of anxiety. At the slightest provocation—particularly when questioned or put under pressure or stress—an icy fury exploded from out of nowhere and completely demolished the self-control that he always prided himself on having. The emotion was very uncharacteristic and had only manifested itself on his return home.

It burned deep inside him—smoldering embers waiting for ignition—and even though he tried he could not extinguish the sparks that flared into being when forced to explain why he was acting as he was or when faced with his own destructive memories. It was an ugly emotion that he was struggling to control and with which he was failing dismally.

Joe felt the now-familiar flare of fear brought on by the direction in which his thoughts were heading. His haunted mind abruptly baulked and shut down and he cleared his throat.

As he made the sound, Katie turned to face him, offering him a slight smile. He saw an expression of sadness in her beautiful green eyes and he winced. He couldn't bear what he was doing to her. He was the cause of the unhappy expression on her pretty face and it made him want to turn and run from the room.

He quickly moved toward her and gently handed her the baby, watching as she tenderly took the gurgling little girl. He saw her smile grow less forced as she gently stroked the baby's soft downy hair.

"Hello, little girl," Katie murmured. "Have you been playing with your daddy?"

Joe watched, his heart aching as Josie waved her little fists in the air and blew a raspberry, causing Katie to laugh aloud.

"All right, I get the message," she continued. "Let's get you fed."

As he stared at his wife and child, struggling to keep his tumbling emotions in check, Katie glanced back at him again, and he noticed unshed tears sparkling in her eyes and a feeling of panic welled up inside him.

"I'll go take a shower before you bathe, Josie," he announced abruptly, his voice sounding hoarse to his ears, and he turned to leave the kitchen.

"Joe."

He heard Katie call his name with a pleading note in her voice and stopped in his tracks, feeling his shoulders stiffen with sudden tension that tightened every muscle in his body.

"Yeah?" he answered.

He refused to turn and look at her and heard a small sob from behind him. He closed his eyes. He couldn't do it anymore. He was done—wiped out—at the end. It certainly wasn't Katie's fault. He knew that. She had every right to be upset, even angry, but his conscience was needling and taunting him, urging him to deal with the escalating situation. The only solution to this, as far as he could see, however, was that he would almost surely deeply hurt and even lose the one person who could help him if he allowed her to.

He waited, the seconds before she replied seeming to stretch into long minutes.

"Nothing," he heard her eventually say and again, felt the guilt and turmoil churn inside him at the tone of defeat evident in her voice.

Joe nodded his head and silently hurried from the kitchen.

Katie heard his footsteps as he crossed the hallway then climbed the stairs to the upper floor. She wiped away the single tear that had trickled down her cheek and sat down at the kitchen table.

"Okay, sweetheart, it's just me and thee," she said, attempting to smile for the benefit of her daughter.

Once Josie had finished her bottle and Katie had managed to get the obligatory burp from her daughter, she took her upstairs to bathe her before putting her to bed.

As she walked along the upper landing, Maggie Anderson came out of her bedroom, saw Katie and Josie, and a smile spread across her face.

"And how's my beautiful little girl?" asked the older woman.

"She's fine," Katie answered, seeing the look of adoration on Maggie's face and feeling a great deal of affection for her mother-in-law. "I'm just going to bath her."

"Please, let Jack and I do that," Maggie pleaded, gently stroking Josie's cheek. "We would love to."

Katie hesitated. "Are you sure?" she asked. "She can be a bit of a handful."

She heard a note of sadness enter Maggie's voice as she said, "Oh, get away with you, honey. She'll be no more of a handful than Joe was at this age. You need to get ready anyway."

Raising a hand, she gently touched Katie's cheek. "Come on. Give her to me."

Katie, guessing that Maggie knew of the problems between her and Joe, rubbed her cheek affectionately against the elderly woman's hand then handed over her child. She watched as Maggie carried Josie back into her bedroom, hearing Jack's voice faintly from inside until the door closed.

Continuing to walk the length of the hallway to the bedroom she shared with Joe, she let herself inside and – as expected – found the room empty with no sign of her husband. She glanced about the bedroom, experiencing a sudden feeling of loneliness.

Since he had returned home, it was rare that she and Joe were ever together in the same room besides their bedroom. He certainly never undressed in front of her anymore and always seemed to find some excuse to leave when she did the same.

She had no idea where he was, and feeling a twinge of sadness, she made her way into the large en-suite bathroom adjoining the bedroom and shut and locked the door. If Joe wanted to avoid her then she had no choice but to accept the inevitable – that that was how it would have to be.

Katie suddenly felt tired and unsure if she wanted to go out that night after all. Everything felt too much of an effort and her heart was not in it, however, she stripped off her clothes and let herself into the shower cubicle. She stood under the hot spray for long minutes – head bowed – trying to find some semblance of enthusiasm for the night ahead.

Forty-five minutes later, she had finished dressing and stood in front of a floor-length mirror staring at her reflection. As she studied the image in front of her, she saw a tall, slim woman with very short, copper-colored hair and clear, green eyes.

Since Josie's birth, her body, while still retaining its slimness, had gained more curves and the tight, dark green, ankle-length lace dress clung to those curves. The silk underlay was strapless with a sweetheart neckline, the sleeves long with the back plunging into a V. She wore high-heeled, black, patent shoes and Maggie had loaned her a pair of emerald and gold earrings that sparkled and glittered at her ears. The only other jewelry she wore was her wedding ring.

Quickly dismissing any negative thoughts that lingered, she turned away from her reflection, grabbed a black patent clutch bag and black lace shawl, and hurried to leave the room. As she reached the door, it suddenly swung open and Joe stood there, his gaze immediately alighting on her.

There was a sharp, intense look in his eyes and her pulse raced faster as the expression in them became smoldering, recognizing the look that he was giving her.

She stared back at him. It was the first time she had seen him in a formal uniform other than desert combats and the sight of him left her almost breathless.

He was resplendent in Marine evening dress with royal blue, high-rise trousers with a red stripe down the outside of each leg, black evening dress uniform jacket, red cummerbund, crisp white shirt with black bow tie and white dress cap. Gold embroidery on red staff sergeant chevrons adorned the sleeves of the jacket and his dress shoes gleamed and reflected the light like mirrors.

"You look—" Joe stopped, cleared his throat, then went on, "stunning."

Katie smiled, welcoming the obvious warm look that she could see in her husband's eyes. She felt a surge of love and pride that this man was hers.

"You don't look so bad yourself," she replied softly.

As Joe continued to stare—his gaze roaming over her—she felt tiny electric shocks titillating the nerve endings throughout her body. A warmth began in the pit of her stomach, spreading outward and upward to her breasts then to her nipples, which immediately hardened into buds of arousal, the delicate lace of her bra caressing them and making them even more sensitive.

"Shall we go?" Joe asked finally, jerking her back to reality.

Katie nodded, and Joe, taking her hand, turned and led the way out into the hallway where Maggie and Jack were waiting for them with a camera, Jack holding a squirming, wide-awake Josie in his arms.

"You both look wonderful," Maggie stated, "and I need a photograph."

"Mom!" Joe exclaimed.

Katie held her breath at the note of impatience in his voice and his hand clenching slightly as it held hers.

"Oh, humor me and go stand by the banister rail," Maggie ordered.

Without making any further comment, Joe silently obeyed and Katie followed him. As she reached his side, he turned toward her, and to her surprise, placed a hand on each of her hips and pulled her toward him, close enough that their bodies touched. Katie glanced up at him, saw that he was looking down at her, and she smiled.

There was a blinding flash as Maggie took a photograph.

"Beautiful," she exclaimed. "Now, go and have a good time, both of you. Don't worry about Josie, Jack and I will look after her. Now go!"

Smiling briefly at his mother, Joe again took Katie's hand in his. They both kissed the soft cheek of their little girl before descending the curving staircase to go through the kitchen and out into the double garage. After raising the electronic door, they climbed into Joe's car then were on their way.

Chapter Two

As they drove the short distance to the hotel, Joe couldn't resist darting sidelong glances at his wife. He had always recognized that she was beautiful but tonight she was irresistible. He had no idea how he could have resisted Katie for as long as he had. Just being near her almost pushed his control to the limits and any resistance he had was quickly unraveling. His see-sawing emotions confused him, his wants and needs turbulent and at war with each other.

He gripped the leather steering wheel until the knuckles of his hands turned white and he took a deep breath, trying to slow the pounding of his heart. He had a sudden powerful urge to pull the car off the road into somewhere secluded and make love to Katie, lose himself in her beauty and the sensations that she always aroused in him. He gritted his teeth and forced his mind to concentrate on the road ahead before he killed them both.

As they reached the hotel and he parked the car, Joe saw Katie looking at the brightly lit building with an expression of excitement on her face. He felt a slight stir of amusement when he realized that she reminded him of a child on her way to a party.

After exiting the car and as they walked across the car park, Joe took Katie's arm and they walked up the wide stone steps to the front entrance. A Marine in dress uniform greeted them politely at the hotel doors, taking the ornate, gold-script invitation from Joe then he inclined his head and pointed a white-gloved hand into the building.

"Just follow the signs, Staff Sergeant, Mrs. Anderson," he announced.

Joe nodded and led Katie into the foyer of the hotel. The first thing he became aware of was noise issuing from wide-open ornate glass doors and they walked toward them, they both paused on the threshold of a ballroom. Katie glanced inside, and Joe watched her, enjoying the expression of awe on her face as she gazed at the throng of men in uniform with their women in glittering ball gowns and sparkling jewelry.

As he went to escort her inside, he felt her pull back on his hand. He turned to her and asked, "What's the matter?"

"I'm just a corporal, Joe," Katie said. "I don't belong here."

Detecting a note of nervousness in her voice, Joe moved close to her, a smile edging onto his face.

"You're also my wife, Katie," he announced gently. "The women here can't hold a candle to you. Believe me."

With that final comment, he took her hand to lead her into the ballroom.

* * * *

After Joe had introduced Katie to his commanding officer and friends and the formal dinner was over, the dancing began and he found them a small table by the dance floor. He held out a chair, and Katie sat down, finally able to take a sip of the red wine she had been carrying around since her arrival.

Sitting down himself, Joe glanced around the ballroom, suddenly feeling uneasy and irritated, the noise of conversation and music deafening, the crowd surrounding him blurring into one mass of kaleidoscopic shifting color. He felt cold sweat bead his forehead and a sense of panic begin to take hold.

He wanted out of this place — needed to be on his own in peace and quiet. As the fear — of what he had no idea — threatened to escalate out of control he felt a hand laid on his arm. He turned to look at Katie and saw a look of concern on her face.

"Joe, are you all right?" she asked, raising her voice slightly above the noise of the music and laughter.

Joe stared at her for a moment, hesitated then answered, "Everything's fine," and turned his attention back to the dance floor.

At that moment, the tempo of the music changed — becoming slower — and couples immediately rose from their tables and moved into each other's arms.

Joe turned back to Katie. "Do you want to dance?" he asked his blue eyes focusing on her face. He managed to smile at her.

Katie nodded silently and Joe — taking her hand — escorted her onto the dance floor. As she moved into his arms, Joe pulled her close, his gaze taking in her sparkling, clear green eyes, her smooth, glowing skin, and moist full lips that smiled at him lovingly with a hint of sensual awareness.

Her perfume was delicate and her eyes glistening. With a wrench that caught at his heart, he committed the way she looked to a small secret part of his mind, a part in which he had stored all his wonderful memories of their time together and that he kept safe from his increasingly destructive thoughts.

He kissed the top of her head, felt her warm body move closer against his, then she softly kissed his neck. He shivered at the gentle but sensual touch of her lips against his skin before pulling her against him even harder. As she rubbed against him, he knew that she had become aware of his erection and received confirmation of this as she raised her face to look at him. Katie licked her lips.

He lowered his head, his mouth inches from her own, the urge to kiss her becoming almost overwhelming, but he controlled himself and grimaced.

"Sorry," he said softly.

"No need to be sorry," Katie murmured. "Do you want to go fool around?"

"Oh, yeah, do I?" Joe answered, feeling himself shudder with anticipation. "Now?"

"What do you think?" Katie responded, her voice sounding husky to his ears. "There's no time like the present."

Joe grimaced again, feeling a little embarrassed. "I think...you'll need to walk in front of me," he said. "I don't want to shock anyone with my...condition."

He allowed Katie — who was laughing softly — to take his hand and he followed behind her as she kept slightly in front of him, shielding him from the view of the other guests. They left the dance floor and as they passed their table, she grabbed for her bag and shawl and they left with unseemly haste, heading for the grounds of the hotel.

Once outside in the warm night air, Joe promptly took Katie off to the right, around the side of the building and into the darkness of the large landscaped gardens. Silently, they hurried toward a black grove of trees.

As they hastened across the grass, Katie felt a warm frisson of sensual desire start to travel down her spine and into her stomach, her legs trembling with anticipation. She was desperate to have Joe make love to her—wanted him so very badly.

Eventually, reaching the trees and ducking beneath low branches, she allowed Joe to guide her among them into the blackness. When they couldn't go any farther, he leaned against the large trunk of a tree and she felt herself pulled—almost roughly—toward him. His mouth unerringly found hers even though it was so dark that their features were merely pale blurs.

Katie welcomed the hot firmness of his mouth and returned the passionate kiss eagerly. She slowly slid her hands up the slope of his powerful shoulders, lingering against the warm skin of his neck before clenching them in his short hair. As his arms tightened around her, the feel of his powerful muscles made her hot with *pure lust*.

As he sensuously entwined his tongue with her own, Katie wondered—in a small part of her mind that hadn't become almost overwhelmed with sexual desire—how she could have let the distance between herself and Joe become so significant. She ground her hips against his—feeling his hardness—wanting him and desperate for him to forget the usual foreplay and make love to her—hard.

Her thoughts disintegrated into sparkling shards of want as Joe began to kiss her neck, lingering at the place where a small pulse beat fast and delicately beneath her skin. He licked a swirling trail along and around it, eliciting a moan from her and sending a series of volcanic shivers rippling through her body.

God, I want him so much.

The words played dimly in Katie's mind as she tossed her head back with reckless abandon, allowing Joe easier access to the suddenly hypersensitive skin of her neck.

Lowering her hands from behind his head, Katie thrust them beneath his open jacket and pulled his shirt loose from his trousers. She felt his warm, smooth muscular back and dragged her nails across his skin, not hard enough to hurt him but with enough pressure to cause him to shiver with delight.

Joe murmured her name then suddenly began to tug at her dress, attempting to lift it.

Katie withdrew her hands from behind his neck when he struggled and she quickly lifted it by its hem, raising the dress to her panty line, feeling the light, ethereal touch of the night breeze on her bare legs, emphasizing the breathless anticipatory rush of waiting to be *fucked* by her husband.

"Please. Fuck me, Joe," Katie murmured.

Hearing her plea, Joe placed a warm hand on her thigh, caressing the silky, soft smoothness of her skin, gently running his fingertips up to her hip, downward and around to the inside of her leg, then moving his fingers upward in light circular motions until he reached her panties. As his fingers touched her through the thin silk, he discovered that she was already hot and moist and when he felt her hips move to press downward against his fingers—welcoming them—he almost tore the delicate material from her in order to be able to thrust inside her.

Joe found Katie's lips again, and he kissed her hard, a small part of his mind wondering if he was hurting her but his control—which he was quickly losing—prevented him from holding back. He rubbed her delicately, the increasing friction causing Katie to moan against his mouth and her hips to thrust gently against his roaming fingers.

Katie moved her hand down to the front of his trousers where his rigid erection strained against the material, the small palm moving up and down, the movements alternating between a sensual rubbing and delicate squeezing of his cock.

His body stiffened in response, his hips involuntarily jerking at her touch so that the friction of her hand increased. He buried his face against Katie's neck, his whole focus under the control of that small hand slowly and delicately manipulating his penis.

Moments later, the fastenings of his trousers were undone and Katie grasped his throbbing, aching dick. The feel of her fingers encircling him caused his hips to jerk toward her, his cock slipping deliciously through her grip. He groaned again, his breathing harsh and rapid.

"Do you want me, Joe?" Katie asked.

Hearing her tone so soft and sensuous and feeling one fingertip delicately circling the crown of his penis, Joe gasped.

"Fuck, yes." His voice sounded husky to his own ears and he tilted his head back, fighting to control himself. "No pun intended."

"Say it to me," Katie ordered, the words said in the same sensuous whisper.

Her grip tightened on him—squeezing—releasing—and squeezing again. Still stroking gently between her legs, her juices coated her inner thighs.

He moaned loudly in response.

"Say it," Katie repeated a little louder, her grip on his cock tightening.

"God damn it! I fucking want you," Joe said through gritted teeth. "I want to fuck you so fucking bad!" His voice rose on the last word.

Unable to control himself any longer, he ripped at her damp panties, tossing the silky material away into the darkness. He clutched her thighs in his hands and lifted her up, promptly swinging her around to rest her back against the trunk of the tree.

In one smooth, powerful movement, he was inside her – deep inside her wet heat – stopping when he couldn't go any farther – moving minutely backward and forward, teasing her and waiting for a response.

Katie felt his pulsating hardness – the tiny thrusting movements – and the instantaneous approach of her orgasm. She whimpered with pure ecstasy, gripping the back of Joe's head and bringing his mouth toward hers in a kiss so hard that it was almost painful.

Her whole body was a writhing mass of sensation and she lifted her hips to meet his thrusts with an equal force of her own as he began to move in and out of her, burying his cock deep inside her then almost fully withdrawing himself.

Their moans were loud and unrestrained then too quickly Katie felt the overwhelming, exploding sensation of her orgasm arrive. Every nerve in her body sparked as her senses spiraled up and out into shockwaves that had the whole of her body quaking. She arched her back, her head thudding into the rough trunk of the tree, internal muscles clenching Joe's cock.

Joe gasped, feeling his cock clench with surprisingly strong, liquid pulses and he climaxed deep inside her. He slammed into her one final time then buried his face against her warm, perfumed neck.

"God," he murmured, his heart hammering against his ribs, his breathing ragged and harsh. "Shit."

They both remained motionless, Joe holding Katie tightly until he eventually straightened, withdrew from her and placed her feet gently on the ground. He reorganized his clothing and Katie pulled down the skirt of her dress.

A small silence stretched between them.

Joe stood with head lowered, trying to control his breathing, a powerful surge of guilt engulfing him.

What in the hell have I done? He'd let the barrier come down, let her creep in beneath his defenses, allowed his powerful craving for her to get the better of him. He had used her, which would only hurt her even more after he carried out his plan. He cursed himself in his mind. *Fuck, I'm the world's worst scumbag.*

Joe abruptly put his arms around Katie again and drew her toward him. Lifting her chin with one hand, he said softly, "Hey. You know I love you, don't you? I'll always love you, Katie. Whatever happens, honey, please don't ever forget that."

At his words, he felt Katie's body stiffen. Putting her hands on his shoulders she asked, "I don't understand, Joe. What do you mean?"

Joe hesitated. "I know I haven't been acting right. I've been a bastard, actually," he continued slowly, "and I'm sorry. I've hurt you and I make no excuses. But please remember how much I love you."

Katie gently touched the side of his face. "I do understand," she replied. "I love you so much. Whatever the problem is, we can solve it together. You just need to trust in me — in us."

Joe sighed, suddenly kissed her gently, then forced a laugh.

"Come on. We need to get out of here. It wouldn't do to be seen sneaking out of a grove of trees. It would be pretty obvious what we'd been up to."

Katie sighed. "If we must," she answered.

With Joe's arm around her—guiding her out from beneath the trees—he and Katie made their way back across the grass to the car park. Joe opened the car door for her then climbed in himself. After starting the engine, he sat in silence, hands clenched on the steering wheel.

Out of the corner of his eye, he saw Katie lean across to him, and felt a hand on his arm, kneading the tense muscles gently.

"Joe, what's wrong? Talk to me, please." He heard concern in her voice.

Joe hesitated, a strangling sensation in his chest that threatened to choke him. He vigorously shook his head and closed his eyes in desperation.

"I can't, Katie," he responded quietly. "If I could I would. I'm sorry."

Nodding silently, Katie withdrew her hand and sat back in her seat. Without another word, Joe put the car in gear and drove away from the hotel.

As they made their way home, Katie felt trepidation as she wondered what was wrong with her husband. She guessed that the barrier was back up and Joe had shut himself away from her again. Their earlier conversation in the grove of trees had struck a chord of uneasiness inside her. Her intuition told her that he had been trying to warn her about something but she had no idea about what.

On reaching the house, Joe drove into the open garage to park the car then both he and Katie got out to go into the house.

"Head on upstairs," he whispered to her, running a finger gently down her cheek. "I'll be up in a minute."

Glancing at him sadly—guessing that he would go into the lounge to sit in the dark to think about whatever was tormenting him—she walked slowly to the stairs and began to climb them. She heard Joe's footsteps cross the tiled hall floor and silence.

After what had happened between them at the hotel Katie had—possibly naïvely—thought that everything would be all right between them. She was devastated that even making love to her had not been enough to bring down—or even destroy—the icy shield that Joe had erected around himself.

On reaching the dark landing, Katie made her way toward the nursery and quietly let herself in. A dim night light in the shape of a fairy lit the room with a soft glow. Making her way toward the cot, Katie leaned over its side and gently caressed her baby girl's face. Josie, clad in a pale pink night suit with rabbits on it, stirred slightly, pursed her bow-like lips, and carried on sleeping.

"What are we going to do about your daddy, little one?" Katie murmured, tears filling her eyes. "I love him so much, sweetheart, but I can't reach him. I don't think he wants to be loved anymore."

A single tear ran down one cheek and dropped into the cot. She straightened up, stepped back and fiercely wiped at her eyes, but the silent sobs continued and more tears trickled down her face. Gulping, she swiftly rubbed at her face, determined not to let the desolate feeling in her heart get the better of her.

She stood with head bowed, still refusing to allow herself the opportunity of howling out her pain like a child as she so desperately wanted to, then straightened up, and turned toward the door. She jerked slightly with startled surprise seeing her husband standing in the doorway of the nursery watching her, head lowered slightly, eyes gleaming beneath the peak of his cap.

She stared at him, waiting for him to speak. There was an expression of pain on his face. He lifted a hand toward her as if he was silently asking for her help. In the next instant, however, the moment of communication was lost. His hand clenched into a fist and dropped to his side. His expression hardened, and he backed away from the door, disappearing into the darkness of the hallway.

Katie heard him walk the few paces to their room, the door open softly then close.

Inside the bedroom, Joe quickly began to undress. After hastily putting on his sleep shorts and T-shirt he hung his uniform in its protective bag, wrapped his cap in tissue paper and put it back in its box, then swathed his spotless gleaming dress shoes in muslin, placing them in the wardrobe. He was just about to get into bed when the bedroom door opened and Katie entered.

She stopped dead when she saw him as though she had not expected him to be there and still awake. Seeing the look of surprise on her face, Joe smiled slightly.

"Hey," he said, walking toward her, "Josie still asleep?"

"Sound," Katie replied, walking past him to go into the bathroom and closing the door behind her. He let her go.

When she came out a few minutes later dressed in a short nightshirt, Joe stretched out a hand and tenderly touched her arm. She turned to face him and he saw her face streaked with tears.

"Come here," he said softly and pulled her toward him.

Katie went into his arms and he enfolded her in a tight embrace, resting his face against her sweet-smelling hair. She always made him feel so content when he was close to her and it was going to destroy him to do what he had to do.

"Katie."

Joe said her name and waited until she lifted her face from his shoulder. He saw a questioning look in her eyes.

He paused before he said, "I love you. I love you so very much."

Katie touched his face, running a finger along his lips. "I adore you," she replied softly in return.

Hearing her voice tremble with emotion, Joe lowered his head and kissed her gently, his mouth moving against hers as though she were as fragile as glass. There was passion in his kiss but it went deeper than that. For the moment, the mental shield that he had erected around his emotions was down—albeit struggling to raise itself—and he was trying to show her with all that he had how deep his feelings for her were.

At last, he raised his head. "Come on," he said, "let's go to bed, it's late. The little one will be howling her head off before much longer."

They went to the bed, folded back the throw, and got beneath the quilt. Katie stretched out to turn off the bedside light but Joe stayed her hand.

"Leave it on," he whispered.

Katie turned to glance over her shoulder at him then shrugged and snuggled down beneath the quilt. Joe spooned in against her back, one hand lifting her nightshirt so that her bare bottom pressed against his groin. His rested his arm across her waist, laying his head on the pillow beside hers.

She wriggled back against him, pressing her warmth against his skin. His response was immediate as she squirmed against him again.

Joe chuckled. "Tease," he growled. "Go to sleep, minx."

Katie put a small fist beneath her chin and closed her eyes. Before many minutes had passed, he heard her soft even breathing and knew that she had fallen asleep.

Joe refused to allow his eyes to close. His emotions in turmoil, he wanted to cherish these last moments with his wife. He needed to feel her warmth against him. It was going to be so cold and empty where he was going and he wanted to watch the way she curled up as she slept.

He could smell her perfume and although he was becoming aroused again, he was determined not to disturb her. If she woke and discovered what he was going to do, he knew his plan would fall apart. Just the sad heartbreaking look she would give him would be enough to stop him in his tracks and he wouldn't be able to leave her. She would unintentionally undermine his decision and if he was ever going to lead a normal life again he had to go ahead with his plan.

Chapter Three

After what seemed like hours, Joe finally glanced at the digital clock on his bedside table and saw that the red digits were reading 0300 hours. Right on cue, a small whimper sounded from the baby monitor on Katie's table.

Unable to stop himself from smiling slightly — it seemed at times as though his daughter had her own timed agenda — Joe carefully and gently moved backward away from Katie, holding his breath as she stirred slightly. Quickly and silently, he got out of bed and made his way to the door, opening it quietly and stepping out into the hallway. He listened for any further sounds of protest from the nursery and when there were none he hurried down the stairs to the kitchen where — his mind comfortably blank with the routine task — he began to heat up a bottle. When he judged the milk was warm enough he hurried back upstairs and went into the nursery.

Josie was awake and kicking in her cot. Placing a small towel over his shoulder, he gently lifted the little girl into his arms and took her to a rocking chair in the corner of the room. Sitting down, he settled the baby in his arms then began to feed her.

Joe marveled at how tiny and perfect she was and at how much she resembled both him and Katie. He committed each of her expressions to memory in case he never saw her again. He adored her and it was going to break his heart to leave her.

Once the baby had finished her milk, Joe got to his feet and, placing her up against his shoulder, he rubbed her back until a very loud burp caused him to laugh gently.

"For a little thing, you sure do make a big enough noise," he said softly.

Josie was already falling asleep as Joe walked her to the cot, but before placing her in it, he stared down at his daughter.

Lowering his head, he gently kissed the fine, silky hair. "Goodbye, my little girl," he murmured. "I love you so much."

His voice choking on the words and with tears he refused to shed filling his eyes, he laid the little girl in her cot then stood staring down at her.

"I'm so sorry for doing this to you and your mom," he whispered, then realizing he was going to break down, he quickly left the nursery and went back in to Katie.

She was still asleep and he went to silently stand beside her, looking down at her sleeping peacefully, a small smile on her pretty face.

"Oh, Katie," he whispered. "What am I going to do to you?"

He stood by the bed for long seconds, heart pounding and threatening to tear apart with emotion. At last, he shook himself. "I love you," he whispered.

He walked back around the bed to the chest of drawers where he stored his underwear and, sliding one of them open as quietly as he could, he lifted up folded garments and drew out two envelopes. He re-closed the drawer and went back to Katie's side of the bed.

Placing one envelope upright against the lamp where she would see it when she awoke, Joe took a deep breath and hurried from the room. Moving quickly, he ran quietly down the stairs and into the kitchen.

He leaned the second envelope against the kettle, where his mother or father would see it first thing, then glanced slowly around the room. His senses drank in all the personal and familiar things that he loved, before he finally straightened his shoulders and let himself into the garage.

Moving with a purpose, he went to a tall metal cabinet in the corner and reaching up to its top took down a small key and unlocked the door. Inside, on the floor, were his desert combats, body armor, boots, webbing with utility pouches, and his large rucksack with his combat helmet resting on top.

Not allowing himself time to think—knowing that if he let one element of doubt enter his mind he would not be able to continue—he took off his shorts and T-shirt. Naked, he immediately began to shiver in the chilly air. His feet burning from contact with the gritty concrete, he quickly clothed himself and finally put on and laced up his well-worn combat boots.

Slowly—and hating himself for doing it—he took off his wedding ring then hesitated, thoughtfully fingering the wide titanium band, gently running the tip of a finger across the warm metal. At last, mentally shaking himself, he undid the chain holding his dog tags around his neck, threaded the ring onto it so it tumbled down to rest next to them then refastened it and put it on back over his head, tucking it inside his T-shirt. Finally, he put his helmet on, shrugged into his rucksack and carrying his body armor in his hand he was finally ready to leave.

Walking back into the kitchen and from there into the hallway, he went to the front door and paused. Turning to look back over his shoulder, he glanced up the stairs to where his wife, daughter and his parents lay sleeping and for a split second, his resolution wavered.

Joe wanted to go back upstairs—climb into bed with Katie—cuddle up to her and make love to her and try to forget about the crazy and cruel stunt he was about to pull.

Torn emotionally in too many directions, he realized, however, that if he didn't see this through, he would end up destroying everything that he held dear. The anger inside him would eat him up and take over every normal human emotion that made him the man that he had once been—was struggling to remain—and he would never be normal again.

Opening the front door, he stepped outside into the warm night air and closed it quietly behind him.

Feeling like a coward for sneaking away in the night like a scavenger, he resolutely stiffened his shoulders and settled his pack more comfortably. Swallowing the huge lump of grief that had formed in his throat and which threatened to choke him, he strode down the path toward the ornate iron gates that protected his parents' property.

Once through them, he turned onto the wide road and marched off into the night without looking back, a cold ring of ice forming around his heart.

Chapter Four

Katie woke abruptly, bolting upright in bed—her heart pounding in her chest—darting her eyes frantically around the dimly lit bedroom. For a few seconds her mind remained blank although an unknown fear tightened her chest and throat.

Something is wrong.

Before she knew what she was doing, she had thrown back the quilt and was on her feet, listening intently to the baby monitor to see if she could hear any noise coming from the nursery. The monitor remained as silent as the bedroom.

She turned to look at Joe's side of the bed and was not surprised to see—as usual—that he was gone—the quilt tossed back, the sheet creased, a faint dent in the pillow showing where his head had been resting beside hers. He was probably downstairs in the lounge, alone in the dark room with his equally dark thoughts.

Katie could hear her breathing, rapid and loud in the silence of the shadowy room. Even though she couldn't hear any unusual sound in any other part of the house, her sixth sense rang alarm bells.

Attempting to calm herself, she eliminated the primary things that could be wrong.

Her baby – the monitor was silent.

Someone has broken into the house. Joe would be on his or her case already.

There was something wrong with Maggie and Jack – again – Joe would know about it.

So, what is it?

The panic was flaring inside her and gaining in strength. She was acutely aware, with an almost primal intuition that all was not as it should be.

Hurrying around the end of the bed, she made for the door. She wanted to shout out Joe's name, have him come to her and soothe her, put his arms around her and tell her that there was nothing wrong and that everyone was safe, that she was imagining things.

Feeling panic-stricken, Katie hurried from the bedroom out into the silent hallway. She made a beeline for the nursery, her bare feet whispering on the thick pile of the carpet, noticing on her approach a faint pool of amber radiance thrown into the hallway by the dim light inside the room. Pushing it open, she moved on tiptoe toward the cot, peering into its depths.

Josie was lying sound asleep, breathing slowly and deeply. Katie had not realized that she was holding her breath until it came out of her in a rush.

My baby is safe – completely at peace – so it's something else.

She glanced around the nursery, peering into the dark corners where the rays from the night light did not reach. Confirming that the room was indeed empty, she turned and left.

Pausing on the long, dark landing, she strained her hearing to see if she could detect any strange, unwanted noise but found only silence, night hanging heavy in the house.

Katie moved back into her bedroom, hesitating on the threshold, searching its shadowy corners. Her gaze came to rest on the bedside table and she saw the white envelope propped against the lamp. She immediately felt her body stiffen and a cold foreboding fill her stomach.

She dreaded the walk around the bed to take up the envelope that seemed to loom like a huge warning sign. She sensed that once she opened it and read its contents it would change her world forever, bringing with it more pain and heartbreak.

Katie stood inside the bedroom door—frozen into immobility—her gaze locked on her table, her mind empty of all but one thought. *What is in that letter?*

Slowly and reluctantly, she moved toward the opposite side of the room. As she approached the table, her footsteps slowed and she gritted her teeth, clenching her fists. Forcing herself to reach forward, she gripped the envelope between two fingers as though it was contaminated and she picked it up.

Her name stood out in black relief and on recognizing Joe's handwriting, a small whimper came from her lips. Sinking down onto the edge of the bed, she clutched the letter in her hand, staring down at it.

Finally, she took a deep breath, turned it over, and ripped open the envelope with her finger. Extracting the single sheet of paper from inside and gathering her strength, she unfolded it and before her courage failed her, began to read.

My darling Katie
By the time you read this, I will be gone, if I can keep my courage and willpower to go.

First, I want to tell you how much I love you. You and Josie mean the world to me and this has been the most difficult decision that I have had to make in my life. I don't expect you to believe me. You have every right to be furious and hurt, and knowing you as I do, I don't expect you to forgive me.

Something happened to me in Afghanistan. I cannot begin to explain it to you, how it has left me only a shadow of myself. What I do know is that the man you used to love no longer exists and I need to resolve that situation. If I'd stayed, I would only destroy what we have between us. I would make your life a misery. The anger and hate would take over and you would come to hate me if you don't already.

I am so sorry to do this to you, Josie and my family. Again, I don't expect you to understand what I have done but know that I do love you and I am doing this not only for myself but also for us. By now, I will be on my way back to Afghanistan. I know I have deceived you and it will probably be impossible for you to forgive me. So be it. It is down to me to have to live with that for the rest of my life.

Take care, my love. I love you more than life itself. Please try to forgive me if you can. I already miss you. You and Josie are my life.

Joe

Katie's hand dropped onto her lap, the letter fluttering from her suddenly lifeless fingers and landing on the carpet at her feet.

Stunned — her mind reeling with disbelief — she remained seated on the bed, gazing almost catatonically at the bedroom wall, Joe's written words swirling chaotically around in her suddenly disorganized mind.

Joe is gone – again!

Back to Afghanistan…to do what? What does he mean by resolving matters? What matters can be so horrible that he would risk his marriage and his own life?

Katie had always believed that Joe's memories of what had happened to him during his last deployment had festered deep inside him, plaguing him, haunting and torturing him, the cause of his anger and his nightmares. The hate and anger born from his capture and the death of his men could have grown into an unbearable force and Joe being the man that he was, he would not be able to sit around without seeking some form of retribution. Whatever his plans were, it was the decision of a man who was struggling to deal with a nightmare.

Katie felt terrified and bewildered. Joe would not only be putting himself in danger but anyone else with him.

What can I do?

If she went to the US Marine Corps and told them of her concerns, they would find Joe, drag him back to the States, and possibly lock him up in a psychiatric institute. He would hate that and loathe Katie for doing it to him. On the other hand, if she left the situation as it was who knew what Joe would do to find resolution and peace from his torment?

Katie bent down and picked the letter up from the carpet. Her hand shook as she held it up to read again. This time the words blurred as tears filled her eyes.

"Oh, my God, Joe," she murmured. "What have you done?" She lowered the letter, her hand shaking.

What should I do now? More to the point, what can I do?

Hot tears began to trickle down her face and she let them come. The wrenching ache in her heart was unbearable and she doubled over, clutching her arms about herself as though to keep herself from falling apart.

She sat where she was for long minutes, conscious that she was procrastinating—wasting time—still in denial that Joe could have left without explanation, leaving behind those who might have been able to help him. She knew that she needed to move, shake herself out of the despair into which she was rapidly sinking.

Getting up from the bed, clutching the crumpled letter in her hand, she grabbed the baby monitor and moved drunkenly to the bedroom door.

Her mind felt shrouded in a fog of disbelief—she couldn't think straight—was barely aware of making her way out into the dark hallway. There, she hesitated and listened for any noise coming from the nursery. Again, hearing nothing, she turned and made her way quietly along the hallway to the top of the staircase where she hesitated again.

The house remained silent throughout and she ran quickly down the stairs and across the hallway to the kitchen. She almost expected Joe to appear from the lounge asking why she was up and wandering about the house in the early hours of the morning but she remained alone and undisturbed.

Once in the kitchen, she went to the cooker and turned on the small light mounted beneath it, slightly comforted by the small pool of radiance. Silently, she went to the kettle to fill it with water and it was at that point that she discovered a second white envelope propped against the appliance, addressed to Joe's parents.

So, he has remembered everyone.

Katie stared at the letter then went to fill the kettle at the kitchen sink, hoping that a soothing cup of tea would ease her confused thoughts and dissipate some of the apathy that had overtaken her since reading the letter.

Plugging the cord into the electrical appliance, she turned it on and, feeling like she was on auto-pilot, found herself a mug and proceeded to put in a tea bag and milk from the fridge. While she waited for the water to boil, she moved to the window and looked out onto the dark garden.

Night, however, pressed against the window and all she could see was her own image super-imposed on the pane of glass. Her eyes filled with tears again.

She had nearly lost Joe once before and now she felt physically sick at the idea that she might have lost him again. Hurt and pain that had only just begun to heal had come flooding back, this time a hundred times worse.

She heard a soft whimper escape her lips and it sounded so forlorn and pathetic in the silence of the kitchen that she pressed her fingers against her mouth.

Only last night, Joe had assured her that he loved her. She could not believe that he had been planning to leave her and Josie all along. It was not the action of a rational man and among the feelings of confusion, anger, and hurt was a sharp gnawing fear that her husband was heading down the road to mental destruction and he was going to get himself killed.

A tear trickled down Katie's face and she uttered another small sob.

How had she not seen that this was going to happen? How could she not have seen what was wrong and attempt to help the man she loved?

Wait a minute. If she was honest with herself — and it was about time that she stopped avoiding the truth — she had known all along, from the time that Joe had returned home, that there was something amiss — his distance from his parents and her — his constant denials that there was anything wrong and his anger, agitation and restlessness. Perhaps she should have tried harder but she had glimpsed the anger behind his calm veneer and had not wanted to provoke that anger. She had taken the coward's way out and now this had happened.

Katie hated herself with a helpless, tortured anger.

I knew. I let it happen and now, it's too late.

Becoming aware that the water in the kettle was boiling merrily and grateful for the distraction, she began to make herself a mug of tea. A few minutes later, clasping the hot china mug and shivering slightly with shock, Katie sat at the kitchen table. As she sipped at the steaming drink, she hoped desperately that the hot liquid would start to thaw the ball of ice that had formed in the pit of her stomach.

She closed her eyes, attempting to blot out the most recent image she had of Joe's face when she had turned to him as he was cuddling her in bed. The memory was too painful to contemplate at that moment and she felt that she would dissolve into a sobbing heap if she couldn't divert her thoughts to something more mundane and trivial.

Concentrating on her drink, it was a few moments before Katie sensed someone standing in the kitchen doorway. For a joyous second, she was convinced that when she lifted her eyes she would see Joe standing there but when she did glance up, she saw the pale figure of Maggie in her nightclothes watching her.

"Katie?"

Although Maggie's voice was quiet, her tone was full of concern.

Katie stayed silent, unable to answer the elderly woman because she would have burst into tears and sobbed like a child.

Maggie stepped into the shadowy kitchen. "Katie, what's wrong? Is it Josie?"

Feeling the tears already close to the surface threatening to spill over, Katie shook her head, swallowed, then replied huskily, "No, Josie's fine. She's sleeping."

"Then what...?" Maggie prompted and a tone of dread entered her voice.

Katie sighed. "Maggie. I don't know how... I'm sorry, but Joe's gone."

For what seemed like an eternity, the words appeared not to register with the older woman. She gazed at Katie, an expression of puzzlement wrinkling her forehead.

"Gone?" she echoed. "What do you mean...gone? Katie, you're scaring me."

Katie pointed a trembling finger to the second white envelope laying on the counter by the kettle.

"He's gone back to Afghanistan," she finally explained softly, her voice breaking and tears beginning to trickle down her face.

Maggie Anderson turned to where Katie pointed and moved to pick up the letter. Remaining silent, she slit it open with a long, neatly manicured nail then withdrew the single sheet of paper. She began reading it. Halfway through, she staggered then dragging out a kitchen chair from the table—its legs screeching across the tiles—she slumped down into it.

Katie watched her, unable to offer a single word of consolation or reassurance.

The letter that Maggie was reading drifted like a leaf down on to the tabletop and she buried her face in her hands, a soft moan escaping her.

Katie put her mug down and stood up to boil the kettle again, placing a gentle hand on the woman's shoulder as she passed by.

After making a second cup of strong tea and handing it to the older woman, she resumed her seat at the table and continued to silently drink her own.

At last, Maggie raised her face from her hands. "I don't understand…" she began. "Why has he done this?"

Katie shook her head. "I don't know any more than you, Maggie. He left me a letter too," she explained, feeling defeated and tired. "He talks about what happened to him on his last tour. He said that if he stayed here, he would end up destroying everything around him, including us and make our lives a misery. He said that he had matters that needed resolving and to do that he had to go back to Afghanistan."

Maggie nodded. "He said as much in the letter to Jack and me." She shook her head. "What can have been so terrible to make him leave?"

Katie sighed, hesitated, then said slowly, "He would never speak about what happened to him. When I brought the subject up, he became angry — more than that — absolutely furious. He suffered terrible nightmares but again, he wouldn't give any details. The only thing I do know is that on a mission, men from his squad died. I think…"

Katie paused, glanced down at her hands clenched on the mug with a white-knuckled grip, then glanced up at her mother-in-law.

"I think he's ill, Maggie. Whatever happened to him out there changed him. Joe thinks that what he's doing is the right thing… That he's protecting himself and us. What scares me the most is that he may be putting not only himself at risk but also the men he'll have in his charge. I don't think he's been thinking straight since he came back. Whatever decisions he makes or is going to make are going to be influenced by whatever is wrong with him."

Maggie shook her head again. "I can't think straight," she said, her voice shaking slightly. "What can we do?"

Katie ran a hand through her short hair. "I don't know, Maggie. I really don't." She paused again. "I thought of going to the USMC. They could get him back from Afghanistan but then that would almost surely mean he would end up in a psychiatric hospital and that would destroy him. It would be like caging a wild animal, and I can't do that to him. He would never forgive me."

At that moment, there was the sound of slipper-clad footsteps shuffling their way across the tiled hall floor and Jack appeared in the kitchen doorway, tightening the belt of his dressing gown. Katie felt a brief painful jolt at how remarkable the likeness was between Joe and his father.

"Is this an early morning girl's chat?" Jack asked. "Or can a man join in?"

The two women remained silent, gazing down at their respective drinks.

Jack gazed from his wife to Katie. "Okay," he said slowly, "are you girls going to let me in on the secret?"

"Why don't you sit down, Jack?" Maggie asked quietly.

"What...?" Jack began, concern now edging into his voice.

"Sit down!" Maggie reiterated. "Please."

Without another word, Jack pulled out a kitchen chair, seating himself beside his wife. Clasping his hands on the surface of the table, he asked, voice devoid of the lightly humorous tone that he had been using, "Now, will someone please tell me what the hell is going on?"

Maggie silently slid the letter across the smooth tabletop to her husband.

Jack looked down at it then sideways at his wife. "What...?" he began.

"Just read it, Jack," Maggie urged.

The kitchen was silent as Jack picked up the sheet of paper and began to read. Katie watched him as he progressed through the letter, the trembling of his hands the only physical sign of his shock at its contents.

At last, his hands fell to the tabletop, the letter from Joe still clutched in his fingers, and he sat with head bowed, eyes closed. He finally opened them and looked straight at her.

"What in God's name is going on here, Katie?" he asked.

"Katie knows no more than we do," Maggie interrupted. "Joe left her a letter as well offering her a basic explanation as he did us."

Jack ran his hands across his face, the gesture provoking in her a surge of grief, as it was so reminiscent of an action that Joe did when he was under stress.

Jack stared at Katie. "You had no idea he was going to do this?" he asked.

His features had sagged and his voice sounded as though he had suddenly aged.

Shaking her head, Katie answered softly, "No," and proceeded to repeat what she had told Maggie just before Jack had arrived in the kitchen.

"Did something happen between you two at the ball last night?" he asked.

"No," Katie replied, remembering with clear-cut clarity how she and Joe had made love in the grounds of the hotel like passionate teenagers.

Feeling as though her emotional instability was about to spiral into hysteria, she continued, "I thought everything was almost back to normal between us. I had no idea he was planning any of this, but I should have known." She slapped the table with the palm of her hand.

Maggie reached for Katie's hand across the table.

"Don't beat yourself up over this, honey," she began, her voice gentle. "Joe has always been good at keeping his worries and problems to himself—dealing with them alone. He has never asked for help."

Katie nodded, noticing that Maggie's face held a strained expression and that she looked ten years older than her true age.

"Yes, I know," she agreed briefly.

"So, what do we do?" Jack asked. "I take it we can't get the USMC involved in any of this? As you said, it could get him into serious trouble but how can we leave him out there?"

Katie remained silent. Her thoughts were scrambled, her emotions in a turmoil. She felt emotionally exhausted and at the end of her strength.

She did have an idea, however, one that was still in its infancy and lurking at the boundaries of her mind. It was risky and probably impossible to put into action. To put it into perspective she needed to bring it out into the open, talk about it to make it clearer in her mind.

"I think there is a way," she began, her voice sounding hesitant to her own ears. "But it's crazy and I think it almost certainly won't work."

Both Maggie and Jack looked at her. "What is it?" Jack asked, clasping his wife's hand on the table. "Any idea, even if it's crazy is better than no idea at all."

"Well, I could volunteer and get redeployed back to Afghanistan," Katie explained quickly, glancing from

Maggie to Jack and watching identical looks of horror cross their faces.

"Katie!" Maggie exclaimed. "No, you can't do that. What about Josie?"

The idea was quickly gaining solidity and Katie continued, "I'm due back off maternity leave in a few days, anyway. For reasons only he knows, I don't think Joe informed the USMC that he and I are married — or he didn't have time to let them know — otherwise I would have been notified of his plans for redeployment, allowances, salary, housing and so on. I can volunteer for another tour of duty out there. I am a CTM. They're always crying out for them overseas for various reasons, battle casualties, or fatalities. I'll be attached to the marines. I might be lucky and be assigned to Joe's squad. Even in the event I'm not, I can try to find him and get him to come home. But, it would mean that you would need to look after Josie for us."

Katie's voice broke as she mentioned her daughter's name but she swallowed and continued firmly, "It won't do my career much good if I get sent out there and it all comes out, but if I can get Joe to come back with me..."

Maggie and Joe looked at each other then back at Katie, both shaking their heads in unison.

"Katie," Maggie responded. "You cannot do this. You'll be putting yourself in danger, risking your own life. You have Josie to consider in all this. If we go through formal channels, Joe will have to come home, regardless of the consequences to his career. If, as you say, he's ill, then that will be the best way forward. We should do it through formal channels."

"Maggie," Katie began adamantly. "The Marine Corp means the world to Joe and he's a proud man. To have anything less than an honorable discharge would kill him. We might just as well put him in front of a firing squad. He would never forgive any of us. My idea probably can't be done but I can at least try."

She paused and swallowed the lump in her throat, eyes filling with unshed tears.

"He's your son but my husband and I love him with all my heart. I *will* do anything to help him. What's happened to him is not his fault. Yes, he's left me, Josie, and you. We are all devastated. But when all is said and done he's our responsibility."

Katie stopped speaking and a heavy silence — full of sadness — reigned over the kitchen.

After a few moments, Jack broke the quiet. "Are you sure about this, Katie? You'll miss six or seven months of your daughter's life. Of course, we would look after Josie as if she were our own, but have you thought seriously about this? Joe is stubborn. You could get another tour of duty out there — find him — and he refuses to listen to you. What happens then? You would be in danger as well as Joe. I think we all need to sleep on this and discuss it at a more sensible hour."

Katie shook her head. "No," she stated. "My mind is made up. That's if the idea is feasible at all. Joe needs our help and I would never forgive myself if I didn't try to do something to help him."

"If you can pull this off we will be eternally grateful," Jack announced softly, and Maggie nodded, again reaching across the table to clasp Katie's hand in her own.

Chapter Five

Katie stood outside the USMC HQ, wondering anxiously — not for the first time — what on earth she was doing back in the sweltering mid-August heat of an Afghanistan summer, having left her four-and-a-half-month-old daughter behind in the States to go chasing after a missing husband who — even though she had been on the base a little over a week — she had seen no sign of.

Once she had joined her new marine unit, after her maternity leave had ended and while waiting for her deployment date, the Marine Corp had put Katie through a grueling six-week training regime. She had learned at her cost that the marines were vastly different to the British army — tougher and harder — and she had had to adapt to new rules and regulations. She had received, however, the benefit of up-to-date, state-of-the-art medical training and, after a period of intense persuasion, they were happy to allow her to redeploy back to Afghanistan.

Her deployment date had taken six weeks to come through which meant a month and a half of being terrified for Joe's safety. She and his parents had fretted daily at his silence, imagining a knock at the front door and upon going to answer it, seeing the straight-backed shadows of the Marine Corp Chaplain and Commanding Officer through the misty glass, there to impart the devastating news that Staff Sergeant Joe Anderson was dead — killed in action.

The last few weeks before shipping out had been a nightmare for Katie. Joe's absence and the struggle to convince the Marine Corp that they *needed* her out in Afghanistan had taken its toll on her as well as Joe's parents. Even the baby had been fractious almost to the point of being inconsolable.

It had almost broken Katie to leave Josie at the airport. It was only the fact that there was the faintest hope she could find and convince Joe that he needed help and bring him home that enabled her to go through security at the airport and board the aircraft on the first leg of her twenty-hour journey.

Since her arrival back at Base Independence, there had been no opportunity to try to find Joe. She had had to go through a tough assimilation, prove her merit and skill on the shooting range, and take part in drills under the heat of the Afghanistan sun. She still had no idea which squad he was with or where he was on the base. To make too many enquiries would have raised eyebrows and triggered far too much curiosity and suspicion.

Being back at the base had brought about a surge of memories concerning her last tour with Joe and it had taken all of her willpower to suppress the sadness she was feeling at her husband's duplicity, the lies and the fact that he had not trusted her enough to ask for help. He had had his orders, his deployment papers and had mentioned nothing.

Now here she was, attending a briefing for her first patrol as a CTM with her new squad and she was nervous. Five days out in the desert with men that she barely knew and who she believed — if past experiences were anything to go by — might not appreciate having a woman with them, was extremely daunting.

She had spent the last month and a half getting herself as fit as she could by weightlifting, running and dieting. She could now hump a fifty-pound pack along with the best of them and they were going to be surprised...and so was Joe when she eventually ran into him.

She was quite happily going to kick him where it hurt the most — husband or not — before flinging herself into his arms and kissing him breathless. He deserved everything that was coming to him.

Glancing at her watch, Katie saw that time was ticking on and she needed to get to the briefing. Clutching her warning order — WARNO — advising her of the upcoming patrol and containing all pertinent information about it in a sweaty hand, Katie stiffened her shoulders, tilted her chin, and walked in through the double doors of the prefabricated building. Once inside, she hesitated.

There were butterflies having a field day in the pit of her stomach and she felt sick with nerves. Steeling herself, she walked slowly along the short, green-painted corridor until she heard voices coming from a room off to her right. Noting that it was where the briefing was to take place, she took a deep breath and stepped through the chocked-open doors into a room where approximately twenty male marines had already gathered.

As Katie appeared, conversation ceased immediately and every male head turned toward her. If she had been in a better frame of mind, she would have been amused at the varying expressions she saw on their faces — surprise, contempt and even some interest and admiration. However, she ignored the reaction and feigning indifference, turned to the front of the briefing room and froze in stunned horror, a sinking feeling in the pit of her stomach telling her that her situation was about to become far more complicated than it already was.

Sergeant Louis Eastman was staring at her with an astonished expression on his face. Beside him, bending over to rest a helmet on a pack was another marine who did not bother to look up as Katie entered.

There was a long silence as Katie's and the sergeant's gazes locked. She watched as his eyes narrowed imperceptibly then he shook his head slightly. Katie stood straight — almost to attention — her chin tilted defiantly in the air.

Sergeant Eastman cleared his throat. "Yes, soldier?"

"Corporal Anderson reporting for duty, Sergeant," Katie answered. "I'm the new CTM." She had not missed hearing the cold unfriendliness in the sergeant's voice.

Within a few seconds of her finishing speaking, there was the loud thump of a helmet dropping to the floor and a muffled expletive in a very familiar voice.

Katie's head turned so fast toward the tall marine who had ignored her entrance, that she cricked her neck painfully. She watched aghast as her husband straightened up and spun round to stare at her.

She quickly took in the newly cropped, almost shorn hair, the deeply tanned face, and the muscles rippling in Joe's arms and chest. He looked every inch a tough, hardened marine but when she finally locked gazes with him, she felt ice creep through her veins.

She had never seen such a furious expression on a person's face before. The color of Joe's eyes was almost black, his features frozen into a grimace with lips thinned and a tic working alongside the scar tracing down his cheekbone. He stood like a rabbit frozen in the glare of a car's headlights and stared at her as though she were an apparition. To those who might have been looking on, he appeared calm if a little pale but his fists — clenched tightly down at his sides — were white-knuckled.

On seeing the order advising him of the imminent arrival of his squad's new CTM, an alarm bell had rung in Joe's mind at noting the name and rank. Not believing that Katie might follow him out to Afghanistan, he had dismissed what he considered to be the impossible.

Now, he felt unnerved at the sight of her and uneasy at the fact that she was standing there with coldness in her green eyes and no warmth or delight at seeing him on her pretty face. *But what did I expect? Open loving arms?*

He knew without a doubt that he was in a deep pile of shit and that he had some fast talking to do. He recognized by the tilt of her chin that she was furious with him and the hurt he guessed she must be feeling had added fuel to that anger.

A part of him could not help but notice how beautiful she looked. Her hair was shorter and framed a tanned face that glowed with health and she had obviously been working out and had toned up considerably. She still had the power to arouse him and he reiterated to himself again that he was in trouble.

After what seemed like minutes, but were probably mere seconds, he said in a voice that sounded husky to his own ears, "Welcome aboard, Corporal. Take a seat and we'll get this briefing going."

He watched as Katie silently turned on her heel, making her way farther into the room to a chair at the end of the first row. He was fully aware that as she moved, all the marines watched her in silence. He noticed that she held a few of their stares until they turned away, then she sat down. She propped her weapon against the side of her chair, took out a small notebook and pen from a pocket on the sleeve of her combat shirt, then stared attentively forward at him, her face devoid of expression.

Joe, noticing the interested, speculative gazes of his men, ignored them and turned away, pulling down a screen with a large topographical map on it. As he turned back to face front, his eyes caught those of his sergeant.

Louis cocked an eyebrow at him as if to ask, *what the hell are you going to do now?*

Joe glared back, feeling disconcerted—an unfamiliar feeling for him—together with a simmering anger at the position in which Katie had placed him. Questions churned in his mind.

Where is our daughter? How did Katie manage to swing her deployment to Afghanistan? Moreover, what the fuck are both of us going to do about being in close proximity to each other on the base and out on patrol?

Conscious that he was wasting time and that his men were becoming restless at the delay, Joe attempted to dismiss the tumbling thoughts in his mind so that he could focus on the briefing.

"Our patrol will be in this area," he began, tracing a red outline on the map with a finger. He continued to speak for the next hour, explaining the mission objectives of the patrol, objective rally points—ORPs—

call signs, friendlies, and enemy hotspots, the marines making notes and scrawling co-ordinates on their maps.

Throughout the briefing, Joe found his gaze drifting now and again to where Katie was making her own notes. She appeared to be struggling to avoid his eyes whenever he looked at her.

Finally, he put his hands on his hips. "Okay, marines. Our call sign tonight will be Charlie. Our staging point is at the motor pool so report to Sergeant Eastman there at 2300 hours. Dismissed."

"Oorah, Staff Sergeant," responded the squad followed by a loud scraping of chairs and thud of boots as they all rose to their feet, picking up weapons and helmets and moving to leave.

Joe glanced once more in Katie's direction. One marine passed by her as she was getting to her feet, stopped and smiled. The young corporal moved nearer his wife, held out a hand and Joe overheard him say, "Dan Reed."

He saw the admiration on the young man's face and unable to stop himself from doing so, closely watched them speak.

Instantly angry and jealous, Joe gritted his teeth. He tried to tell himself that it was only one of his men introducing himself and he should be grateful that at least one member of the squad was making an overture of friendship toward her. He also had no right to expect her to consider his feelings after what he had done to her, but the smile that Katie had given the young marine once belonged solely to him.

Oblivious to his surroundings, Joe continued to watch the couple, unable to drag his eyes away from the evolving scene, berating himself for eavesdropping on their conversation but continuing to do so anyway.

He saw Katie was still smiling, albeit a small one, and shaking the proffered hand.

"Katie…Anderson," Joe heard her reply briefly.

As if he was watching a scene unfolding in a play, Joe heard another marine yell, "Come on, Danno. Drag yourself away, why don't you?"

"Yeah, yeah, butt out, shithead," Corporal Reed responded then said to Katie, "Anything you need, give me a shout."

"Thank you," Katie answered. "I'll do that."

Watching Corporal Reed as he walked away, Joe said to Katie in a hard, cold voice, "Corporal Anderson, stay behind."

He watched as she turned to glare at him then nodded. "Yes, Staff Sergeant," she replied and remained where she was, folding her arms.

Joe turned to Sergeant Eastman and with a gesture, indicated that he should leave. Louis Eastman glanced from Joe to Katie, shook his head, then walked out of the briefing room, closing the doors loudly behind him.

Katie waited for the blow up to occur, anger already welling up inside her. She refused to lower her eyes and raised her chin defiantly as Joe approached swiftly. She was startled when he reached her and grabbed her upper arms as though he was about to shake her. His voice sounded furious when he spoke.

"What the fucking hell are you doing here?" he asked. "Why couldn't you have just stayed away, Katie?"

Katie wrenched her arms free and took a step back. "Wouldn't you have just loved that?" she snapped, hurt at his words almost choking her. She could feel the heat mounting in her cheeks. "Who the hell do you think you are anyway?"

"I'm your husband," Joe answered, a cold sharpness edging into his voice.

Clenching her fists at her sides, Katie snapped back angrily, "No, Joe. You lost that privilege when you walked out on me and your daughter!"

As soon as she said the words, she instantly wished that she could retract them when a look of pain filled Joe's eyes.

For a moment, he appeared lost for words and lowered his head. He remained silent for a few seconds then raised his gaze to look at her.

"You don't understand..." he began.

"No, I *don't* understand, Joe," Katie rejoined, her voice trembling. "I don't understand at all because you never took the time to tell me. When I asked, you refused point blank to discuss anything with me."

Once she had started to voice her pain and hurt, there was no way she could stop or back down and she felt physically sick with the notion that their marriage was falling apart.

"You never gave me a chance," she continued. "You planned everything in secret. You lied to me then you just left me and Josie, even after..." Katie almost choked on the words. "Even after we made love on the grounds of the hotel at the Marine ball the night you left. You even said that you loved me. How could you do it, Joe? You kept everything locked up inside you. Your parents even tried to help you but you refused all our help."

She felt tears fill her eyes—helpless to prevent it from happening—and knew that she was about to cry. But if she started she would not be able to stop. She took a deep shuddering breath, trying to control herself and bit down hard on her lip. She was damned if she was going to cry in front of him.

Joe continued to stare at her in silence. He ignored her plea for an explanation and asked quietly, "What are you doing here, Katie? You left Josie. Where is she?"

"Oh, please. What the fuck do you care?" Katie spat sarcastically, anger overtaking her again at his refusal to answer her. She felt her heart breaking at the harsh, cruel way they were speaking to each other.

"Give me some credit for having as much intellect as you. She's safe and staying with your mum and dad. We talked at length and they agreed with what I was doing. What business is it of yours anyway?"

The muscles in Joe's jaw clenched, a sure sign that she was getting to him and he was becoming angry again.

"Well hell, Katie. Sorry for shitting on your parade but it *is* my business. However much you suddenly appear to hate the idea, we are still married so that still makes you my wife. That means this, sweetheart. You stay away from my men, you hear, because they sure as hell don't need any distractions from a pretty face. They have a *job* to do. I have a *job* to do and I'm gonna keep it that way."

Katie uttered a gasp of anger at the insinuation in his statement. "I hope you're not implying that I'm going to waste my time mucking around with your men. No, Joe. *You* stay off *my* case. Whether you like it or not, I'm here, so deal with it. If you don't like me talking to your men or them talking to me, again, bloody deal with it. In case you've conveniently forgotten, I have *my* career in the army as well with *my* job to do. I'll stay out of your way if you stay out of mine. I'll also obey *your* orders. Just don't make me a scapegoat for all the problems that you feel you need to resolve."

Again, she could not stop the sarcastic-sounding words she threw at him. With shoulders heaving, she finally lapsed into silence, staring at him and noticing that his body was now rigid with anger.

Joe put his hands on his hips. "Fucking A you'll obey my orders—to the letter, lady. I'll treat you the same way as I treat my men, and you'll carry out the same duties as well. You chose to come out here with some crap idea of being a heroine. So be it. Just don't expect to come running to me if you get your pretty ass tangled up in any problems. It's a long time for these men to be out in Afghanistan. You might find yourself with a few situations that you can't handle."

Katie stared at Joe. It was as though she were hearing a complete stranger and was astounded at the cruel way they were speaking to each other. She knew she had to get out of the room before she broke down. Her eyes brimming with tears she said in as steady a voice as she could manage, "Is that all, Staff Sergeant? Can I go now?"

Joe swallowed, nodding. "That's all, Corporal," he responded quietly. "Report to the motor pool at 2300 hours with full equipment."

Katie nodded silently and, retrieving her weapon, she stalked past her husband and slammed her way through the doors of the briefing room. For a second, she thought she heard Joe call out her name but continued walking—back ramrod straight and head held high—hopeful that she was showing nothing of the heartbreak that was almost tearing her apart. She was almost running when she reached the exit and rushed out of the building.

Once outside, she stopped in her tracks and lowered her head, hearing herself uttering soft, hurt-sounding sobs.

I can't believe what just happened. She wished she had never started this. She wanted to be back at home with

Josie, Maggie and Jack. However, it was too late. The damage had already begun.

Straightening her shoulders, she strode away from the USMC HQ back to the accommodation tents. She would spend her downtime getting her equipment ready and try to get a couple of hours of sleep before making her way to the motor pool. She had to get herself together and try to forget about the confrontation with Joe so that she could focus on her job.

* * * *

Back in the briefing room, Joe remained standing where Katie had left him — body tense, fists clenched on his hips, head bowed, taking deep breaths in an attempt to bring his anger under control.

He had no idea what had possessed Katie to volunteer for deployment back to Afghanistan, leaving their baby behind. He was furious at her arrival and not just for personal reasons. She was a distraction and not just to himself but to his men. Their close proximity and the hostility between them would create unforeseen difficulties and he now felt an enormous responsibility to keep her safe.

Joe shut his eyes tightly as if by closing them he could dismiss what had just occurred between himself and his wife. The cruel words they had spoken to each other still rang in his ears and for a second he thought of running after her and taking her in his arms. He immediately dismissed the thought, convinced that it would just make matters worse and, with Katie's stubbornness, would serve no purpose.

Suddenly aware that he needed to get moving, Joe turned to retrieve his rucksack. On catching sight of his helmet laying on the floor, he bent to retrieve it, missed on the first grab, and in sudden fury, managed to grasp the innocent item and hurl it with tremendous force at the wall. It hit with a resounding crack, fell to the floor and bounced, coming to rest at his feet, rocking slowly.

"Fuck!" Joe yelled. "Fuck! Fuck!"

* * * *

On reaching her new quarters, Katie ducked through the entrance and went inside. The female accommodation at Camp Roosevelt was a lot bigger than that at Camp Churchill. In the week she had been in country, she had made friends with the other women, her usual practice and an easy task for her, but it was a different set up from that on Camp Churchill.

The American women tended to be more laid-back, more vocal and Katie had noticed that there were cliques, which had never happened on her last deployment. The women were friendly enough but she found herself holding back from becoming too involved with them.

Now, on entering the tent she greeted those present before going to her bed space.

Tossing her helmet to the floor, she lifted up her medical pack and placed it on the bed. Opening it, she rechecked the medical supplies stored inside. When she was satisfied that all was in order, she placed it back on the floor before making sure that she had her basic field equipment in a small pouch on the front of her body armor. Again satisfied, she collected her shower kit from her locker and went out back to the shower tents. It was the last opportunity she would have to take a shower for five days. She would be lucky to even have the opportunity of having a wash on patrol and she was not looking forward to that.

Once she had taken a long hot shower, she went back into the tent to her bed and lay down on her sleeping bag to get some sleep. As soon as she closed her eyes, she remembered the argument between herself and Joe in the USMC HQ. She moaned silently, wishing she could take back some of the harsh words that she had thrown at him.

Thoughts rocketed around in her mind, making her sleepless and restless.

She loved him so much, what had possessed her to be so hurtful? He might even think that she hated him for what he had done and she had no way of retracting her words.

God. She was a wimp. He deserved everything he had gotten from her.

So, why do I feel so guilty?

Katie's emotions reeled backward and forward between love and hate.

She'd seen an obvious look of pain on his face. Why? She didn't understand. He had left her and Josie with no explanation and no warning. He deserved her anger and he deserved to be hurt. But—and there was a big one in all this—she still loved him.

No matter what he had done to her and their daughter, he was still her husband and he must have had his reasons for doing what he had, as cruel as those actions had been. She had put her life on the line in an attempt to find out his reasons and until she had discovered them, she had no right to judge.

Katie tossed and turned for a long time, wanting to sleep but her mind too chaotic, her emotions a tumbling, churning mess. Finally, still unused to the change in time zone, she dozed which led to a deeper sleep haunted with black, writhing shapes and mumbled argumentative words.

The alarm on Katie's watch woke her at 2200 hours. The tent was in semi-darkness, some of the women already asleep, others watching films on laptops, typing or listening with headphones to music on iPods.

Katie rose from her bed and began to dress for the patrol. Her uniform consisted of combat trousers and combat shirt, thick thermal cotton socks, combat boots, body armor, limb protectors and gloves. She clipped the pouch containing her personal role radio — PRR — to her front, put on the headset in its harness, combat helmet, then slid the last piece of her uniform — a white armband with a red cross on it — up her arm. She finally slung the heavy medical pack onto her back then picked up her weapon.

Once she was fully dressed, she felt hot and uncomfortable. It was going to be hell having to wear and carry enough equipment and supplies to double her weight but she would never complain and give her new squad the satisfaction of thinking that she couldn't cut it.

Katie saw that it was fast approaching 2230 hours. She had a long walk to the motor pool so decided that it might be advantageous for her to start out now. Not wanting to disturb those women already asleep, she quietly left the tent and went out into the night.

Once outside, she took a deep breath. It was a beautiful, hot night and quelling her nervousness, she felt a twinge of excitement as she looked up at the vast expanse of black, star-studded sky.

Chapter Six

Setting off, Katie walked away from the tents and turned onto the main Camp Roosevelt road leading to Camp Churchill. As usual, the base was a hive of activity, with torchlight flickering here and there as personnel made their way about the camp, the roar of aircraft engines and the whup-whup of helicopter rotor blades slapping at the air as they took off from the distant airfield. In the background, was the constant— almost comforting—thud of generators keeping the electricity going.

As Katie walked along briskly—boots kicking up clouds of shimmering dust and sand—she kept an eye on the time and eventually turned onto the long road leading to the motor pool, breathing easily and glad that she had made the effort to keep fit.

She was halfway along the road when she heard somebody call out from behind her. Startled that someone knew her, she stopped and turned around to see Corporal Dan Reed jogging toward her.

"Hey," he greeted, grinning at her as he reached her. "Need some company?"

Katie hesitated, aware that for her to turn up with a man would send Joe into a tailspin, but then she dismissed the thought.

So what? She was not about to isolate herself from anyone because Joe had said so and because he might not like it. He would have to deal with it.

"Yes, thanks," she replied and they both continued on with the walk toward the motor pool.

"So, where are you from?" Dan Reed asked.

Reluctant to answer or get into a conversation with the young corporal and reminding herself to be careful about what she did say, Katie replied, "I'm originally from the UK but due to family reasons I transferred from the British army to the US marines. I've lived in Virginia for the last year or so."

"Nice place," Corporal Reed responded.

Katie nodded. "It is. Where are you from?"

"Chicago," Corporal Reed answered. "My family is there."

Katie and was grateful when a few meters ahead, the glare of the security lights of the motor pool came into view, and there was no need for her to answer any further awkward questions. There was a milling group of marines and Joe and Sergeant Eastman were standing nearby. Taking a deep breath and preparing herself, she followed Corporal Reed across the road and joined the other members of the squad.

As she arrived, Joe gave her and the young corporal a hard, interrogative stare—as though he had been watching and waiting for her, his expression one of anger—then dismissed her and turn to continue to speak to his sergeant.

Turning away, Katie acknowledged some nodded greetings from a number of marines but noted that the majority of the men still ignored her. She guessed that they had never had a woman go out with them on patrol before or perhaps had never had a female member on their squad period, and they were both unsure of how to treat her and how to deal with her.

She mentally shrugged. *That's their problem. I'm here to do my job and to rescue my husband.*

Corporal Reed remained standing beside her as though he had labeled himself her protector. As nice as he was, Katie felt uncomfortable knowing that Joe was well aware of the young corporal's attention.

She watched as Joe turned to face them and stand motionless, hands on his hips, facial features taut and grim.

"Okay, marines, listen up."

The men instantly became silent and attentive, and Katie received the impression that her new squad respected her husband and paid attention to what he had to say. She felt an unwanted surge of pride at Joe's obvious leadership skills and a pang of loss that this man might not be hers anymore.

"The patrol is a go, no abort given. An LMTV will be here in twenty, so go for a smoke, get your equipment sorted out, and collect your rations and water from over there." Joe pointed to a Land Rover idling nearby. "Okay, get moving."

As he finished speaking, he turned his back on Katie to speak to Sergeant Eastman, and Katie—glaring at him—wondered if he could feel the daggers that she was throwing at him with her gaze.

Corporal Reed said, "The Old Man seems a bit uptight tonight."

It wasn't a direct question but a statement, and Katie—startled at the comment—shrugged.

"I don't know the man so I can't say," she lied, hopefully convincingly.

"Yeah," Corporal Reed continued. "He's usually a pretty okay guy, jokes and mucks around with us guys, but tonight he looks like he's pretty pissed at something."

Everyone waited in line at the Land Rover to collect extra meals ready-to-eat — MREs — and bottles of water, placing the rations into already bulging packs. As they were finishing, a truck pulled up beside them, engine rumbling.

"All right, let's move!" Sergeant Eastman yelled. "Load up!"

Keeping her eyes away from Joe — determined not to glance in his direction — Katie joined the line of men at the rear of the two-and-a-half-ton truck who were waiting for the tailgate to be unlocked and lowered. Each marine then hoisted himself onboard. Corporal Reed was directly in front of Katie and once he had climbed aboard, he turned and reached down a helping hand to her.

Grateful for the assistance, Katie put the toe of her boot into a metal groove at the base of the tailgate and, grasping Dan's arm, boosted herself up into the interior of the truck. As she was halfway up, she felt a hand on her backside give her a final push. It startled her and once she was inside, she spun round to see who it had been and saw that it was Joe.

Flushing slightly, she said stiltedly, "Thank you, Staff Sergeant," and sat down on the bench beside Corporal Reed, turning her gaze away from her husband and pretending to study the interior of the truck. She rested her weapon across her thighs, leaning forward slightly — as were all the others — their rucksacks too heavy and cumbersome to allow anyone to settle back comfortably against the canvas sides of the truck.

Joe and Sergeant Eastman were the last to board, seating themselves directly opposite Katie, which made her feel distinctly uncomfortable. Turning her gaze away, she heard the tailgate crash into place and lock, the engine rev up, and the truck pulled away, making the short journey to the first checkpoint. Katie glanced out of the back of the truck at the receding lights of the base and felt her nerves kick in.

This was her first patrol with her new squad and she was not embarrassed to admit to herself that she was terrified. There had been no time to get to know the other marines—to *bond* and gain their trust and respect—of paramount importance if they were to watch each other's backs in a hostile situation. She tried to remind herself how she had dealt with her fears when involved in firefights on her last deployment. The situation was no different now and she needed to clamp down on any panic before it began to get out of control.

She turned away from her view of the receding base, glanced down at her hands clenched tightly on her weapon then looked up, straight into Joe's eyes as he stared at her intently from beneath his helmet, head lowered so that no one could see where his gaze was directed.

Katie lowered her own head and stared back—unflinching. Their eyes locked for long seconds—neither backing down—until the truck jolted to a halt at the first checkpoint and Katie eventually turned away. As she did so, a marine seated two persons away from her suddenly asked in a sarcastic tone, "You gonna be able to save our lives, Corporal Anderson?"

As the truck rumbled off again, Katie leaned forward, angered at the question, and focused her gaze on the man who had asked it. As she glared at him, he began to look distinctly uncomfortable.

"If you get shot or blown up you'll find out won't you?" Katie eventually responded and her answer caused a few chuckles to come from some of the other men.

Joe immediately went on the attack at the unfortunate marine.

"Shut that crap up, Murray. I hear you say something like that again, I'll kick your ass from here to Hell. Understand me?"

"Yes, Staff Sergeant," Lance Corporal Murray replied, and turned to study his weapon rather intently.

Joe glared at the unfortunate marine for a few more seconds, then he turned his head to look out of the back of the truck.

She wondered — with some confusion — what her husband's game was. It was as though he was two different people. On the one hand there was the man who had callously walked out on her and his daughter, who had planned the whole thing in secret over a period of weeks, probably almost as soon as he had returned from Afghanistan because he would have had to obtain his orders and have his flights arranged, all without a word to his family.

The other Joe was the one that she remembered, the one who couldn't keep his eyes off her and who defended her at the slightest provocation. She didn't understand him but promised herself that eventually she would get him alone and find out if it was the last thing she did.

The truck stopped abruptly at the second checkpoint and Joe got to his feet.

"All right. Five until we offload. You know what to do. Let's get to it."

Everybody began to move, the men tightening the straps of combat helmets, readying their weapons and shifting equipment into positions that were more comfortable. The truck rumbled on for a few more minutes then came to a stop. The driver jumped down, jogged around to the back of the truck, unlocked and dropped the tailgate.

By virtue of her seated position at the rear of the truck, Katie was the first to stand up and jump down, landing lightly on the hard, dusty ground. She immediately raised her assault rifle and moved off the road onto the baked, hard-packed sand and dust of the desert. She faced outward, socking the buttstock of her rifle into her shoulder, and sighting along it, watching for any movement or telltale sign that there was someone in the area that shouldn't be there.

Her surroundings felt surreal, as though at any moment, the protective bubble encircling her would burst, and she would be plummeted into a harsh reality.

The desert was silent. No wind soughed through the hidden rocks and no animals scurried for shelter at the appearance of the intruders into their territory. It was hot, the air laden as it always was with dust, and Katie found it difficult to breathe, as though her lungs could not draw in enough oxygen to sustain them.

A full moon hung in all its bloated cream glory against the black backdrop of the night sky, surrounded by a powdered sugar coating of stars. The glow threw shards of luminous light on the surrounding terrain, creating areas of shifting shadows and blackness among the rocks that would keep the squad on an even higher level of alert than usual.

In the open, the moonlight made parts of the desert sand look like ice and created a hazard of exposure and vulnerability. If there were any insurgents waiting for them in the pockets of darkness, Charlie squad would not be able to see them.

Katie hastily pulled down her night-vision goggles, her surroundings instantly bathed in green and she waited patiently. Behind her, she could hear the continuous muffled thud of boots as the men landed on the road and moved to their patrol positions. As they formed up, she found her own place behind the pointman and coverman and silence fell.

As she waited, from out of the corner of her eye, Katie noticed Joe come to stand beside her. She was as aware of his presence as ever and with a sad feeling realized that no matter how he had treated her and Josie she still loved him — would always love him.

He glanced at her and Katie's heart suddenly skipped a beat. She had not meant for any of this to happen and now felt desperately guilty and uncomfortable at putting Joe in the dangerous situation where he had a job to do and her presence might make things very difficult for him. He needed his full concentration and she promised herself that she wouldn't create any problems for him or endanger the lives of him or his men.

She turned her head to return his stare and nodded in an attempt to reassure him, expecting him to return the gesture but he stared at her for a few seconds more before turning to face front without responding, leaving her feeling slightly hurt.

I can't blame him, though. After the things I said to him following the briefing, I'm surprised he's even taking the time to look at me.

Joe raised a hand and gestured for the patrol to move off.

Katie tried to concentrate on the task at hand. She followed the man directly in front of her, placing her feet slowly and carefully where he had already trodden, trying not to raise any dust clouds which could alert the enemy — if they were nearby — to the patrol's presence, also ever mindful that somewhere on the dark ground could be the small piles of rocks or disturbed earth that denoted the presence of mines or improvised explosive devices — IEDs.

* * * *

Charlie patrol marched for two hours unimpeded, keeping to a well-used path running parallel to the road until finally it turned and moved off into the desert, the terrain becoming more uneven and rock strewn.

Katie, unused to marching long distances over such rough ground with a heavy equipment, found herself sweating freely even though the temperature had dropped a few degrees and some of the stifling heat had abated. The webbing on her shoulders began to dig in and chafe and she felt tired, uncomfortable and thirsty.

At 0200 hours, they came on a small semi-circular outcrop of rock and Joe raised a hand, bringing the men to a halt. Katie heard his voice come quietly over her PRR.

"All on this net...take fifteen."

The squad broke formation to rest, leaning or crouching against the rocks. Embers of cigarettes glowed in the dark, and the men took on water or chewed on some of the rock-hard candy bars that came with the MREs.

Raising her night-vision goggles, Katie found her own space against a boulder a few meters distant from the others. Struggling out of her pack, she let it drop to the ground then took off her helmet, wiping a gloved hand across her forehead. Bending over, she placed the helmet on the ground, extracted a bottle of water and took a long gulp, sighing blissfully as the coolness of it ran down her throat. She was just screwing the top back on when someone tapped her on the shoulder.

Turning, Katie saw a marine standing behind her, shuffling awkwardly from one foot to the other.

"Yes?" she enquired.

"My buddy has a bad foot and needs you to take a look at it," the man explained quickly.

"All right," Katie said, noticing that the man's eyes did not meet hers and with some amusement realized that he was nervous. "Let me just get my equipment."

She once again picked up her medical rucksack, slinging it over her shoulder then turned to the marine.

"Lead on," she said and took one pace when Joe's voice from close by said, "Helmet, Corporal."

Katie stopped dead, stared at Joe through the murky darkness for a second then said, "Sorry, Staff Sergeant," and grabbing her helmet from the ground, slammed it onto her head in a fit of temper, mumbling a swear word beneath her breath. She knew full well she had just acted like a petulant child and that Joe had probably heard her insulting remark quite clearly.

Ignoring him, Katie followed the marine along the line of reclining men until she reached the last man. A young private sitting on the ground had removed his boot and sock and glanced up at her as she stopped near him. A wary look appeared on his face at the sight of her and she sighed inwardly. Anyone would think that she was about to do something illegal to him.

After removing her helmet, Katie placed it and her pack on the ground then crouched down beside him.

"What's the problem, Private?" she asked.

The young marine cleared his throat, tried to speak but couldn't.

Katie's mouth twitched in a smile. "Come on," she coaxed gently. "I don't bite. I know what I'm doing. Trust me."

The man sitting next to the private jabbed him in the ribs and hissed something at him.

The young marine's mouth opened and closed like a fish, then finding his voice he replied, "I've a blister on my heel, Corporal. It's busted open and fucking hurts like hell."

"All right," Katie responded, her tone brisk. "Mind if I take a look?"

The private shrugged and thrust his foot almost in her face, nearly causing her to over-balance.

Flinching slightly and feeling a little put out, Katie removed her combat gloves and delved into the depths of the little pouch on the front of her body armor. She unerringly found a pair of nitrile gloves and while pulling them on, moved a little to the right so she was better able to see the injured limb and said to anyone within earshot, "Can someone shine some light here, please?"

Within seconds, someone had aimed a red torch beam at the outthrust foot, and Katie, grasping the limb, turned the ankle slightly and was able to see a large open blister with blood drying around the outside on the young marine's heel.

"How long have you had this, Private? It's not a fresh blister."

She glanced at him and saw that he had the grace to look sheepish.

"Coupla days," he answered sounding evasive.

Katie shook her head. "You should have had this seen to before we left base. Never mind that now. Where are your socks?"

The private produced thick combat socks and Katie felt them.

"Soaking wet," she said. "Right. This is what you need to do. Put on fresh socks, which I'll dust inside with medicated powder. I'm not going to clean the blister because it's clotting nicely and that will stop any further bleeding. I'm going to put on an antibiotic dressing and a second padded dressing on top of that. It will prevent the wound from rubbing against your boot and making it worse. I'll dust your boot as well. Is that acceptable to you?" She glanced at the marine, waiting for a response.

The private nodded and retrieved a spare pair of socks which he handed to Katie. She took out a small plastic sheet and the requisite medical supplies that she would need. She sprinkled medicated powder into each sock and laid them down. Then placing an antibiotic impregnated dressing on the raw area of skin and patting it gently into place she folded up a large square of gauze, laid it on the wound, and wrapped surgical tape around both the ankle and foot to keep it there. She then dusted both the private's feet with medicated powder.

"Okay, Private, you can put your boots and socks back on now."

Katie returned her equipment to her pack then addressed the young marine.

"Now," she continued, "you need to keep your socks and feet as dry as possible. That dressing will not stay on forever so I'll check on it in a few hours. If you have any swelling or the pain increases before then, shout."

She smiled at the private, grabbed her equipment, then straightened up.

The marine nodded. "Yes, ma'am." And she heard a new respect in his tone.

Katie turned and began to walk back along the line of marines, noticing that she was now receiving nods from a few more of the men. It was as she was walking back to where she had intended to rest that she heard, "Corporal Anderson, a word."

Chapter Seven

Sighing, Katie turned. Joe was standing a few meters away with his arms folded. She walked briskly over to him.

"Yes, Staff Sergeant," she responded coolly.

"What's the problem with Private Bradley, Corporal?" he asked.

He was studying her face intently and flinched, an expression of guilt crossing his face. She wondered what he had seen in hers, and she was fed up with the charade she and Joe were playing with each other. She was tired and hot—the temperature was unbearable even this late at night—and she was unhappy at the hostility flaring between them.

She moved so that her back was toward the rest of the squad and brushed back her damp curly hair. Trying to keep her voice steady, she replied wearily, "Private Bradley has an open blister on his ankle, Staff Sergeant. I've treated it but I suspect he's had it for a few days and ignored it. I've told him that I'll need to review it in a few hours but to report to me if it gets any worse in the meantime."

Joe glanced over to where Private Bradley was sitting then turned his gaze back to Katie.

"Is he going to be okay to continue on with the patrol?" he asked.

Katie nodded. "He should be as long as we keep on top of the pain and prevent infection," she answered, forcing her tone to remain completely neutral, reflecting none of her inner turmoil.

Joe nodded. "Okay, that's fine," he said then murmured, "Are you okay, Katie?"

Katie hesitated, unsure of to how to reply and finally she decided simply to speak the truth.

"No, I'm not all right," she answered quietly. "I don't think I'll ever be all right again."

Her voice trembled slightly and she swallowed, biting her lip to stop herself from crying. "I'm not as tough as I thought I was."

Joe pushed his helmet to the back of his head then wiped his face.

"God, Katie," he said quietly. "I'm sorry about all this. I should've known you'd not sit back and take it — that you'd end up out here. I really have made a fucking mess of things."

Katie nodded, not letting him off the hook. "Yes, you have."

She stared at her husband, determined not to allow any of her true feelings to show. Nonetheless, a small amount of warmth stole into Joe's eyes and he even smiled slightly.

"Stubborn, aren't you?"

Katie raised her chin. "You should know," she replied, her tone sounding a little short and chilly.

Joe hesitated. "Look. We'll talk soon and I'll try to explain why I did what I did. It might not make sense but you deserve that much. And…" But he didn't complete the sentence.

Katie nodded then turned away. "That's fine, Staff Sergeant. Thank you."

Joe watched his wife walk away.

"By the way, Corporal, when you're on the move, wear your helmet at all times," he added.

Katie glanced back over her shoulder. "Yes, Staff Sergeant," she said again, her voice stilted and because nobody could see, she gave him the slightest of smiles.

Joe read some of the hurt at his dishonesty and betrayal evident in the wistful look. His heart ached watching the slim, straight back and the proud, stubborn way she held her head as Katie walked away. He wished he could turn back time.

However, would I have done things any differently?

"Shit," he murmured to himself.

He thought not.

Katie made her way back to the shelter of the rocks and was about to sit down when she heard Joe give the order to move out. She sighed and murmured, "Damn!"

She had not had a chance to rest, let alone eat, and she was tired. Fastening the chinstrap of her helmet, she again heaved her rucksack onto her back, grimacing at its weight. She knew that the patrol was going to have to quicken its pace because dawn was only a few hours away and they had to reach their first ORP, an unused compound already searched and used by previous patrols, by first light. It was another ten clicks away and they needed to set up operations and while away the daylight hours before continuing the patrol that night to reach their primary destination by the early hours of day two.

The squad formed up and moved out from the low outcrop of rock onto the exposed desert. The temperature had dropped even further and a slight breeze had sprung up, a fact Katie was thankful for as it chilled the perspiration on her face and went some way to cooling her body.

The patrol moved onward carefully and in silence, resting every so often. Dawn broke with the moon seeming to drown in a flaming aurora of colors on the horizon and at last, Joe raised a hand and everyone dropped to a knee—still alert—aiming their weapons out to either side.

Katie heard Joe speak into his radio from her position close by. After he had done so, four marines joined him then after a few minutes' conversation he gestured for the rest of the squad to gather around him.

"Okay," he said quietly. "I'm taking a small recon team to scout out the ORP. Sergeant Eastman, set up security and keep your eyes peeled. The terries could have come back and planted more IEDs. Get a couple of guys out using the mine detectors but I don't want them any farther out than the perimeter."

Sergeant Eastman nodded and moved away to comply with the order while Joe and the four marines moved off.

With dawn spreading across the sky, the outline of their figures was barely visible, moving among the rocks and boulders that formed the surrounding landscape. She tried not to stare but it was hard to watch her husband disappear into what could be enemy territory.

She and Charlie patrol waited patiently, some of the men taking the opportunity to drink water, eat rations or smoke cigarettes. There was some murmured talking but for the most part, everyone remained silent.

A short time later, the pointman reported someone approaching and their level of alertness increased. Katie sighed with relief when Joe and his men re-appeared in their midst where he reported that the area was clear and they could proceed.

The patrol formed up again, the men eager to reach the compound and settle down for sleep. Katie was equally as eager. Her feet burned in her boots and her legs and shoulders ached. All she wanted to do was lie down on her pad and sleep for a few hours undisturbed.

The squad finally neared the compound, a ragged oval, sand-colored sprawl of small buildings with an inner courtyard, the whole separated and encircled by a narrow no-man's land and a three-meter high outer wall of dried mud.

Hunkered down at a safe distance, Joe ordered two two-man teams, each equipped with a handheld standoff mine detection system—HSTAMIDS—to sweep the perimeter of the compound, including all windows and doors.

Other patrols had used the compound for downtime, but insurgents were notorious for re-infiltrating cleared buildings and replacing mines and IEDs already removed. Katie was relieved Joe was not about to take any chances.

The squad waited out in the open, tension elevated because of its exposure, an opportunity for the insurgents to mount an ambush. They pointed all weapons out onto the surrounding terrain with everyone focused intently on the heat-hazed distance.

At last, after several minutes, a transmission received via the PRRs gave the all-clear then the squad entered the compound to begin to set up headquarters within the central courtyard.

As the huge orange sun began to heave itself into the sky and the temperature began to rise, the marines began building makeshift shelters from various pieces of scattered wood lying on the ground and lengths of material each man had brought with him for that purpose.

With shelters erected and sleeping pads put down on the hard dusty ground, the men crawled beneath them, most appearing to immediately fall asleep. Others remained on watch in the hot sunlight, having climbed up onto a ledge halfway up the three-meter outer perimeter wall, leaning against it to watch for any sign of the enemy.

Katie had not thought to bring anything with her to build her own shelter — the idea had never crossed her mind — so she proceeded to search the compound until she came across a building where the roof jutted out slightly, creating shadow on the ground that would shield her from the sun.

Pulling a sleeping pad from her rucksack, she spread it out on the hard ground. Taking off her helmet, she dragged her pack to where she could use it to rest her head then she put on her sunglasses and finally took a long drink of water. She glanced around the courtyard, searching for Joe.

Some of the men were staring at her with what she could only interpret as interest — much as any man would stare at a woman — and she felt uncomfortable. This was turning out to be a little more difficult than she had anticipated as she was obviously getting attention from the men.

She saw Dan Reed seated on the ground beneath a shaded lean-to at the opposite end of the compound talking to Joe, Sergeant Eastman and two other marines. They were studying maps and making notes,

Joe occasionally talking into the handset of a portable radio. Dan raised a hand when he noticed Katie watching and she nodded in response.

Having drunk her fill and feeling exhausted, she made sure her weapon and helmet were within reach so that she could grab them quickly and she laid down.

It was so good to relax. Even though the temperature had risen some degrees and the ground beneath her sleeping pad was hard, she was so tired that these small issues were trivial in comparison to how exhausted and drained she felt. Turning on her side, she watched Joe until eventually, before a few minutes had passed, her eyes grew heavy and she drifted into a much-needed sleep.

* * * *

Only a brief time later, someone shook Katie's shoulder and called her name. She moaned in response and opened eyes that felt dry and full of grit. She was disoriented at first because someone had erected a lean-to over her after she'd fallen asleep and now she was lying in shade. Outside the canopy, it was broad daylight, the sun glaring in its intensity.

She saw Corporal Reed crouched beside her. Groggily, she sat up.

"What's the problem?" she asked, rubbing at her eyes, feeling sweat dampening her face and her T-shirt clinging to her upper torso. She grimaced and would have given anything to be able to have a long, cool shower.

"My buddy is sick," Dan Reed announced, rising to his feet. "You need to come and take a look at him."

"Okay," Katie replied, now wide-awake. She crawled out from beneath the lean-to and scrambled to her feet. "Lead me to him. What's wrong?"

Remembering the order from Joe to wear her helmet, she grabbed it, put it on then picked up her pack and weapon, slinging one over each shoulder. Together, she and Dan walked hurriedly away from her lean-to.

"What's wrong with him?" she asked again.

Dan tipped his helmet back. "He developed a pain in his gut about an hour ago and started throwing up. The pain has gotten worse and now he's real sick."

Katie glanced at her companion, concerned. "Does he have a fever?" she asked.

"I don't know, Corporal. I haven't asked him."

"Okay, I'll check him over," Katie said, keeping anxious thoughts about what might be wrong with the marine to herself.

Corporal Reed led her across the compound toward a lean-to where a young man was lying down. As Katie drew close, she saw him tossing his head from side-to-side and heard him moaning softly. His hand was lying protectively across his stomach.

Katie ducked beneath the makeshift canopy and knelt down beside the marine. Turning to Corporal Reed, she asked, "What's his name?"

"Lance Corporal Bob Harris," he answered.

Turning back to the sick man, Katie placed a hand on his shoulder and gently shook it.

"Bob. Bob, can you hear me? Can you open your eyes for me?"

Lance Corporal Bob Harris groaned again but obeyed. His eyes were glazed and full of pain, his face glistening with sweat and very white.

She placed the back of her wrist on his forehead, noting he was extremely hot, then she picked up the hand that wasn't lying on his stomach, felt his pulse and discovered it was fast and slightly shallow.

She didn't like where this was going at all.

"Bob, I'm sorry but I need to ask you a couple of questions. Try to answer them for me. Have you been vomiting?"

The lance corporal nodded, "Yes," he replied, his voice sounding hoarse.

"Did the pain start in the middle of your stomach and move to the right low down?" Katie asked.

The lance corporal nodded again and Katie's concern increased. She was almost positive that the marine had appendicitis and she had nothing in her medical equipment to treat it. She turned to Corporal Reed.

"I'm sure it's appendicitis," she said. "I need to speak to the Staff Sergeant and radio the base. I want you to sit beside him and keep him company. Talk to him and try to keep him awake."

She crawled outside the lean-to and Corporal Reed took her place. Katie searched the compound for Joe and eventually found him in the exact same place she had seen him before. She began to jog toward him, ignoring the slow whistles from some of the men as they watched her as she passed.

Joe watched her approach and as she reached him, he frowned. "What's the problem, Corporal?" he asked.

"I need to talk to you, Staff Sergeant," Katie answered, her tone cool. "It's an emergency."

"Sure," Joe agreed, setting down his map and getting to his feet. He gestured for them to move a short distance away from the others. Turning to her he asked, "What's up?"

Keeping her voice low, Katie explained, "I believe Lance Corporal Harris has acute appendicitis. I need to radio the base to get some advice on what to give him to relieve the pain and we'll need to order up a medevac."

"I see," Joe said. "You're sure it's appendicitis?"

Katie nodded. "He has all the symptoms, and they're typical of acute onset," she replied. "It could be dangerous if we don't move quickly on this."

Joe nodded, "Okay. Let's get you through to the base. You can use the radio."

He went back to the main transmitter, took the handset from one of the marines and spoke into it, announcing the base call sign. He listened then handed it to Katie.

"You're through to the CTH, Sergeant Webster."

Katie glanced at him and saw the warning look in his eyes. She nodded slightly, accepting that she had to be careful about what she said, pressed the button on the side of the handset and spoke, "Sergeant Webster?" then released the button.

"Corporal Walker, is that you?" the sergeant asked, using her maiden name which Katie did not correct, wanting to avoid any complicated questions that might arise. Even though the sergeant was probably extremely curious as to why she was back in Afghanistan with a US marine squad, it was not evident in his tone.

"Yes, Sergeant," Katie replied, hurriedly. "I need some urgent advice from one of the surgeons. Is anyone around?"

Sergeant Webster's voice was business-like when he replied. "Good to hear your voice again, Corporal Walker. Wait one and I'll get Major Macintyre."

Katie waited impatiently, glancing over her shoulder to where the sick man was lying under the lean-to. A few minutes later, a Scottish voice spoke from the receiver.

"Corporal Walker. How are you? Couldn't stay away from us then?" it asked.

"Fine thank you, sir," Katie replied, feeling slightly impatient. "Sir, I have an emergency here. I believe a young marine has appendicitis. I need some advice on what to give him and we need a medevac out here."

"Right-o," the officer said, his tone brisk. "What are the symptoms?"

Katie quickly listed the symptoms and waited for confirmation of the diagnosis.

"Good call, Corporal," Major Macintyre finally said. "But you canna give the wee laddie anything for the pain, I'm afraid, until we assess him here at the CTH. While I think your diagnosis is perfectly correct, it could be other conditions as well. You can only make him as comfortable as possible. No liquids, but try to keep his temperature down. I'll order up a medevac and get it out to you as soon as possible. Pass me back to Staff Sergeant Anderson and I'll get the necessary co-ordinates from him."

Katie turned to Joe and handed him the handset. "Major Macintyre wants to speak to you. I need to get back to my patient."

Joe took the handset and Katie hurried back to the young marine. There was a small crowd gathering and Corporal Reed joined her outside the lean-to.

"How is he?" Katie asked, stooping slightly to see into the shelter.

Corporal Reed tipped his helmet back on his head and wiped the sweat from his face.

"He's in a lot of pain," he answered. "Can't you give him something, ma'am?"

Katie shook her head. The sun beating down onto the back of her neck had started to make her feel slightly dizzy.

"I can't," she answered. "He's not allowed to have anything, including water. It will make him vomit. Any painkiller will simply depress his central nervous system. A medevac will be here soon."

She crouched down, moved awkwardly beneath the canopy and studied the young marine. His pallor was marked and sweat beaded his forehead, trickling down the sides of his face to soak the sleeping pad. Katie placed the back of her wrist on his skin and winced at the heat of fever coming from his body.

"Corporal Reed," she called and Dan Reed crouched down to peer in at her. "Can you ask the Staff Sergeant if he could come over here?"

Corporal Reed nodded and rose to his feet. Katie opened up her pack and removed a sealed combat casualty blanket, ripping open the plastic packaging with her teeth, shaking it out and spreading it over the patient. She then took out a bottle of water and a square of gauze. Turning back to her patient, she shook him gently.

"Bob? Bob, can you hear me?"

Lance Corporal Harris' eyelids fluttered and he moaned but remained unresponsive. Katie put her hand beneath the blanket and placed two fingers on his limp wrist to check his pulse. It was still fast and fainter than before. Katie tried to quell her rising anxiety.

She saw a pair of dusty boots and combat-clad legs appear then Joe crouched down. Without acknowledging his presence, preoccupied with attending to the sick man, Katie opened the water bottle, poured some of the liquid onto the gauze and gently wiped the sweat from the lance corporal's face. Once she had finished, she looked at Joe.

"How are you doing?" he asked softly, his voice barely above a whisper.

Katie wiped the perspiration from her forehead. "I'm all right," she answered, suddenly wishing that he would take her in his arms.

Joe gazed at her then cleared his throat. "How's he doing? Problem?" he asked.

"Yes. His condition is deteriorating rapidly," Katie responded. "He's unresponsive and we need that medevac as soon as possible."

"It'll be here in about ten minutes. I've sent some men outside to lay down some smoke and escort the CTT here. It won't be long. Hang in there."

Katie nodded and turned back to her patient. Pouring more liquid onto the gauze, she bathed the lance corporal's face again.

"I have to get back," Joe continued and Katie barely acknowledged him.

Joe rose to his feet, straightened then ducked down again. "The medevac is almost here. They made better time than I thought they would," he announced.

Katie, hearing the distant sound of a helicopter, knew the combat trauma flight—CTF—was close.

"Good," she replied, feeling a surge of relief that help was almost with them.

Joe hurried away and Katie turned back to the young marine, noting he was completely comatose now. She could hear the approaching helicopter's engines getting louder until, as it reached almost overhead, the noise became deafening. It then moved away a short distance and she heard the noise from the rotor blades change pitch as it came in to land. She crawled out from beneath the lean-to to wait for the combat trauma team—CTT—to arrive.

A short time later, three members of the medical team appeared, jogging through a ragged hole in the courtyard wall, carrying a stretcher and an Emergency

Medical Carrier—EMC—and accompanied by two marines. The group approached the lean-to where Katie was standing.

She briefly explained the symptoms to the CTT doctor then stood back to allow them access to the sick lance corporal. She had done her bit for him and could do no more.

Waiting patiently while the CTT tended to their casualty, checking his vital signs and stabilizing him, Katie wanted desperately to go to Joe but had to stand and watch—with some relief—as they lifted her patient gently onto a stretcher. The patient couldn't have been an easy weight to carry but two of the CTT each took an end of the stretcher and, with the assistance of the two marine escorts, moved off, heading back to the Chinook helicopter.

Katie watched the group disappear out of sight and wiped a hand across her damp face. She was perspiring heavily and the flies were driving her mad. The courtyard walls reflected the sun blindingly, the rays bouncing off them with searing brightness. She was desperate for sleep and, grabbing her equipment, she started back toward the lean-to and her sleeping pad.

Chapter Eight

"Corporal Anderson."

Joe's voice sounded from behind her, and with a sinking feeling that sleep was drifting farther and farther out of reach, Katie stopped in her tracks and turned to face her husband.

Despite her tiredness and the almost stupefying heat, she couldn't help but feel warmth flood her body at the sight of him. Clad in combat trousers and T-shirt, body armor and dusty combat boots and helmet, he was the epitome of a strong, tough marine. Even the stubble on his jaw line and the scar on his face added an element of danger to his persona and Katie felt angry with herself for the strong surge of emotions that he always seemed to trigger in her.

She had an idea that no matter what situation they both found themselves in—even if it was hostile—his closeness would always stir up unwanted images of making love with him.

She longed to run into his arms, have them close around her and hold her tight, have his mouth come down on hers, feel the sexual frisson that never failed to burn between them. She loved him so much.

Now she faced him, trying hard to quench the longing she had for him and the wish to regain what they'd had.

"Yes, Staff Sergeant," she said, forcing a coldness into her tone.

Joe saw the look of longing on his wife's face and understood what she was feeling. Katie always wore her heart on her sleeve, try as she might to hide it, and her brilliant green eyes were expressive and showed every emotion.

He also saw the conflicting emotions of pain and grief that he was causing her and he shifted uncomfortably, wanting to take her in his arms but fully aware that an Afghanistan compound was not the time or the place and that until the situation was resolved between them, there might never be another.

He cleared his throat. "Corporal, I need to show you around the perimeter, give you a clear idea of where the men are positioned in case anyone is injured in an attack. It will save you time and energy searching for them."

Katie nodded, "Fine, Staff Sergeant, just let me put my gear down."

Joe nodded, watching her as she continued to make her way to the lean-to. He had heard the appreciative whistles and ribald remarks made by his men as she had jogged across the courtyard to tell him of his sick man and while he knew that it was 'men being men', the jealousy ate away at his insides, made stronger by the fact that he was unable to put them all straight on the fact that she was his and it was 'look but not touch' – and maybe not even look.

When Katie rejoined him, he led the way across the courtyard to the jagged, debris-strewn hole in the wall where it appeared as though an explosion had occurred, demolishing part of it.

They moved through the gap out onto the wide, uneven path that encircled the entire compound, a no-man's land separating the wall of the courtyard from the perimeter. Joe calmly and quietly explained, as he would have done to any new member of his squad, the positions of his men and in what direction the enemy could possibly come from.

They'd walked for about ten minutes when Joe suddenly stopped at a heavy wooden door set in the inner wall and turned to her.

Katie glanced at him, her eyebrows raised questioningly.

"I want to show you one of the rooms that the Taliban used for hiding weapons and explosive caches," he explained, responding to her silent query. "The room has already been searched and any evidence taken away."

Finishing the brief explanation, he pushed on the door and, with some effort, managed to open it a meter or so before it wedged into the dry earth. Without a further word, he slid his way through the narrow opening and beckoned Katie to follow him.

Once inside the white-walled room with its dry mud and sand floor, sunlight filtering in through two glassless windows looking on to the inner courtyard, Joe dropped the veneer of a staff sergeant carrying out one of his responsibilities and turned to face Katie.

"Are you all right?" he asked.

Katie shrugged. "I'm okay I suppose," she replied.

Joe could detect no emotion in her voice and he stood in silence for a minute or two staring at her, trying to gauge her mood and feeling uneasy at the way she was looking at him. Suddenly feeling a surge of impatience, he took two paces toward her.

"Katie…" he began.

He stopped dead in his tracks as Katie held up a hand, palm outward in a warding off gesture.

"What the hell do you think you're doing, Joe?" she asked.

She was still staring at him, her green gaze holding a sharp and evaluating expression.

At her question, Joe instantly felt the increasingly familiar flare of irritation begin to churn in his stomach and behind that a faint feeling of panic.

Don't do this, Katie, he thought. *Don't push me. Leave things alone. You don't want to go there.*

He felt the muscles in his body tense. "What do you mean?" he asked and cringed when he detected the ice-cold tones of his voice.

"You know exactly what I mean. Don't play games with me, Joe. I'm too tired at the moment to take any bullshit, even from you. I want some answers about what the hell you're doing back out here," Katie responded.

Joe stared at her and remained silent.

Please, Katie…I love you, but please…

"Let me remind you of what you've done, as you seem to be finding it so difficult to remember," Katie continued. "We are married and we have a daughter. You have parents who are sitting at home worrying themselves sick at your absence. You left in the middle of the night, leaving us letters saying that you had issues that needed resolving. You told us nothing, Joe. You made plans, and you slunk away without so much as a goodbye. What the hell is so bloody important that you could do all that?"

Joe felt as though a metal vice was encircling his head and tightening, millimeter by millimeter. His chest ached with tension and he suddenly found that he was struggling to draw air into his lungs. The irritation was quickly turning to anger, the flight or fight mode—inherent in every human—taking hold as he was backed into a corner.

You'll regret it, Katie, a small voice, almost pathetic in its pleading, sounded inside his mind. *I'll come out fighting.*

"I told you once and I'll tell you again," he suddenly answered. "I don't want to talk about it. Cut me some fucking slack, will you?"

"You're going to have to talk about it, Joe," Katie continued. "Do you honestly think that what you've done or what you're doing is…normal?"

Katie's voice was softer but Joe's arms dropped down to his sides, fists clenching as the embers of his anger flared brighter and rational thought began to dissipate, replaced by the only defense mechanism he had left in the throes of his emotional conflict.

He gritted his teeth. "There's nothing wrong with me, Katie," he snapped. "I have to sort this out myself. I don't need you banging on at me all the time because you're just making things fucking worse."

As he finished speaking, Joe realized he had involuntarily thrust his head forward in an aggressive manner.

Back off, Katie. For God's sake, back off. Back off!

"You need to get a grip, Joe," Katie continued. "What are the issues that you say need resolving? Is it something that happened to you when you were captured?"

Agitated with her questioning, Joe put his clenched fists on his hips.

I need to get out of here. Get out of here. Out. Of. Here.

The words sounded like gibberish in his mind.

"Leave it," he suddenly ordered, a helpless feeling that he was losing his grip on reality nearly overwhelming him.

"Joe..." Katie began again.

Without being able to stop himself, Joe lunged toward her.

"I said, fucking *leave it*, for God's sake!"

He heard the words with the small part of him that was still rational, spat with such hate and fury that he was suddenly terrified.

Joe stopped his forward motion as Katie staggered back from him. He saw the terrified expression on her face and realized what he had been about to do. A sick feeling of horror welled up inside him.

Fucking hell. I was about to...

"Oh, my God, Katie," he began.

At that moment, someone came through the open door and as both Katie and Joe turned, they saw Sergeant Eastman standing staring at them, a look of annoyance on his face.

"What the fuck is going on here?" he asked, looking from one to the other.

Both Katie and Joe remained silent and when he received no response, Louis Eastman strode toward them. He turned to Joe.

"This has got to stop, buddy," he announced. "You are seriously jeopardizing this patrol and the men. Whatever the issues you have between you, get them sorted or fucking put them away until we get back to base. I shit you not, pal. I *will* get you taken back. You are showing all the signs of not being able to command crap. Give me one more excuse to call base and get you removed."

At his final word, a heavy silence fell and he and Joe glared at each other, any friendship they had once shared forgotten at that moment.

Joe shifted his gaze to Katie then back to his sergeant.

"Fuck you both," he spat, his tone full of hostility. He thrust his way past his sergeant, and strode toward the door, forcing his way through the gap and disappearing.

At his leaving, Katie felt her legs sag and she staggered, feeling tired, both mentally and physically. Putting a trembling hand to her forehead she murmured, "Jesus."

Sergeant Eastman touched her arm. "Are you okay, Katie?" he asked.

"Yes, but for a minute before you arrived…"

Katie's voice trailed off into silence, then she said with a note of desperation in her voice, "Louis, I'm so afraid that something is wrong with Joe."

Louis' hand dropped from her arm and he nodded. "Yeah, I know," he agreed. "I noticed there was something up as soon as he arrived in country."

"Do you have any idea what happened to him when he was captured?" Katie asked hopefully.

Louis shook his head. "Nope. He's never spoken about it. Whenever I brought the subject up? Well, he turned into someone I didn't recognize."

"Oh, God," Katie murmured. "I don't know what to do. He needs medical treatment—counseling—but I can't make him listen. Louis, aside from the death of his men, I think something terrible happened to *him* on his last deployment and I think he might have developed PTSD as a result. I'm not a doctor or a psychiatrist but I did a course on it during my training so I know a little about it. He has all the signs and symptoms. He won't admit it though and until he does, nobody can help him. I think he's out here to seek some sort of revenge."

Louis Eastman nodded in agreement. "My thoughts also," he replied. "God help him. Look, I'm not about to report the poor son of a bitch. All I can do is keep an eye on him and cover up his mistakes. By rights, I should get on the radio and get him medevacked out of here as a psych case, but I can't do it. He's a good man, one of the best, and at the moment, the men respect and trust him. He's just gone off the rails a bit. You need to do your bit, Katie. Keep an eye on him, and try to get him to open up about what happened. That'll be the first step in making him admit that something is wrong. Now, we have to get out of here otherwise there'll be more shit happening."

Katie nodded, feeling only slightly relieved that Louis Eastman was going to help her with Joe. She followed him out of the room into the harsh sunlight and, in silence, they retraced the path back to the hole in the wall and through that into the courtyard.

Sergeant Eastman went to join Joe, leaving Katie to go to her lean-to, to retrieve her pack. Collecting it, she turned to search the area, found who she was looking for and walked over to Private Bradley. He glanced up as she approached and gave her a small nod.

"Private Bradley," she began, "how's your foot?"

"It's doing good, ma'am," the young marine answered.

"I need to take another look at it," Katie continued briskly. "Remove your boot and sock."

She knelt down on the hard ground and while Private Bradley unlaced his boot, removed it then took off his sock, Katie withdrew the medical equipment she would need and laid it out on the ground. As before, she dusted the private's sock then turned her attention to the injury. She unwound the surgical tape, removed the dressing and lifted the marine's ankle so that she could take a good look at the blister. It was healing well and Katie glanced at the young man.

"It's looking good," she commented. "Now, you still need to keep a dressing on it. If it hurts, I'll pad out your heel again so it won't rub. Is that all right?"

Private Bradley nodded and Katie proceeded to put another clean dressing on the blister, padding it out slightly, and she wound a length of surgical tape around the ankle. Having finished, she got to her feet.

"Remember," she reiterated. "If you get any pain when walking, come and see me." She offered him a smile then turned and walked slowly back to her lean-to.

Almost asleep on her feet, she slipped the strap of her weapon from her shoulder and propped it against the side of the building. Sinking to her knees, she crawled beneath the canopy. It was only marginally cooler there but she didn't care.

By now, feeling completely exhausted, lightheaded and sick, she took off her helmet and lay down, resting her head on her pack. It didn't matter that parts of it dug into the skin of her face and were full of lumps and bumps. Groaning softly, she closed her eyes and instantly fell asleep.

Chapter Nine

An hour later, following the briefing, Joe decided that it was time to check out the men on watch at the wall and obtain updated reports from them. He also secretly wanted to see Katie. He had watched her lie down and was aware that she was probably asleep because she hadn't moved in some time.

He walked up the compound and as he neared Katie's lean-to, he slowed his pace, still glancing around the courtyard as though he was inspecting security. His anger had gone as quickly as it had occurred, leaving behind an emptiness inside him that made him feel physically sick.

His gaze turned to where Katie was lying and he felt a terrible longing to crawl beneath the awning and cuddle up beside her. He saw the peaceful look on her face, the way she had curled into fetal position and her usual sleeping pose with one small fist thrust underneath her chin.

A part of him wanted to say to hell with the obsession that was eating away at him, to admit to Katie that he felt as if the anger burning inside was spiraling out of control and he would end up doing something he would regret. He was confused—felt as though elements of his life were disintegrating and he could do nothing about it.

Subconsciously, he knew that his wife and Sergeant Eastman were perfectly correct in their assumption that the death of his men and his capture on his last tour had deeply disturbed him and that he did indeed require psychiatric counseling, but to admit to this consciously and to actively seek help went totally against his pride and dignity.

Joe continued walking on past his wife, struggling to strengthen his resolve and draw on his remaining inner strength to continue—rightly or wrongly—with what he had come out to Afghanistan to do.

Hastening through the gap in the wall out to where members of his squad were keeping watch, he then climbed up onto the ledge and walked along it, talking to his men, making sure that they had ample water and ammunition. At one point, he stopped and leaned on the rough wall, raising his small binoculars to look out onto the panoramic vista of the desert in all its dry, arid glory.

The sun was beginning to lower itself on the horizon now that it was early afternoon, the harsh, searing rays decreasing in intensity. The sky was pale gold, turning the ochre and dun colors of the barren desert into a shifting miasma of warm tones. Lone scrubby trees stood outlined against the horizon and there was a marked absence of human and animal movement, a good thing for Charlie patrol.

Finishing his survey of the area, Joe lowered his binoculars and rested his elbows on the wall. Still looking out onto the surrounding landscape, his mind again drifted away from the task at hand and he saw

Katie's face superimposed on the golden horizon like a mirage.

He tipped his helmet back onto his head and closed his eyes, feeling weary and heartsick. For the first time in his life, he felt isolated and alone—set apart from his men—some of whom he had known on past tours, particularly Louis Eastman. He felt like everything that he had ever been as a man was crumbling into ruins.

Joe opened his eyes, bowed his head and focused on the pitted and gouged sand-colored stone of the wall. He ached inside for his wife—for what they had once had. He grieved for himself and for his dead men and he blamed himself entirely for their deaths.

Joe ran a hand across his face. The trigger in his mind—something that prevented him from delving too deeply into his memories—snapped the mental shield back into place, and he was catapulted back from his thoughts to reality. Jumping down from the wall, he continued his methodical and intensive patrol around the outer wall until once more he arrived back at the gap leading into the courtyard.

Stepping through, he began to walk back to where he had left his equipment, wanting to check in with the base for any change in Intel. As he approached Katie's lean-to, he saw that she was awake and that she wasn't alone. He recognized Corporal Reed as her companion and noted that the two were conversing intently. He saw that Katie was smiling at the young marine and Joe was instantly and irrationally angry and jealous. Eyes narrowing, lips thinning, he paced past his wife, his stride like that of a lion who has sighted prey. As he passed, his gaze never strayed from Katie, interpreting the expression on her face as interest and animation for the young marine with her.

He noticed Corporal Reed glance at him and nod a greeting, which he ignored, then saw Katie finally notice him. The look of undisguised fear on her face made him experience a rush of satisfaction, which turned quickly into a sick guilt at the content of his thoughts.

What the fuck is happening to me?

Joe hastily turned his face away and went on his way back to the radio, trying to get a grip on his feelings. He felt as though he was drowning – suffocating with anger and confusion. To someone who had always had his life strictly under control and had never suffered any conflict while out in the field, his situation now felt like a nightmare.

Reaching the radio, he sat down and picked up the handset. Pressing the button, he uttered his call sign and password, then spoke at length with his squad leader at Base Independence. After receiving the updated Intel, he ended the transmission and turned to Sergeant Eastman.

For a moment, the two men stared at each other then Joe said casually, "Son of a bitch! We've got trouble."

Louis Eastman raised a questioning eyebrow. "Yeah?" he responded just as casually.

"Intel says that the satcam has spotted hostiles heading our way – about a dozen of 'em. They're a couple of clicks away for now but we need to move out damn quick. Our orders are to avoid contact. Our primary mission objective remains the main compound. Get the men grouped for a briefing, Sergeant."

Sergeant Eastman nodded, got up and strode away. Reaching the center of the compound, he stopped.

"Okay, gentlemen and lady," he said in a loud voice, glancing in Katie's direction. "Get yourselves over to the Staff Sergeant for a briefing." At his final word he turned on his heel and went back to join Joe.

Those marines who had been sleeping—now having been nudged awake—rose to their feet, darting surreptitious, puzzled glances at each other. Normal procedure was a briefing directly before they moved out on the evening patrol, not some hours preceding it. They realized that it now appeared there might be a problem looming on the horizon.

Chapter Ten

Joe frowned at the meandering approach of the marines.

"Move your asses," he yelled out, his voice hard. "This isn't a goddamn fucking tea party."

The men responded to the order by quickening their pace and gathered around their staff sergeant and sergeant in a half circle, serious and quiet now as they sensed that they were about to be told something that they might not want to hear. Katie and Dan joined the end of the group and waited patiently.

Joe cleared his throat, immediately aware of Katie's presence and avoiding looking directly at her, said, "Okay, Marines. Intel has advised that a group of hostiles are heading this way…"

Swear words and questions immediately hurtled his way, effectively cutting off the rest of his sentence.

"Let's have some hush for the Staff Sergeant, shall we?" Sergeant Eastman shouted and there was immediate silence.

"The enemy is about two clicks distant—for now," Joe continued. "We've been ordered to avoid contact with them. Our primary objective remains the Taliban compound. We need to move out...now. After leaving this compound, the patrol will be out in the open with no cover except a tree line a click from here. In other words, ladies, we will have our balls hanging out in the wind. We will move in teams of four, the first team as fire team one. You've done it before so you know the drill. Corporal Anderson."

He turned to face Katie, finally focusing his gaze on her.

"You'll move out in the second group of four, fire team two."

He turned back to the squad. "I cannot emphasize enough the need to stay focused, stay alert. Concentrate on where you put your feet and on your fields of fire. The EOD team has already been here on a sweep and IEDs and mines have been removed or detonated but that doesn't mean to say that the bastards haven't been back and planted more. You have ten to get your equipment ready and your asses over to that hole in the wall. Get moving, Marines. Dismissed."

"Oorah, Staff Sergeant."

The marines chanted the inevitable mantra and scattered back to their shelters. Without wasting any time, they quickly began packing away their equipment.

Katie hurried back to her own lean-to, swiftly began to fold it away, then checked to make sure that the most important items in her rucksack were easily accessible.

She hastily retied her boots then thrust her arms through her pack's webbing. Lastly she pulled on her combat gloves then picked up her weapon.

She felt the weariness in her body, the heat, stiffness and aches and pains in her legs that, despite her rigorous training sessions, were unused to the long march and the rough sleeping arrangements. She was ashamed to admit to herself that she was finding the patrol tough but she wouldn't give up or let something beat her, so she straightened her shoulders and moved off to join the rest of the squad, making their way toward the mustering point.

As she reached the men, Katie became aware of the heavy silence among them. There was a marked absence of the loud jocular humor that had been prevalent for the better part of the day. About to enter into a situation where their lives depended on their focus and concentration, each man had taken on a different persona. The hot air seemed to tingle with emotional pressure and an aura of restlessness indicated each marine was clearly aware of what could happen once they left the confines of the compound but they were eager to get moving, despite the danger.

The soldiers gripped and re-gripped weapons with their gloved hands. They shrugged and writhed their shoulders to ease the fit of body armor, and there were quiet bursts of static from PRRs as they were checked to make sure the radios were operational.

Katie stood alone — uneasy and nervous — shifting her booted feet aimlessly in the sandy dust. The tension among the squad was palpable about her and she grasped her weapon more tightly in response. The palms of her hands were damp inside her gloves.

She was grateful when Dan came to stand by her side. She glanced at him and smiled slightly, noting that his face was gleaming with sweat, his dark eyes intense and even his usually humorous expression was now one of sharp concentration.

Dan returned her smile briefly, nodded then asked quietly, "You okay?"

Katie nodded and answered with a voice that shook slightly. "Nervous."

The corporal glanced around him and nodded. "Yeah, you and everyone else," he replied.

At that moment, Joe and Louis Eastman joined them.

"Okay," Joe announced in a low but carrying voice. "Listen up. Group up into two formations, one-meter between each man, fire team one to move out first. Go as fast but as carefully as you can. Any questions?"

There were shakes of heads and the men moved restlessly, eager to get on with the mission.

"Okay, let's move out."

As they exited through the jagged hole in the courtyard wall, the marines formed up into two lines as ordered and began to move off along the pathway between the perimeter wall and the inner. They moved silently, with only the faint sound of boots thudding on the hard ground and occasionally a dull clink as a weapon came into contact with body armor.

After a few minutes, an opening appeared in the outer perimeter wall and the line of marines walking along that route stopped before exposing themselves in the opening. The second line of marines walking the inner wall moved to stand hidden at the farthest edge of the opening.

Joe made his way to the front, closest to the exit, then crouched down to minimize his exposure to enemy eyes and with binoculars up, peered out so that he could survey the landscape. He was not happy with what he saw.

The terrain between the compound and the tree line was flat with no cover whatsoever. The only protection they might have when reaching it, was lost in a rippling heat-haze, making spotting movement of hostiles difficult. He scanned the land slowly from left to right but all appeared silent and deserted.

Joe turned to the squad and, making a hand signal that ordered them to go down on one knee around him, said quietly, "Listen up. It's all clear. Fire team one, you're up. The rest of you stand by with weapons live so we can give them cover. Fire team two, wait five then go."

Every man nodded and the first four men edged toward the opening in the wall. There was no hesitation as they stepped out from its protection and began to walk slowly and carefully away from the rest of the squad, weapons raised, eyes intently surveying their surroundings for hostiles and the ground for signs of IEDs, anti-personnel mines or explosives of any kind.

"Okay," began Joe. "Fire team two, you're up."

As he spoke, his eyes met Katie's. He did not want to send his wife out to cross that bit of land—every fiber in his body was screaming in protest—but there was nothing he could do about it. To single her out for special treatment would be to cause all kinds of damage to the morale of his squad.

Taking a last glance at fire team one that was now some fifty-meters away, he said, "Fire team two, move..."

There was the sudden nightmarish sound of a single gunshot, which cut off the rest of his sentence. It whip-cracked out of the tree line in front of them, shattering the silence.

Out of the corner of his eye, he saw Katie jump, obviously startled, then he watched in horrified silence as one of the leading marines in fire team one seemed to stumble, attempted to remain upright then fell backward onto the hard ground, shockingly still. The three remaining marines threw themselves flat onto their stomachs, bringing their rifles up, facing toward the tree line, waiting for orders.

"Fuck!" Joe exclaimed vehemently.

The marines behind the compound walls ducked but shouldered their weapons and shuffled closer to the opening.

Joe thumbed his radio. "Sitrep?" he demanded harshly.

There was a burst of static then a voice replied, "Douglas is down, Staff Sergeant. He ain't moving. We need the medic out here."

For brief seconds, Katie felt her heart leap into her mouth. A sudden terror threatened to choke her and she wanted to scream out a fear-filled refusal to expose herself to an onslaught of bullets from an unseen enemy intent on destroying her. Then her courage, commitment and dedication to her job suddenly overpowered the fear, squashing it into submission, and she turned to look at Joe, waiting for him to give her orders to go to the casualty. She was astonished to see him shaking his head.

"Copy that. Negative. Bring Douglas back in."

There was an instant response. "No can do, Staff Sergeant. I can see from here that he's bleeding like all hell. The medic needs to get her ass out here and check him out before he can be moved."

Beginning to feel annoyed, perceiving her position as the squad's CTM being disregarded for purely personal reasons, Katie shuffled forward nearer Joe.

"Staff Sergeant," she began.

Joe appeared to ignore her attempts to get his attention.

"*Staff Sergeant Anderson.*"

Katie spoke loudly and firmly and moving her weapon, managed to knock his, which was lying across his knee. Joe's head whipped around and she was shocked to see how pale his face had become, teeth clenched together, jaw rigid.

Enunciating the words slowly and clearly, Katie said, "I need to get out to the casualty, Staff Sergeant. He needs emergency medical treatment."

As she spoke, there came a volley of gunfire from the tree line and she and the surrounding marines flinched and ducked. There was a ferocious fusillade of return fire from fire team one as they lay flat on the ground beyond the compound then everything fell silent again.

Katie stiffened her back, keeping her eyes on Joe, waiting impatiently for him to make his decision.

Sensing that the men about her were glancing at each other, questioning looks on their faces as though they were becoming aware of what might be going on between her husband and herself, she snapped, "Staff Sergeant! We're wasting time. I have never disobeyed an order in my army career but I will now."

Her foremost thought was to get to the wounded marine who — as the seconds and minutes of the golden hour ticked by — could be dying or worse...was already dead.

Long, interminable seconds passed and eventually Joe nodded. Thumbing his PRR, he said in a harsh voice, "One of you, get your ass back here. The medic is coming out and needs some cover."

Katie watched as the man closest to the compound began to slowly and carefully edge his way backward on his stomach. Immediately when he began to move there was further gunfire from the trees which raised small fountains of dust and sand close by him, causing him to stop his movements immediately. Once he had done so, the shooting ceased.

When there were no more bullets ricocheting around him, he began to move again. There was another single gunshot but this time the two remaining members of fire team one returned fire and the marine began to swiftly crawl backward again, head low, trying to keep himself as flat to the ground as possible, clouds of dust partially obscuring his movements.

Joe turned to the rest of the squad. "Right, fire team two, wait out. The rest of you men go with Sergeant Eastman and get up on the ledge. I want covering fire on that tree line. If anything moves, knock it out. Let's go."

As Sergeant Eastman moved away at a run with the rest of the marines, Joe remained crouched down, surveying the men out on the terrain. The marine who was on his way back to collect Katie had almost reached the outer wall and in a few minutes, he was up onto his feet and running to join them. Once inside, he leaned against the inner wall, panting.

"How's Douglas?" Joe asked him.

Eventually regaining his breath, the marine answered, "I think he's screwed. He hasn't moved since he went down."

"All right." Joe turned to Katie. "You stay low, Corporal. Kowoski will cover you all the way and the others will when you reach them. Get Douglas stabilized then all of you get back here pronto."

Katie nodded. She leaned her rifle against the wall, took off her combat gloves and straightened up, taking out a pair of nitrile gloves and putting them on in preparation for dealing with the casualty. She moved closer to the opening in the wall but remained out of sight of the enemy.

Turning to the marine who had now regained his breath, Joe asked, "Ready, Corporal?"

The marine nodded and Joe turned back to Katie. "Okay, Corporal, get ready to move out."

For a split second, their eyes met then her escort edged in front of Katie to the opening.

"Okay, ma'am. We need to move fast and slicker than shit off a hot plate," he said. "Keep beside me until we get to my buddies then we'll cover you while you sort out 'ole Douglas there. Try and watch where you put your feet and you shout real loud when he's ready to be moved."

Chapter Eleven

Katie nodded again, for the moment speechless with fear, then the corporal was jogging out of the compound, and she instantly moved by his side.

At their appearance, there was an immediate response from the tree line ahead of them. The bullets were wide of the mark but still close enough to cause the fear inside Katie to bloom into something bordering on terror. She picked up speed, her boots thudding on the hard ground, her heavy pack pounding her back.

The air was stifling. The blood pounded in her ears and her breath hissed harshly through her clenched teeth. Sweat bloomed beneath her helmet and began to trickle down her face, the salty wetness running into her eyes and stinging them, blinding her so that she could hardly see in what direction she was running.

Gunfire now began to come in continuous bursts from the enemy in front of them and the marines lined up along the compound wall returned fire. The noise was tremendous but all Katie could hear was her own guttural panting and someone screaming, "Go," from behind her.

Ohmygod, ohmygod, ohmygod!

The words in her mind seemed to pound in rhythm with her boots slamming on the hard ground and she wanted to scream, to let out a howl of primal terror.

The distance between herself and the downed marine seemed endless. A heat-haze shimmered all around her, rippling the air. Dust from her own and the corporal's thudding boots obscured her vision as it plumed up from the dry ground in clouds. She stumbled and almost went down but the corporal beside her grabbed her arm and dragged her upward, almost wrenching her shoulder from its socket.

"Move it!" Katie heard him scream and she lengthened her stride, realizing that she was alone, the corporal having thrown himself to the ground. She almost leaped the last few feet to the casualty, landing with a jarring thump alongside him, pain blooming along the left side of her body as her hip and rib cage slammed into the hard ground. Dust billowed up around her, and she choked and spat gritty sand and sticky clods.

Breathing harshly, she shrugged out of her med pack, throwing it down beside her. Turning to carry out an assessment of the injured man, she was horrified to see that a vast pool of dark blood had seeped into the sand and dust beneath the still figure.

"Douglas, can your hear me?" she shouted, shaking the man's arm vigorously, raising herself up slightly so that she could look at the marine's face. As she took in the pallor of his skin, her heart sank.

The man was unconscious and when she placed her hand briefly against the skin of his hand, it was cold and clammy. She pressed nerveless fingers against his carotid pulse and felt a faint, weak hammering. The man was still alive but barely.

"Fuck!" she spat out.

Moving quickly, keeping her head as low as possible without impeding her actions, she carried out a skillful full-body assessment, searching for injuries that might not be obvious externally. She finally tore open the man's body armor and after wrenching up the saturated bloody combat shirt and T-shirt, the wound immediately became obvious.

The lower right side of the man's stomach was nothing but a huge, deep penetrating wound in which Katie could see part of the internal organs and gleaming wet tissue and muscle. Blood was still pumping in slow thick spurts from deep within the wound and she immediately knew that there was possible damage to the main femoral artery. The man was bleeding out. He needed a blood transfusion immediately and to be medevacked out of the field back to the combat trauma hospital—CTH.

Katie immediately pressed the button on her PRR and said forcefully, "Staff Sergeant, we have a Cat A— urgent status here. We need an immediate medevac. He's bleeding out."

Seconds later, Joe answered, "Roger that, Corporal. Medevac is on its way. Estimated time of arrival is— three zero—thirty minutes."

Katie pressed her PRR again. "I don't think we have thirty minutes, Staff Sergeant."

Knowing that time was of the essence to prevent the rapid onset of shock, Katie began pulling out packets of hemostatic dressings and gauze, scattering them on the ground beside her. With hands that trembled only slightly, she tore open their protective coverings and combining the two in layers four deep, laid them in an overlapping pattern on the wound, completely covering it. Pressing down hard on the thick pad and gently using her fingertips to press it into the depths of the wound, she hoped that the blood clotting agent on the dressings would reduce, or even completely stop, the flow from the damaged artery.

Still keeping pressure on the wound, she used her teeth and free hand to tear off long strips of surgical tape to fasten the pad to the skin of the stomach. Maintaining the pressure for the rest of the two minutes for the clotting agent to start to work, with her other hand she pulled out an abdominal tourniquet. Shaking the long body strap loose, she laid the pressure pad across the man's stomach, and quickly pulling her left hand free, released pressure on the wound.

She flung the strap to the far side of the man's body and after struggling for a minute or two, managed to rock him from side to side, thrusting her arm beneath the still body and grasping the end of the strap, pulling it back toward her. She was then able to draw the end up and over to fasten it together on top of the pressure pad, rather like the seat belt on an aircraft.

She then unclipped a small pump bulb attached to the pad, similar to that used with an old-fashioned blood pressure cuff, and began to pump it quickly. A small gauge set into the tourniquet showed a dial in increments of ten pounds and precious seconds passed before she was satisfied that the pad was tight enough around the man's body when the gauge showed it steady at eighty pounds.

She stared intently at the dressings, watching the dark crimson stain, which had already seeped through, to see if it had continued to increase in size. It did not, confirmation that the arterial bleed appeared to have stopped with the aid of the anticoagulant impregnated in the hemostatic dressings and tourniquet.

Almost not daring to breathe, praying silently that the bleeding would remain completely stopped, Katie took out a plastic packet containing an unused single eighteen-gauge large bore catheter. Tearing it open, she tapped the back of the man's hand and managed to raise a vein just long enough to insert the sharp needle into it.

Happy to see the red of arterial blood back up into the needle, she screwed on the tubing then attached a five-hundred mil bag of plasma volume expander. She finally taped the tubing to the man's arm to prevent it from tearing out of its entry point and turned the drip to push the fluid into the casualty's body to replace the blood loss and reduce the chance of shock. Additional fluids such as antibiotics and lactate ringers would have to wait until she could treat her patient under less hostile conditions. Placing the bag of fluid onto the casualty's chest, she spoke into her PRR and said, "All on this net...ready."

Numb with shock and exhaustion, without a clear thought or plan in her mind but unable to waste time waiting for someone to come and assist her, Katie awkwardly shrugged into her pack. Mindful to grab the injured man's weapon so that the enemy could not get their hands on it, she rose to a low crouch, grasped the injured marine's webbing with her right hand and reaching out with her left hand, she dug her fingers into the hard ground, clawing with them to wrench her body forward, stopping to drag the casualty along behind her.

Repeatedly she pulled herself forward then dragged the casualty, aware of the pain at the edges of her mind as sharp stones and abrasive sand ripped at and rubbed the skin raw on her fingers and the palm of her hand and the solid weight of the man tore at her shoulder muscles. It was almost beyond her capabilities, but inch by inch, gritting her teeth, barely aware of the tears trickling down her face, her mindset reduced to a small tunnel of determination and perseverance, she continued on.

A cloud of dust surrounded her, blinding and choking. The pain in her right shoulder screamed for rest and a seething mass of pain clenched her hands.

When she felt as though she couldn't go on, she suddenly felt the dead weight of the man ease and the speed of her movements increased as one of the marines of fire team one joined her in dragging his injured colleague along the ground. The remaining two members, together with the marines lined up along the perimeter wall, opened fire in an attempt to keep the heads of the enemy in the tree line down, preventing them from firing back.

The marine assisting Katie raised his head. "On my shout we get up and drag this guy back to the compound like fucking hot shit," he shouted. "You grab the IV and we move like our asses are on fire."

Katie nodded and took the IV bag from the casualty's stomach. The second she had done so, her companion screamed, "Go."

Without thinking, her mind mercifully blanking out any thought of how exposed she was, Katie straightened up and ran as fast as she could—hand gripping the injured man's webbing. The resultant tilted weight tore at her right shoulder muscles. Air whistled in and out of her lungs. Sweat stung in her eyes. Her mouth was dry.

She couldn't contemplate the damage that the rough handling might be doing to the abdominal wound suffered by the marine so she focused her attention on the nearing compound wall, pulling the man behind her with what little strength she had left.

Ten meters from the perimeter wall, the fourth member of fire team one joined them and two more marines came running out from the opening. They pushed Katie aside roughly then took the injured man from her, ripping the IV bag from her grasp, lifting him up then ran the rest of the way to the safety of the compound.

Katie stumbled the last few meters through the gap, exhausted and completely out of breath, tripped and slammed against the inner wall of the compound. She found herself pressed against the rough powdery stone, her right cheek resting against the wall, unable to get her breath, feeling nausea roil through her stomach.

Turning, she leaned her back against the solid surface, her whole body trembling violently, pumped full as it was with adrenaline but weak with exhaustion and for brief seconds she felt as though she were going to pass out. She stood spread-eagled, eyes closed, willing the sparkling blackness behind her eyelids to dissipate and the fog in her brain to clear.

Someone thrust an open water bottle into her hand and she took a large mouthful, closing her eyes and swallowing the cool liquid. Finally, regulating her breathing, she opened her eyes and glanced straight into Joe's face. He was staring at her intently with such a look of horror in his gaze that she would remember it for as long as she lived.

"In one piece, Corporal Anderson?" he asked, appearing to enunciate each word carefully with an intense control. Katie believed that she was the only one who heard the slight tremble in his voice as he asked the question of her.

Katie nodded. "In one piece, Staff Sergeant," she replied softly, but there was no time to reassure him any further.

Glancing around, she searched frantically for the casualty and saw that he was lying on the ground surrounded by the marines who had escorted her back to the compound. She straightened up from the wall, tried to force words from her dry throat and found that she couldn't, coughed then shouted, "Get him into the courtyard."

He was lifted into the air and borne away at a run. Katie's shouted order had gone unquestioned. As she followed them at a jog, forcing her tired body to co-operate, she turned and shouted over her shoulder, "We need that medevac *now*."

Entering the courtyard, Katie made her way to where the casualty was lying on a sleeping pad. She flung her rucksack to the ground, dragged off her helmet and, letting it fall, dropped to her knees beside it.

Without raising her head, she ordered, "I need some help here. Somebody get his combat shirt and T-shirt out of the way to give me a clean area to work in."

While she pulled out medical supplies, scattering them on the dry ground, one of the marines who had helped carry the man into the courtyard knelt down on the opposite side to Katie and quickly began to push the man's uniform up his chest as far as it would comfortably go.

The injured man remained unmoving and unresponsive. Conscious of precious time ticking on, Katie checked the pad of hemostatic dressings that she had applied earlier and saw with a sense of desperation that dark red blood saturated them, the life-giving fluid still oozing slowly and steadily out of the young man.

"Oh, fuck!" Katie exclaimed.

With no time to think or finesse her movements, she quickly took out another bag of plasma volume expander and deftly changed the bag, which was now almost empty. She then took out a bottle of sterile water, a bottle of dry powdered antibiotics, a small plastic container and a sealed hypodermic syringe. Ripping open the sealed packet containing the syringe, she proceeded to draw up ten ccs of water and squirted it into the small plastic container. She then sprinkled the required amount of antibiotic powder into it, quickly mixing the contents together to form a white milky substance. Drawing up all of the liquid into the syringe, she injected a small amount into the hub of the catheter at its entry point into the casualty's hand, waited for two minutes, then injected some more. After waiting for the final amount of time to pass, she injected the last of the mixture.

She then flushed the hub site through with sterile water and, extracting a bag of lactate ringers, proceeded to connect it to a shorter length of tubing before attaching it to the hub. She turned the drip to a fast flow-through then pumped up the abdominal tourniquet until the gauge showed one-hundred pounds.

Once again, Katie placed her fingers against the man's carotid pulse, noting that it was still rapid and faint. As she did so, the marine suddenly opened his eyes and looked directly at her.

Her heart thundering painfully with compassion, she watched as a tear trickled from the corner of the man's eye. He tried to speak, failed, then finally, after licking his dry, cracked lips whispered, "Don't let me die."

Katie took his cold hand and squeezed it gently.

"Hey, Marine," she replied soothingly. "Nobody is going to die. You're going to be fine. Stay with me. Keep talking to me. Come on. You can do it."

She became aware of the sound of boots coming up behind her and one of the marines with her asked quietly of the new arrival, "What's going on out there?"

"The Staff Sergeant has ordered an air strike. Gonna blow the bastards to hell," came the quiet reply from behind Katie. "How's old Dougie doing?"

There was no answer forthcoming to the question from Katie's companions and when she glanced up, she saw the marine who had been assisting her shaking his head silently.

"Don't you do that!" she exclaimed angrily, and turned back to her patient, furious at the negative atmosphere around her.

She saw that the young marine had begun to tremble violently. Keeping hold of his hand, she used her other to pull out a folded combat casualty blanket which she shook out and draped over him. It was as she was doing this that Katie sensed a change in the man's breathing.

His chest began to spasm, his breath hitching in and out of his open mouth as though he could not draw enough oxygen into his lungs. Katie's sixth sense sprang into action and went onto high alert. She knew instinctively that the marine before her was dying. Despite having done the best she could for him, she was fully aware that she did not have the equipment or medical supplies to treat a wound of this magnitude in the field, and it filled her with frustrated helplessness and grief. She watched with silent, suppressed horror as the man struggled to take a deep breath, saw it slowly hiss out of him then his chest was still.

No, Katie wailed silently.

Dropping the man's hand, she crawled up and positioned herself to the side of his head. She quickly checked his carotid pulse again and finding none, tilted her head down to watch for the telltale sign of the rise and fall of the casualty's chest. Seeing no movement, Katie raised the man's chin gently with one hand while pushing down on the forehead with the other to tilt the head back. She pinched the man's nose shut using her thumb and forefinger, the heel of her hand on the forehead maintaining the head tilt with her other hand remaining under the chin. Again, she watched to see if the opening of the airway would initiate breathing and whimpered quietly when the marine's chest remained still.

Inhaling normally she immediately gave two full rescue breaths while maintaining an airtight seal with her mouth against the man's mouth. Each of the two breaths lasted for one second in duration and she kept a sideways glance on the chest to see if her efforts were encouraging it to rise. Thereafter, she immediately started chest compressions, not bothering to take the time to check for a pulse or for signs of blood circulation.

Kneeling at the man's side near his chest, with the middle and forefingers of her hand nearest the legs, Katie located the notch where the bottom rims of the rib cage met in the middle of the chest. Placing the heel of her hand on the sternum next to the notch, she placed her other hand on the top of the one that was in position and keeping her fingers up off the chest wall, she interlocked her fingers. She brought her shoulders directly over the man's sternum and pressed downward, hard and fast, keeping her arms straight. After each push, she relaxed the pressure, allowing the chest to return to its normal position.

While doing CPR, Katie's mind closed itself off from the noise of her surroundings. The heat from the sun covered her in a heavy, all-enveloping humid blanket, sweat trickled down her face, her shoulders and arms ached from the chest compressions, and the hard ground stung her knees. Worst of all was the coppery smell of blood stinging her nostrils and the vise-like grip that her emotions had around her heart.

Desperate to initiate some sign of life into her patient, all thoughts and sensory perceptions in her mind dwindled down to a tunnel where she was completely focused on resuscitating the man—to get his heart beating, enabling the life sustaining blood to flow through his veins long enough for the CTT coming in on the medevac helicopter to get to work on him.

She was barely aware of two jets screaming in at low level overhead or the harsh crump of exploding missiles in the tree line where the enemy lay hidden. She neither heard the subdued cheers coming from the marines lining the perimeter wall at the sight of the thick black smoke curling up from the enemy hotspot nor of the sound of boots as some of the marines came back into the compound and immediately joined the silent group around the dead marine. She remained intent on the task at hand until suddenly someone placed their hands on her shoulders.

"Corporal Anderson."

Shrugging off the offending hands and ignoring the voice, Katie kept up the CPR.

"Corporal Anderson. Katie."

The voice seemed loud in the silence that reigned now that the jet engines had dwindled into the distance, their task completed, and the gunfire having ceased now that the enemy had been destroyed, but the hands were stronger, trying to pull her away from her job, distracting her and preventing her from trying to save this precious life.

Eventually the hands tugged hard enough that Katie toppled backward onto her backside. Immediately she sprang to her feet, fury boiling up inside her. She spun round to confront the man who had torn her away from her responsibility and commitment to the casualty and came face-to-face with Dan Reed.

"How dare you..." she began angrily.

Reed backed away and said gently, "Katie, he's gone. Leave him be."

Silenced, shocked out of her tirade, Katie turned to look down at the injured man and shook her head in denial.

"But...he can't..." she began.

Grief and guilt welled up inside her and conscious of the surrounding marines staring at her, possibly condemning her and blaming her for their friend's death, she turned on her heel and strode away from an atmosphere that was now heavy with death and sorrow.

Chapter Twelve

Entering the courtyard carrying Katie's weapon, Joe immediately saw her hurrying down the courtyard, heading toward the far corner away from the group of marines surrounding the casualty on the ground. He noticed her bowed head and slumped shoulders and immediately guessed the reason.

He strode across to his men and questioned one of his more senior marines. The man confirmed what Joe had thought and after ordering the dead man's face covered with the casualty blanket and advising that the medevac would arrive in a few minutes, he picked up Katie's rucksack and began to head in the direction she had disappeared in.

After a few paces, he stopped and crouching down undid the fastenings and withdrew two bottles of water, a towel and a spare T-shirt. As he withdrew the last item, two glossy photo-sized pieces of paper came fluttering out. He grabbed for them and froze.

The first one was of him and Katie on the night of the Marine ball a few months previously. It was the picture that his mother had taken while they were standing on the landing of his parents' house.

Joe gazed with fascination at the way Katie, clad in the clinging dark green lace dress, was gazing up at him, a brilliant smile on her face and at himself, in formal marine dress, looking down at her, a small smile on his face and his hands on her hips. With a jolt, he remembered that it was the night he had left her, Josie and his parents. The guilt at his duplicity and the remembered pain at leaving his family surged up through his stomach and into his heart.

He turned to the second photograph and this time a small groan escaped him. It was a picture of his daughter. He drank in the frilly pink dress, the little white socks, pink shoes and the tiny pink bow in her hair and felt the grief beginning to strangle him.

His mind going blank, he thrust the photographs back inside, replaced the bottles of water and other items he had extracted and turned again in the direction in which Katie had gone. He slowly began to walk across the courtyard to find her.

He immediately became aware of a familiar figure in front of him, heading in the same direction, and his body tensed with the now-familiar anger.

"Corporal Reed," he called.

Dan Reed turned. "Staff Sergeant?"

"Where do you think you're going?" Joe asked, trying to keep control of his voice.

"I thought that Corporal Anderson—" Dan replied but Joe quickly interrupted him.

"I don't think so," he exclaimed. "Get out to the perimeter wall and relieve one of the guys out there."

"Staff Sergeant, I really think that Katie—Corporal Anderson—needs some assistance," Dan continued.

Joe saw the stubborn expression appear on the corporal's face and held the young man's gaze with his own.

"That's an order, Marine, not an invitation. Stand down."

Corporal Reed still hesitated, then nodded and said, "Yes, Staff Sergeant," and moved off toward the gap in the wall.

Joe stared after him, his body relaxing slightly, fully aware that he himself had overstepped the mark by giving the young marine an order purely for personal reasons.

Shrugging, accepting that the incident had now passed and that he could not rectify it, he continued on across the compound toward its corner where he had seen Katie disappear. As he approached where he thought she was, he saw her, almost concealed by a brick wall jutting out from a building.

She was sitting on the ground against the wall of a building, knees bent, elbows resting on them, hands dangling loosely between her legs, head lowered.

He slowed his pace, hesitant to disturb her with his presence. Completely withdrawn into herself, he reached her side before she became aware that he was there. At last, as if sensing him, Katie glanced up and his heart ached for her when he saw the grief-stricken expression on her face.

Her hair was wet, sweat plastering curls to her head, her face covered in dust and dirt. There was a smear of blood on her chin, bloodstains on her combat shirt and body armor and congealed crimson liquid sheathing her hands as though she were wearing gloves.

Joe dropped her rucksack to the ground, leaned her weapon against the wall and crouched down beside her.

"Hey," he said softly, "how're you doing?"

Katie tried to smile at him but a soft sob escaped from her instead.

"I've been better," she answered and Joe heard such a forlorn tone in her voice that he wanted to take her in his arms.

"I've brought your gear. I thought you might want to clean up," he explained quietly.

Katie nodded, glanced down at the ground then back at him.

"I couldn't save him, Joe," she murmured. "I tried, but I couldn't save him."

Seeing a single tear trickle down her face, Joe responded gently, "Oh, honey. You did everything you could and more."

"I wish I could believe that," Katie said. "I bet his family and friends won't think so."

Her tone was so wistful and sad that Joe stretched out a hand and touched her arm, rubbing the material of her combat shirt gently and tenderly.

"Listen to me, Katie. You risked your life to stabilize the guy and you got him back in one piece. You did all that you could. His injuries were just too bad. Nobody is going to hang you out to dry for that. It's tough and at the moment it hurts. Believe me, I know. It will pass and you'll learn to accept that you can only do so much. You have to know your limitations, sweetheart."

He continued to stroke her arm in an attempt to reassure and comfort her.

Katie glanced down at his hand then looked back at him.

"Really?" she asked.

Joe nodded, seeing a faint look of hope on her pale face.

"Really," he confirmed, "Now, the medevac will be here in a few minutes. Do you feel up to getting yourself cleaned up and speaking to the CTT when they get here? They'll need a report from you."

Katie glanced at her bloodied hands. "I guess I look a fright," she said.

"No," Joe answered briefly, "not to me, you don't." He straightened up. "I'll leave you alone for a bit. Come over when you're ready, okay?"

Katie raised her head for a moment. She and Joe stared at each other in silence then he smiled gently at her. "I'll see you in a minute," he repeated and, turning, walked away, leaving her alone.

Striding along with his head down, thinking deep thoughts about his wife, Joe was unaware of his surroundings until Louis Eastman's voice interrupted his reverie.

"How is she, Joe?"

Joe came to a dead stop and glanced up to see his sergeant standing directly in front of him. He raised an eyebrow enquiringly.

"How is Katie?" Sergeant Eastman asked again.

Joe tipped his helmet back on his head and sighed.

"Pretty cut up about things," he answered at last, "She's just cleaning up, then she'll have to make a report to the CTT when it comes in."

"It must be tough on her," Louis Eastman responded, "first time and all that."

Joe nodded in agreement. "Yeah," he answered. "But she's tough. She'll get through it. She just needs time."

He cocked his head at the sound of a helicopter approaching at low level. "Get the men together, Sergeant. I need to radio the base, see what they want us to do. There might be a mission abort."

Sergeant Eastman nodded and strode off and Joe continued making his way back to the radio, his mind back on his duties.

Back at the rear of the courtyard, Katie watched Joe as he walked away. She desperately needed him at that moment and the look on his face had confirmed that if it had been at all possible, he would have taken her in his arms and comforted her. Nevertheless, that had been impossible and now she was left feeling more alone than ever.

She glanced abstractedly at the blood lathering her hands and knew that she needed to get herself moving. Isolating herself and dwelling on what had happened was not the way to get through this deep but brief emotional crisis.

Ripping off the bloody nitrile gloves, she turned to her pack and took out two bottles of water and a towel and began to blindly clean her face and hands. She winced as the cleansing revealed torn and abraded skin on her left hand and she realized that she herself needed first aid treatment for her own wounds. The gloves hadn't been able to protect her completely from the rocky terrain.

Knowing that the CTT would be nearing their location soon, she paid particular attention to getting her grazes and cuts as clean as possible before she took out some antibiotic ointment, gauze and a bandage from her medical pack. She hastily smeared the ointment on the palm and fingers of her hand, placed the gauze in position and skillfully wound the bandage on, fastening it securely with the elasticized gripper fastenings. Finally, she took off her body armor and combat shirt then, while keeping watch for anyone approaching, she quickly took off her damp T-shirt and put on the spare one.

She tried to sponge the blood from her shirt before giving up and putting it back on. With no hope of washing the blood from her body armor, she had no choice but to wear it with the smears of red still adorning it. Again, she did her best to try to wash the blood away with water but gave up. Quickly bundling her dirty T-shirt back into her pack, she replaced the medical supplies she had used and got tiredly to her feet.

Reluctant to return to the rest of the squad, she hesitated. She knew that she was being unreasonably paranoid about what the rest of the men might be thinking about her or blaming her for but it was taking what little courage she had left to join them.

Hearing the sound of a helicopter approaching, she knew that the decision was out of her hands. She picked up the rucksack and shrugged her arms through its webbing. She groaned from its weight and when she bent down to pick up her weapon, she almost toppled forward.

With the noise of the medevac helicopter growing closer, Katie stiffened her shoulders and her resolve and left her sanctuary, walking back out toward where the squad were milling around the courtyard.

As she walked slowly to join them, she felt her shoulders slump and became aware that her feet were dragging in the dust. She wanted to hide, not have to face the report she had to give to the CTT about the death of the marine and to have to face the possible condemnation from the rest of the men. She knew that she was being ridiculous but was unable to convince herself otherwise. She wished that Joe was with her to offer moral support but knew that she had to face this alone if she was ever going to put the incident behind her. Drawing on the remains of her courage, she straightened her shoulders and lifted her head.

She was surprised to see that it was dusk, the sky bathed in glowing orange, gold and red as the sun sank down behind the distant mountains. Torch beams were flickering around her and someone had lit some white chemlight glow sticks and laid them at strategic points around the main area of the courtyard.

As she approached the main squad, a marine came toward her and as they passed each other, Katie couldn't help but glance at his face. She was quite shocked when, instead of the reproach and accusation she was prepared to see, he nodded at her and said, "Ma'am," and continued walking on.

Other marines packing their equipment turned at her arrival and also acknowledged her presence with nods and small smiles and Katie knew with a profound sense of relief that there was nobody within the squad holding any blame against her for the death of their friend.

Reaching a pile of equipment piled in the center of the courtyard, Katie came to a stop. The sound of the helicopter was louder and Joe suddenly stepped through the gap in the wall.

"Okay, Marines, gather round!" he shouted.

The squad responded to the order and as they joined him, Joe continued, "The medevac will be here in five. I want four men outside the walls laying down some smoke and setting up a perimeter around the bird when it lands. We don't know if there are any more hostiles around. They might come back for their buddies. I want six more of you men to pace the perimeter of the compound. Stay close to the walls. There may be mines. A second bird will vector in, in about thirty minutes to extract us. We're going back, ladies, so you can get your beauty sleep. Now let's move it. Stay frosty. Keep your eyes peeled. Sergeant Eastman?"

The usual marine mantra erupted as Joe turned as his assistant patrol leader joined him. "Take the men out beyond the wall and set them up."

Sergeant Eastman nodded and suddenly yelled out at parade ground volume level, "Okay, let's move it. Grab your weapons. We're not here for our health. Move it, Marines, double time."

He started jogging toward the courtyard wall and ten armed marines followed him, boots thudding on the hard ground, their combats merging into the fading light.

Katie, alone for the moment and not sure what to do with herself, heard the approaching helicopter at a point almost overhead and glanced up to see the red winking landing lights and the dim pale red glow from the cockpit as the Chinook neared the compound then veered to the right.

She next saw a pillar of red smoke rise into the air as the marines laid down the markers for the landing zone and the Chinook begin to descend out of sight beyond the low buildings, its huge pair of rotor blades creating a billowing cloud of dust and sand that obliterated the huge helicopter's dim outline.

A few moments later, Katie saw the CTT approaching her through the encroaching darkness. She stood to attention as the officer in charge came to stand in front of her, and Katie saluted him. The remaining members of the CTT moved toward the body of the dead marine. Averting her eyes, Katie focused on the man standing in front of her. Beyond him, she could see Joe standing watching.

"Corporal Anderson," the officer began, and Katie nodded. "I'm Captain Milligan. You have a report for me?"

Katie nodded, cleared her throat and hesitantly began to describe what had happened, the treatment she had given to the dead marine, the dosage for each separate medication and the result. The officer took some notes, accepted her own brief written report that she had hastily completed when she had been alone after Joe had left her and once she had finished, he nodded.

He remained silent for a few minutes and then said, "Your report is perfectly reasonable in difficult circumstances. You may not feel it now, Corporal, but good job." He nodded at her again, turned, sighted Joe and went toward him.

Katie heaved a huge sigh of relief at discovering that she had done everything that had been in her power to do and with that relief, a sudden wave of exhaustion swept over her. Her limbs suddenly trembling and her head swimming she found that she desperately needed to sit down. Turning, she walked to the wall of a building, took off her pack and dropped it to the ground. Sighing wearily, she slid down the wall until she was sitting on the sand. Leaning her head back against it, she closed her eyes.

Having finished his debrief with the CTT officer and saluting his departure smartly, Joe turned to watch as the body, now encased in a bag on a stretcher, was carried respectfully out of the compound. Within a few minutes, he heard the medevac helicopter's engines rev up to full power, the two enormous sets of rotor blades tearing at the air, then watched as it rose gracefully into the sky and, banking slowly, sped off into the now-dark night.

Once its lights had disappeared, Joe turned back to see where Katie had gone. He saw her sitting on the ground leaning against a wall and to his intense irritation, saw that Corporal Dan Reed was crouched beside her.

"For fuck's sake! God damn it!" Joe exclaimed under his breath, anger at the young marine's constant attention to his wife building up inside him. He had every intention of going over to them both and sending the young corporal away with a flea in his ear when Sergeant Eastman came jogging back into the compound.

"The medevac got away safely, no problems," Louis Eastman volunteered. He glanced up when Joe failed to answer him. "Crap," he muttered when he saw that Joe's full attention was on Katie and the young corporal. Turning back to Joe, he was just about to make a comment about the situation when Joe suddenly said in a voice that seethed with fury and violence, "Louis. Will you please get that fucking kid away from my wife before I take him out?"

Immediately realizing what he had just let slip, Joe shoved his helmet back on his head, turned, and noting the shocked expression on his sergeant's face, said angrily, "Shit, you weren't supposed to know that."

Louis nodded his head. "No, I don't suppose I was," he said quietly. "Kindly enlighten me."

Joe sighed. "It's kind of complicated," he responded at last with an evasive note in his voice. "We got married a couple of months ago. We have a daughter back in the States but we sorta split and here we are."

He studied Louis Eastman's confused expression. *Oh, shit. I'm screwed.*

"You sorta split. You have a daughter and you're here. Katie is here?" Louis asked. "Joe, what the fuck is going on?"

Turning back to watch Katie and Dan Reed carefully, not taking his eyes off them for one second, Joe shook his head.

"I don't want to go into it now. I'll tell you one day. But for now, give that dickwad a duty, send him outside the wall, anything... Just get him the hell away from my wife."

Louis moved closer to his friend. "Take it easy, Joe. He's just a kid. I'll move him on."

With that the sergeant turned and shouted at Corporal Reed, "Reed, get your butt over here."

Chapter Thirteen

With the exception of the six marines forming a security perimeter around the Chinook that had arrived for their extraction, Katie and the rest of the squad filed up the ramp of the helicopter into its interior. They were unusually silent with none of their crude humor in evidence, a haggard weariness showing on some of their faces.

Shrugging out of their equipment, they took their respective places in the metal bucket seats and, placing their rucksacks between their legs, strapped themselves in. Once settled, many of them leaned their helmeted heads back against the metal skin of the helicopter and closed their eyes.

Katie found her own seat and buckled in. She could hear Joe yelling orders outside then he and Sergeant Eastman came jogging up the ramp, followed by the remaining contingent of the squad. The ramp rose automatically and the night sky was obliterated, leaving them in the dim, artificial light of the helicopter.

Katie was surprised when Louis Eastman took the seat on her left and Joe the one on her right. Joe barely acknowledged her, but once he had buckled himself in, his leg came to rest against hers. She could feel the warmth through her combat trousers and, as tired as she was, it sent tingles through her body. She pressed her own leg slightly against his and felt a warm joy when she received a response.

"Hey, Sarge."

Dan Reed's voice sounded above the noise of the helicopter engines. "Play fair."

Katie glanced up and saw Dan looking at Sergeant Eastman, gesturing for him to move. She felt the muscles in Joe's leg tense then a marine two seats down from them said, "For fuck sake, Danno. Why would the lady want you slathering all over her? Sit down, why don't you?"

"Yeah, give her a break, Danno. We'd all like to get back to the fucking base some time tonight," voiced another marine.

Sergeant Eastman lifted a gloved hand and, raising one finger, pointed to the empty seat opposite them. "Sit," he ordered.

Muttering under his breath, Dan Reed obeyed, slamming his pack onto the metal plating of the helicopter floor between his legs and sitting back, strapping himself into his seat.

Katie gave him a brief smile then leaning back against the cold metal skin of the helicopter, closed her eyes. She heard, as per normal procedure, the engines start to rise in pitch, the rotor blades speed up, then with barely a jolt, they were in the air.

Katie's whole awareness centered on the presence of her husband seated beside her. He dominated her thoughts. The feel of his leg against hers and the flexing of his muscles through his combat shirt as his arm touched her body sent shivers down into her stomach.

In her depressed frame of mind, she just wanted to say to hell with keeping up the charade of not knowing each other and snuggle into him. Holding her breath, she edged slightly toward him, millimeter by millimeter, coming to rest more firmly against his arm.

Joe seemed to acknowledge her action by pressing his leg imperceptibly against hers. Feeling a good degree more relaxed at his closeness, Katie rested her head back again, difficult because of her helmet but more relaxing nonetheless, and she closed her eyes.

As cold and noisy as it was inside the helicopter, Katie dozed, physically and emotionally exhausted. Gradually the gentle maneuvers of the Chinook and her own deepening sleep caused her body to relax and she slid sideways until her helmeted head came to rest on Joe's shoulder.

Feeling her there, Joe smiled inwardly. She would be mortified that the whole squad would see her sleeping against him but if he was truthful with himself, it felt great to have her snuggled into him and he could care less who saw them. She felt soft and warm and he had an almost insane urge to put his arm around her and pull her close but realized that that was out of the question.

After a further thirty minutes of flying time, the Chinook started its descent into Base Independence and eventually touched down on the helicopter apron. At the slight thud of the landing gear hitting the concrete surface, Katie jerked awake to find her head resting comfortably on her husband's shoulder. Her face immediately burned with embarrassment and she raised her head hastily.

Straightening her helmet on her head, she said quietly, "So sorry, Staff Sergeant. I'm afraid I... er...dozed off."

"No problem, Corporal," Joe replied equally quietly and left it at that.

The ramp lowered and the marines began to unbuckle themselves from their seats, shrug on their rucksacks and collect their weapons, to file slowly out onto the helicopter apron.

As Katie stepped out of the Chinook, she thought tiredly that it had never felt so good to be back at the base with its almost comforting smells of aviation fuel and oil, the noise of the generators and the bustling of personnel.

She followed the marines across the apron — taking a deep breath of the chilly night air — to where two Bulldog armored personnel carriers — APCs — waited to transport them back to Camp Roosevelt. As she approached one of the vehicles, she was stopped by a familiar voice calling out, "Corporal Anderson."

Turning, she noticed Joe walking toward her and stopped to wait for him.

"Hey," he said quietly when he reached her side.

Katie nodded and smiled.

"There's no need for you to attend the debriefing," Joe went on. "Go get some chow and sleep. You look all in."

Katie gazed at her husband's shadowed features. "I don't understand," she began. "When will we see each other?"

Joe hesitated, glancing down at the ground. Eventually looking back at her he finally answered, "I don't know. I have a lot to do over the next few days. Scuttlebutt has it that there's going to be some kind of a big mission and I have to attend a shit load of briefings. I'll try and find some time — "

Katie interrupted him with a small harsh laugh. "I'm sorry?" she queried. "You'll try and find some time to see me?"

The trauma of the last few days and the weariness she was feeling combined with Joe's seemingly callous statement about finding time to see her—his wife— caused tears to spring to her eyes and she lifted her chin stubbornly.

Joe tried to apologize. "Katie, I didn't mean it like that. I will see you, I just don't know when."

Resentful at the part that she was finding herself having to play through no fault of her own, heartsick at the hot and cold actions of her husband and finally out of patience and understanding, Katie had had enough.

"I tell you what, Joe," she snapped in a voice that, while low, was cutting. "You come and find me when you can allocate some time for me in your social calendar. Until then, screw you and leave me alone."

Without seeing what reaction this final remark had initiated, Katie turned on her heel and went to the second APC. The doors were standing open and as she reached them, she tossed her pack into its interior. Dan Reed, seated closest to the doors, leaned forward, reaching out a hand to assist her and without hesitation, knowing that Joe was watching, Katie grasped the young marine's hand and climbed into the vehicle.

Joe stood where he was for a brief moment, alone and hurt at the unexpected altercation with Katie. He couldn't believe that the hostility between himself and his wife had reared its ugly head again. He was well aware that his careless statement, spoken in all innocence, had hurt Katie and he cursed himself inwardly at his lack of thought before he had opened his mouth.

Feeling as though he could kick hell out of something, he strode around to the passenger side of the first APC, climbed into the passenger seat, slammed the heavy door shut, locking it viciously, and turning to the driver snapped, "Get the fuck out of here."

Chapter Fourteen

Katie sat on the edge of her camp bed, staring unseeingly at her boots. She was both physically and mentally exhausted and her stomach roiled with nausea, adding to her low mood and unhappiness.

The tent around her was alive with women preparing for their night out at the PX, their laughter, joking and loud conversation proclaiming their high spirits. She herself felt distanced from the buoyant humor. She had neither the energy nor the enthusiasm for joining in. If she was honest with herself, all she wanted to do was curl up on her camp bed and wallow in her misery, howl out her sadness for all to hear.

She missed Joe, craved to hear his voice, feel his arms around her, experience the safety, protection and love that he brought to her whenever he was with her.

He had not been in touch with her since their return from the patrol two days previously and the harsh words spoken between them. She regretted losing her temper with him, had eventually realized that it had been her own stupidity at misunderstanding what he had said that had created the argument. She had not given him a chance to defend himself, had just left him alone, so had not even had the opportunity to say goodbye to him that night. Her loneliness at being without him was almost a physical pain inside her but her innate stubbornness and pride prevented her from going to search him out to apologize.

As intolerable as her situation already was, it had been compounded by another problem which she had never in her wildest dreams thought could happen. She was certain she was pregnant again. With all the situational stress she had been subjected to over the previous weeks, she thought that the absence of her monthly was the result but the nausea had started the day after arriving back from patrol as had other symptoms, and after doing the mathematics, she now felt she could not sink any lower in spirit.

She was thousands of miles away from her infant daughter whose absence she could barely tolerate. She was redeployed to a combat zone where she had no business being and after the fraught events both personal and in combat recently, she realized it had been a futile belief on her part that she could persuade Joe to give up his vendetta and come home. Now, to make matters considerably worse, she was pregnant.

She knew that her options were severely limited. She could see the base doctor and immediately be sent home, leaving Joe here to carry out whatever he intended to do, or she could keep her pregnancy quiet for as long as she could, hoping and praying that the strenuous exertion of patrols, the heat and the persistent daily stressors would not bring on a miscarriage.

Common sense told her that she should just go home. What purpose was she serving by being in Afghanistan? The antagonism, which kept flaring between her and Joe—hurtful to them both—was causing irreparable damage to their marriage. If it went on, they would end up hating each other, destroying everything that had been between them.

Joe was never going to quit until he had made peace with himself and the demons inside him. Katie had to stay by his side and pick up the pieces, if there were any pieces to pick up, and yet, to be so near him and yet so far was torture.

Each time she stepped outside the tent she searched for him, waiting for him to appear with the easy grin on his face that she loved so much and the warm look in his eyes that was reserved purely for her. However, he never appeared. She saw him neither in the mess nor anywhere about the base and she wondered over and over again if he was avoiding her.

She needed to see him—to speak to him—tell him about the baby before it was too late, try and resolve matters between them.

A movement beside her on the bed jerked Katie roughly from her thoughts. Looking up, she saw that it was a woman called Lou who had joined her. The two had struck up a friendship and although not close, they got on well. Lou reminded her of Wanda, a close woman friend from her first deployment to Afghanistan and with who she still remained in touch. A lance corporal aircraft technician, Lou Weber was a tall stocky woman of twenty-five, jovial and good-natured.

She smiled at Katie, revealing sparkling white teeth and said, "Now, Katie Anderson. I don't know what devils you may be wrestling with but some of us are hopping off to the PX for a night out and you are coming along, no arguments. You've been like a zombie since coming back from that patrol, so a night out will do you good."

Shaking her head negatively, Katie opened her mouth to refuse the invitation but Lou interrupted, "I'm not taking no for an answer. Go put some lippie on or do whatever you have to do to get yourself dolled up in this godforsaken place then we'll be off."

Lou got to her feet, winked at Katie and sauntered off to join other women who were putting final touches to make-up and changes of uniform.

Katie stared after Lou for a minute, ready to jump to her feet and firmly refuse the invitation when suddenly she paused. The thought of spending a night alone in the tent with nothing but her anxious thoughts about Joe and her situation to keep her company was something she couldn't deal with. She needed an opportunity to relax, to be with loud, noisy people out for a good time.

Just one time she wanted to be able to dismiss all the anxieties and fears that had been welling up inside her, strangling her enthusiasm and love for life over the last few days. If Joe was at the PX tonight, that would be an added bonus. If he wasn't? Well, she would try and find out where his tent was and talk to him, whether he liked it or not.

"Come on girl. Get that butt of yours in gear. You've got five minutes," Lou suddenly shouted to her.

"All right, all right," Katie called back, smiling a little.

Quickly she got out her make-up, applied some mascara and some gloss lipstick, fluffed up her short hair, grabbed her flashlight and joined the group of laughing women waiting to leave.

"Helluva good decision."

A woman called Jessie acknowledged Katie's arrival in the group and smiled at her.

"Okay, ladies, let's get going and have some fun," Lou called out and there were loud catcalls and cheers in response.

The women moved out of the tent into the sultry evening air. The moon was full, the stars powdering the black sky like a scattering of diamonds. It was warm and a soft breeze stirred Katie's hair.

The night caused such a powerful nostalgia within her that she suddenly wanted to run back inside the tent, bury herself in her sleeping bag and cry out her heartache. She couldn't do this without Joe. It wasn't within her capabilities anymore. She didn't have the strength.

Lou nudged her arm. Katie glanced at her and managed a small smile. Straightening her shoulders, she felt a surge of determination that she was not going to hide away and that she would make every effort to forget about her problems for that night.

It appeared that everyone on Camp Roosevelt had had the same idea of letting their hair down and Katie and her companions joined a crowd of other men and women heading for the PX.

Katie initially allowed the other women to make the conversation but felt herself relaxing slightly and even experienced a small rise in her spirits. For tonight, at least, she would try to forget her problems, attempt to erase Joe from her mind.

If by some luck he was in the PX, she would attempt to get him alone and tell him about her pregnancy. Feeling a little calmer now that she had some form of plan—mediocre though it was—Katie forced herself to join in the conversation swirling around her. She was even able to laugh at some of the ribald jokes that were Lou's forte.

Eventually, they arrived at the PX, along with what Katie thought looked like half the base. Entering through the main doors, she had to reach down inside herself for an ironclad control to stop looking around for Joe but found that she was unable to stop herself from doing so. She didn't see him among the crowd and was disappointed and saddened.

The women entered the main room of the PX to find it almost full with loud boisterous service personnel and they had to wend their way through laughing men and women to the counter where they ordered cans of Coke. Once they had their drinks, they fought their way to a space alongside one of the walls.

Sipping her drink, Katie remembered the last time she had been there. She and Joe had let the whole of the base know that they were an item. They had danced, had almost made love against a wall and Joe had declared that he wasn't ever going to let her go. Katie felt the sharp sting of tears in her eyes caused by the pain of the memories that the place was stirring in her.

Lou glanced at her friend, nudged her and smiled. "Hey," she said, raising her voice slightly above the noise. "No tears, okay?"

Katie smiled, swallowed and nodded. "No tears," she reiterated.

A few minutes later, music blared out and people began to drag tables and chairs to line the sides of the room leaving a large space in the center. Men and women began to dance to the heavy beat, whooping and cheering, the noise level rising deafeningly.

Grabbing Katie by the arm, Lou yelled exuberantly. "Come on, honey. Let's do it."

Almost dropping her can, Katie laughed, quickly placed it on the floor and followed her friend out to join the other women who were already dancing. As soon as she began to dance, Katie felt herself relax even further. She loved to dance and she was good at it.

For the next few minutes, she almost forgot about her problems, losing herself in the thumping music and when the track finished, she stayed where she was, waiting for the next one to start.

Joe Anderson stood at the counter with Louis Eastman and Corporal Reed, waiting to be served cold drinks. His struggle to stop himself from staring around the room to see if Katie was there was failing dismally. His longing to see her was becoming all-consuming, however, there was a small part of him that hated the inevitable resurgence of the powerful feelings she was always able to arouse in him.

From out of the corner of his eye, he saw Dan Reed suddenly straighten abruptly, his attention diverted toward the dance floor. The young corporal hastily put his Coke on the counter and, turning to Joe said, "Excuse me, Staff Sergeant," and move — somewhat eagerly — toward the dancers.

Joe turned to watch him go and immediately noticed Katie. His eyes narrowed as he watched the young marine make a beeline toward his wife. He glared as the unsuspecting corporal tapped Katie on the shoulder as she danced with her back to him. Katie spun round, recognized who it was and directed one of her brilliant smiles at Dan Reed. He said something to her, she inclined her head and they began dancing to the heavy beat together.

Joe felt a tic start to beat alongside the scar on his face and a slow, cold rage began to build up in the pit of his stomach. He watched as the young marine moved closer to Katie and put a hand on her waist, bending his head toward her when she said something to him and laughed. Katie herself put one of her hands on his arm and to Joe it appeared that she was very receptive to his attentions. He clenched his fists and the sound of the music began to fade as the fury threatened to explode out of all proportion to the situation.

He took a step forward, so angry now that he wanted to go and punch the young marine who had had the audacity to saunter up to his wife and dance with her. All reason was leaving him. The fact that Corporal Reed had no idea that Katie was his wife was the furthest thing from his mind.

Louis Eastman noticing his friend's body jerk forward and his posture become rigid, obviously realized in which direction his gaze lay and exclaimed, "Fuck!" beneath his breath.

He grabbed Joe's forearm in a steel grip.

Joe stared down at the hand on his arm, began to shake it off when Louis said, "Leave it, Joe."

Joe glanced back at Katie then at his friend. He remained silent, not even arguing with Louis' order.

"Leave it, Joe," Louis repeated. "It means nothing. He's a kid wet behind the ears and you beat the crap outta him, you're *finito*. Listen, pal. Katie loves you. I have never seen anyone love someone as she loves you. I'm not normally a mushy guy, but I speak the truth when I say she adores you. Now, leave her some space and chill."

Still digging his fingers into the flesh of Joe's arm, inflicting the pain so it would penetrate through Joe's apparent fog of aggression, Louis held his gaze.

After long minutes of thinking that his friend was going to ignore him, Louis felt the muscles in Joe's arm begin to relax bit by bit. At last, he felt able to release his arm but he didn't trust his friend anymore.

He watched carefully as Joe turned to focus his gaze back on Katie and the corporal. Outwardly, he looked nonchalant and emotionless, but having known him for so long, Louis could feel the tension thrumming in his friend's body and he was gritting his teeth with what appeared to be an ironclad control.

Dancing and laughing with the young marine corporal, Katie felt flattered by the obvious admiration in the young man's eyes. He was good-looking with black cropped hair, dark eyes and a muscular physique.

In different circumstances, she might have been attracted to her admirer but her heart belonged only to one other. It was when she glanced over her partner's shoulder that Katie abruptly stopped dancing.

Joe was standing at the counter with Sergeant Eastman, and he was staring at her. She could quite clearly see that his face was devoid of expression but even across the few meters of floor space, she noticed the cold look in his blue eyes and the obvious tension in his body.

Their eyes locked and held but Joe's expression did not change, then he did something that stunned Katie into flight mode. He turned his back on her without the slightest acknowledgment of her presence.

Katie felt every atom in her body crumble into a devastating sadness. She suddenly needed to get out of the PX, away from the suddenly stifling room and the noise and heat. She wanted to hide in a corner and cry out all her hurt. It had suddenly become too much for her and the sight of Joe so near to her but turning his back had created so much pain inside her that she needed to escape to be on her own to deal with it.

Forcing a smile onto her face, Katie shouted to Corporal Reed, "I'm sorry, I have to go. I don't feel well."

Dan Reed responded immediately, "Let me see you back to your tent."

Katie held up a hand. "No thanks, I'll be fine, but thank you, Dan."

She turned to the dancing Lou and repeated her lie about feeling ill. Lou stopped dancing and touched Katie's arm. "Will you be okay?"

Katie nodded. "I'll be fine," she replied then quickly moved away from the dancing people and headed as fast as she could toward the doors.

Turning at that moment, Joe saw Katie leave. He made a move to go after her but again Louis grabbed his arm. "Leave her, Joe. Let her go."

Joe looked down at the fingers grasping his arm. "She's my wife," he answered and gave Louis such an icy look that it was clear he immediately knew that he was overstepping the boundaries of Joe's patience.

Removing his grasp, he shrugged. "Your funeral, pal," was his final remark.

Chapter Fifteen

Thrusting her way through the crowd loitering outside the doors of the PX, Katie hurried a few paces distant from the building, looking wildly around her for a secluded place where she could go to regain her composure.

Without fully realizing the direction she was going, she turned to her right and strode around the side of the building, finally remembering that this was the place where she and Joe had kissed on the one and only time they had both come to the PX together.

Tears started to roll down her cheeks as she hurried along the side of the building to the patch of blackness where the security lights did not quite reach. Out of breath, she finally stopped, one hand resting on the wall, bent over slightly as she tried to control the sobs that threatened to spill out of her. She raised a hand to her mouth to stem the soft whimpers but the tears fell harder and she began to cry in earnest.

Following behind her, Joe saw Katie's shadow, heard her soft crying and stopped a few meters away from her. All jealousy and anger fled as he listened to her grief and pain. He had done this with his callous and selfish disregard for her feelings. Not wanting to scare her, he called her name softly.

He saw her head jerk up and she spun around. "Joe?" she queried.

Hearing the fear in her voice, Joe swallowed, feeling a surge of guilt.

"It's me," he replied and began walking slowly toward her.

He stopped a foot away from her and they stared at each other. Then suddenly — without any hesitation, as though both had had the thought at the same time — Joe walked the final foot to Katie, she moved toward him then she was in his arms, crying as though her heart would break.

Joe hugged her tightly. "Katie, please don't cry like that. It's killing me."

Her whole body was shaking and trembling and heard her sobs smothered against his shoulder. The crying had a weary tone to it and he realized that she was exhausted.

He hugged her tighter, whispering, "Ssshhh, it's okay. I'm sorry. I'm so sorry, Katie," but was unsure as to whether his words were penetrating the storm of tears.

Katie cried for a long time but eventually her sobs started to taper off and at last, except for her shoulders hitching with stray sobs and some slight childlike sniffing, she was quiet although she didn't move.

Waiting for her to calm down and regain her composure, Joe continued to hold her, enjoying the feel of her body in his arms and catching the clean smell of her hair. After a few more minutes, Katie drew slightly away from him, wiping one hand across her face.

"I'm sorry," she murmured. "I don't know where that came from."

"Hey," Joe said trying to get her to raise her down-turned face. When she didn't respond he said firmly, "Katie, look at me."

Almost reluctantly, Katie raised her face. Her expression was one of such sadness that Joe wished he could kiss away her unhappiness.

"Don't ever be sorry for being upset," he continued gently. "Are you going to tell me what the storm was about?" *As if I didn't know,* he added silently to himself.

Glancing away from him then back again, fresh tears glimmered in her eyes, and at first, he thought that she was going to refuse to answer him then she swallowed and said in a small voice, "I miss you and I miss…Josie."

Speaking the name of their daughter caused her voice to tremble and she coughed and continued, "I don't know what the hell I'm doing here anymore, or where I'm going and…and…" Her voice trailed off into silence.

Joe watched as a tear trickled down her cheek and the way her bottom lip trembled slightly brought a clear picture of Josie to mind as she did the exact same thing when she was about to cry her heart out.

He realized that if he and Katie did not sort out their marriage, if he did not sit down, talk to her and give her the explanations that she was entitled to then it might just as well be over between them.

He wished that things had been different. If they were both back in the US, there might have been a chance for them to talk and heal their marriage but what he had to tell her was going to be the final straw.

He'd had no choice in the matter. The decision had come from higher up the USMC chain of command and he felt at that moment that he should never have married her. Katie deserved better, far more than he could give her out here in Afghanistan. She needed to go home, get back to their daughter, and let him do his job without his mind constantly on her and their problematic marriage.

Joe cleared his throat, well aware that the next few minutes were going to be the worst ones of his life.

"Katie," he said gently but with determination.

Katie glanced up at him, her eyes luminous in the dim light, her cheeks still wet with tears, a questioning look on her pretty face.

"We need to talk," he continued, his eyes studying her and wishing that he could just grab her hand and run away from their situation.

Katie tilted her head back slightly. "All right," she agreed softly.

Joe hesitated then said huskily, "The squad is going to be pulling out of Base Independence. We're going to be relocating to Forward Operating Base Nowazad. There's been an increase in insurgent activity in a very large compound in the local area and Command think that something big is brewing. The British army will be joining us, then we'll be mounting a search and destroy mission against any terries that are in the area."

"I see," Katie said, "When will we be leaving?"

Joe glanced over her head, a lump of emotion threatening to choke him.

"I'm going to ask for your transfer out of the squad so you can go home."

Katie stared at him then stepped back, Joe's arms dropping away from her waist to his sides.

"What?" she asked.

Joe saw the look of shock and disbelief on her face and let her go, knowing that to keep her in his arms was tantamount to cruelty.

"The mission is going to be dangerous," he continued. "You're my wife, Katie, and I love you. I want you out of harm's way."

Katie stood in silence, still staring at him.

"You and I have had some…issues lately, and I've got to focus on this mission, get my men through it in one piece. I can't lose my concentration again, be distracted by personal problems and our confrontations. My squad leader has heard scuttlebutt that I haven't been doing my job properly. If I don't get my shit together, I'll be shit-canned. I love you, Katie, but I don't know if it's enough to get things sorted out between us. We can't focus on our jobs if we're always fighting and I can't afford to get any more of my men killed because of it." Joe lapsed into silence feeling the world's worst bastard.

He knew what he had done to her but there was nothing he could do to take back the words he had just uttered. To alienate her was to save her life and if he had achieved it by being cruel, then he would have to live with it. Watching her, he knew how much he loved her but there was nothing that he could say.

Katie felt each one of his words pierce her like a hot nail and her world crumbled around her. She couldn't believe that Joe—the man who she had thought loved her more than anything—was requesting that she leave, was saying that his love for her wasn't enough and that he thought more of his career than he did of her. For him to say that he needed her to be out of his hair so he could concentrate on a mission was tantamount to telling her that he didn't want her around because she was a nuisance.

Trying to quell the devastating hurt that she felt, she stood staring at him while the tension and silence stretched out between them. She was relieved to feel a hot anger surge up and override the pain that was coiling like a live wire in her stomach.

"You bastard!" she exclaimed, an icy venom in her voice.

"Katie…" Joe began.

Katie stepped back, holding up her hands in a warding off gesture.

"Don't Katie me," she snapped. "No more. This is the third time you've done this to me, Joe, so no fucking more. First you go missing — all right, through no fault of your own — then you fuck off in the middle of the night for your own personal, *important* reasons and now this."

She paused, breathing rapidly, tears filling her eyes.

"Let me get this straight if I may," she continued, her voice trembling slightly. "You want me out of your hair because you consider me — our marriage — a nuisance. It's too inconvenient for you. You need to get yourself and your men through this mission and you'd be only too happy to have me out of the way." Her voice was rising with fury, and she clenched her fists, trying to regain control of her temper.

She moved farther away from him. She didn't know what to do. The hurt was so real and overwhelming that she wanted to run and never stop. Shaking her head and willing the tears to stay away, she said coldly, "You know what? I understand totally. One thing that might put a spoke in your mighty wheel, though, is that you try to get me transferred and I'll pay a visit to your CO. I'll spill the beans, Joe, about your — how shall I put it — *problems*. Then I'll have *you* transferred with me. If I go, you go."

She watched Joe straighten up, tension evident in his body and she heard the anger in his voice as he said, "Try it, Katie, and you'll find that you've made yourself an enemy, even though I am your husband. Don't ever threaten me."

"Then from now on, leave me alone," Katie spat angrily, the grief nearly choking her. "I *will* be going with you when the squad moves out. You have my word on that."

When Joe responded, his voice was icy and abrupt, "Okay, have it your own way."

Knowing that it was over and there was nothing left to say, Katie took another step back from him, feeling that the farther she moved away from him, the more distant her marriage became. She clung onto her control by a thread.

"Best of luck, Joe," she whispered, the threatening tears almost strangling the words. "Congratulations. I'm no longer your responsibility." And with that last heartfelt remark, she turned and began to walk quickly away from him.

Before she reached the end of the wall, she was running—heart pounding—tears streaming down her face—the pain of loss almost unbearable.

She ran until she felt sick, oblivious to the camp personnel around her—of the strange looks she received—intent only on getting back to her accommodation. She knew that even there, she would have no place to hide to lick her wounds and that the women in her tent were bound to notice that there was something wrong. She had to grit her teeth—face the situation head on—and draw on all her courage and reserves of strength to deal with the situation the best way she knew how. It was going to be the hardest thing that she had ever had to do and seeing Joe and being near him in the future was going to be torture but she would do it. She had to.

Panting heavily, a stitch in her side, she reached her tent and stopped outside. She wiped her wet face, smoothed back her short hair and straightened her shoulders. She had never felt less like being among people than at that moment.

She was just about to enter the tent when a voice said behind her, "Corporal Anderson?"

Spinning around she saw a marine who she vaguely recognized as a member of Joe's squad standing behind her. He silently handed her a sheet of paper, gave her a half salute, about turned and disappeared into the darkness.

Standing where he had left her and staring down at the piece of paper, Katie gritted her teeth, wondering what it was all about. She eventually sighed then went into the tent. Avoiding the stares of the other women, she went to her bed and, sitting down, opened to read the print on the paper. It was a copy of a brief email with a WARNO attached to it regarding the upcoming move to the FOB and stating that there was a briefing at 0900 hours the next morning at the USMC HQ.

Katie let the hand holding the note fall onto her lap. Bowing her head, she wondered if there had ever been anyone who felt as bad as she did right at that moment. She was empty inside, as though Joe was dead and gone forever. In a way, she was glad she felt nothing. It would make it that much easier to see him tomorrow at the briefing, that much easier to treat him like a stranger.

Letting the sheet of paper float down onto her sleeping bag, she stood up, tiredly collected her usual shower kit and slowly made her way through the other women, forcing herself to answer greetings and smiles as she headed for the shower tents.

Having hung the obligatory notice on the outside of the shower, she went in, undressed and turned on the water. She stood under the hot spray, letting the soothing warmth pound the top of her head, eyes closed.

She allowed the memories to come — images of her and Joe when they had first met, of the first time they had made love, their wedding day and their daughter. She put a trembling hand on her lower abdomen. There was no obvious sign as yet that she was pregnant — stomach still flat, her body still slim.

She would never tell him now about their unborn child. Again, she would give birth on her own, as she had with Josie. Joe might just as well *be* dead.

Suddenly Katie was crying — quietly at first — then, as the emptiness inside began to disperse, she sobbed as though her heart would break, bending double in the shower, hands covering her face, body shaking as though she were freezing cold, although the icy feeling was deep in her heart. She felt lost and alone. Joe had carved out a dark space in her heart that would never heal and she had no idea how she was going to carry on without him.

She cried so violently that she grew dizzy and sick and had to prop herself against the canvas sides of the shower to prevent herself from falling, gagging and choking on emotion that was like a physical lump in her throat. That was when she knew that if she didn't calm herself, her hysteria could possibly result in a miscarriage, and the loss of another life would be the end of her.

Raising her face to the water pouring from the showerhead, she let the fluid play onto her hot face, washing away the tears. Gaining some control over her emotions, she quickly washed herself, concentrating on showering then drying once she had finished.

Dressing in her nightwear, she collected her toiletries and went back to her bed space. After folding her uniform and stowing her toiletries in her bedside locker, she sat down on her bed feeling apathetic and lonely. The tent was dim with many of the women asleep or busy with other things. She wished that she had someone to talk to but then thought nobody would want to hear about her heartbreak.

She lay down on her bed, dragging the sleeping bag up over her. Closing her eyes, she tried to sleep but her mind instantly darted back to the incident at the PX and to her confrontation with Joe. She remembered every word spoken between them and her heart ached. The tears welled up in her eyes again, only this time she was determined not to give in to them. No matter how much she hurt, the time for crying was over.

She needed to get through the rest of her deployment, look after the little one inside her and get home in one piece. What would happen then she had no idea. She felt as though she were in limbo, not knowing which direction she needed to go. She should take one day at a time, drawing on every ounce of courage she possessed and hoping and praying that she would be able to get through the rest of her deployment with her sanity intact.

Katie tried to relax, concentrating on each part of her body, but her mind wouldn't focus. She needed to freeze her feelings, quench every single emotion she had in relation to Joe—her love for him and their disastrous marriage. She had an unborn life inside her and she needed to protect it and herself. To do this she had to focus on her role and the upcoming mission, which, if Joe's words were anything to go by, was going to be extremely hazardous.

Clenching her fists, she put them over her eyes, trying to blot out the images of her husband, but the pictures refused to go away. She felt a tear trickle from the corner of her eye and a small, silent sob escaped her.

No...I will not cry.

She bit down on her lip hard, the pain distracting her from the tears that she wanted to shed. She tried to relax, to sleep, and eventually she dozed, jolting awake a few moments later then dozing on and off throughout the dark hours of the night.

Chapter Sixteen

Katie jerked awake at the first muted ring of her watch alarm. She had finally drifted off into a deep sleep at around 0400 hours that morning and the two hours that she had rested had just made her feel worse. Her body ached, her mind felt wrung out and exhausted. She was tired and her spirits had never been so low.

Sitting up in bed, she glanced around the dim tent. Nobody was stirring yet. All the women were still sleeping peacefully. She wished there was noise and bustle, something to distract her from how bad she felt, but all was quiet.

To keep thoughts of the previous day at bay, she collected her toiletries and, climbing from her sleeping bag, made her way wearily to the shower tents. She steadfastly refused to allow herself to think anything, blanking her mind and concentrating solely on her actions moment by moment.

She showered slowly, washed her hair, then toweled it and herself dry. Once again dressed in her nightwear, she wandered back to her bed space and dressed herself in combat trousers and shirt. She methodically laced her boots then found herself sitting on the edge of her bed staring into space.

Thoughts of Joe and their marriage kept trying to infiltrate her mind and she struggled to remain composed. She decided to make her way to the mess. The walk to Camp Churchill would do her good and she had to eat. There was no point in allowing her mood to affect her appetite because that would only be detrimental to her own health and that of her baby. Picking up her weapon, she slung it over her shoulder then left the tent, pausing outside the tent flaps.

The early morning was fresh and warm, with a deep blue sky littered with wispy clouds and the sun a pale yellow orb, its stifling heat not yet in evidence. Katie glanced around her, restless and unable to concentrate. She wanted to run as far away as she could from everything, but she gritted her teeth, straightened her shoulders and started to walk to the main road leading from Camp Roosevelt to Camp Churchill.

She concentrated on putting one foot in front of the other, keeping her head lowered, oblivious to other people around her and the military vehicles moving up and down the road. She found herself wanting to look around for Joe but knew that this would serve no purpose except for making the pain inside her even harder to bear. The less she saw of him, the better, although that was going to prove extremely difficult with the briefings and their future mission. They could not avoid being in each other's company and she dreaded the situation with every fiber of her being.

Approaching the mess, Katie felt nervous.

Will he be in there? What will happen when we see each other?

She almost stopped in her tracks, ready to turn around and escape back to her tent, but that would be putting aside the inevitable. Gathering what remained of her courage and confidence, she continued on, hoping and praying that she could get inside quickly, thereby avoiding meeting anyone that she knew.

Pushing open the doors, she went inside the mess, the odor of cooking food instantly assailing her nostrils. The smell immediately made her stomach churn and she felt a pang of anxiety, wondering if she was going to have to turn and run outside to be sick. The sudden surge of nausea begin to fade when Katie swallowed and she continued on her way to the food counter.

Taking a tray, she avoided the cooked food and went immediately to the cereal shelves. After selecting her breakfast and a bottle of orange juice, she turned to make her way to an empty table near the doors and sat down facing the room, propping her weapon against her chair. She stubbornly refused to search the room for her husband but concentrated on eating her cereal instead, her appetite almost non-existent but knowing that she needed to keep her strength up.

Seated some distance away with Louis Eastman, Joe had seen Katie come in. Unable to resist staring at the door—knowing he had been waiting for her to appear—he had still been startled to see her, having wrongly assumed that she would remain in her tent licking her wounds, but then he had harshly criticized himself for the thought. Knowing Katie as he did, he should have known she wouldn't hide away. She was courageous, determined and stubborn. He was shocked to see how pale and tired she looked and again berated himself for the thought.

How else do I think she is going to look, happy and laughing with not a care in the world?

His own emotions were at an all-time low. Whatever words he had spoken to Katie the night before had not been out of a lack of love. He loved her and his commitment to her had been the underlying factor leading to their confrontation. He had to live with the hurt he had caused her — not for the first time — but he wondered if there was ever going to be the faintest chance that he could pick up the pieces of their marriage.

She sat down and her attention was wholly on her meal. She did not even bother to look around the mess with her usual alertness and interest. He wondered if it was because she just wanted to eat and get it over with so she could leave.

Out of the corner of his eye, he noticed some members of his squad enter the mess, and he recognized Corporal Dan Reed, who had shown so much interest in his wife. He felt a wave of annoyance as the young corporal saw Katie sitting alone, and he and the rest of the men headed toward her table.

"Hey, Andy."

Katie, hearing a male voice using an unfamiliar name, almost glanced around her to see who the Andy was but raising her gaze, she saw Dan Reed together with half a dozen other men standing beside her.

Forcing a smile of greeting onto her face, Katie asked, "Andy? Who's Andy?"

Dan Reed answered her smile with one of his own. "You're one of us now so you get to have a nickname," he answered. "This bunch of rugrats is Nuts — whose name will prove self-explanatory once you get to know him" — Dan, jerking his thumb at the rest of his companions, continued with his introductions — "Mental, Mattie, Bones, Womble, Slither, Neanderthal and the shit ugly one on the end is Shrek. And as you assholes already know this is Andy, our medic."

All the men nodded in Katie's direction, offering her friendly grins, then they all propped their weapons against chairs and the table and ambled off to get their breakfasts.

Dan Reed sat down in a chair beside Katie and asked, "Are you okay?"

Pushing her cereal bowl away, Katie kept the smile on her face, even though her jaws were aching from the strain.

"I'm fine," she replied. "To what do I owe this honor?"

"Breakfast then the briefing," Dan answered, "Want to come with us?"

Hesitating, Katie eventually nodded. It would be good to walk into the forthcoming briefing with someone and not alone as she had expected to.

Dan stood up again. "Let me go get some chow and I'll be back. Don't go away."

Katie, watching the young corporal move away to the food counter, wished with all her heart that she was free to indulge in the young man's interest but she couldn't. She was a one-man woman and suspected that she would remain that way indefinitely, probably for the rest of her life.

She sighed and rubbed a hand across her forehead. She was so tired and wished more than anything that she could just go back to her tent and sleep the day away. The arrival of the men back at her table loaded with their breakfasts and drinks interrupted her thoughts.

As though they sensed her despondent mood, they began to crack jokes, rib each other and act like a group of juveniles in a school canteen. Katie's smile became more natural and when Dan rejoined the table, he had a wonderful sense of humor, and Katie even laughed at some of his jokes.

Joe couldn't stop himself from occasionally glancing over at Katie. He couldn't help but notice the unhappy expression on her face, but her smile flashed now and again and he felt glad that she wasn't alone, that his men were looking after her.

He still felt unhappy with what had passed between them the previous night. Through his own misguided conceptions, he had perhaps lost the most important thing in his life and if he was honest with himself — and it was about time that he was — he was beginning to deeply regret the decision he had made.

Katie finally looked at her watch. "I hate to spoil the party," she began, "but it's coming up on 0845 hours."

Dan rose, bending down to take her bowl and empty bottle of juice. "Yep," he agreed. "Best not piss off the old man. Come on, ladies. Let's get."

Scraping back chairs, the men all rose, picking up their weapons and slinging them over their shoulders. With Katie among them, they deposited their dirty crockery and utensils on the racks then left the mess.

Feeling her stomach clench with nerves at the looming briefing, Katie kept her mind distracted by focusing on the conversation of the men. They included her in their conversation, chatting to her about her family life and her army career.

They reached the USMC HQ just before 0900 hours and made their way to one of the briefing rooms. Just before she entered the double swing doors, Katie hesitated.

She felt sudden panic at knowing that soon she would be face-to-face with Joe and was unsure if she had the strength to go through with it. Dan, preceding her through into the room beyond, turned on noticing her absence and came back to her.

"Hey," he said quietly, "You don't look so hot."

Katie managed a small smile at him. "I'm fine," she responded and followed him into the room where they took their seats in the center row of chairs. Having seated herself, she took out a notebook and pen from the pocket on the sleeve of her combat shirt and waited for the briefing to start. Her heart pounded unevenly and she had an anxious feeling in the pit of her stomach.

Her head jerked up as the doors swung open and Joe and Sergeant Eastman entered. Katie focused briefly on her husband. His eyes searched the room then found and caught her gaze. He stared at her for long seconds then his glance moved on.

"Good morning, Marines," he announced. "Now, listen up. We have a lot to get through in a short space of time."

Joe turned away and pulled down a topographical map before facing forward again.

"I take it you've all seen the WARNO?"

He waited for the group to acknowledge his question before he continued. "Okay. You'll know then that we're moving out to FOB Nowazad. The FOB is located two hundred kilometers out, or for those who don't yet have a decimal mindset, one hundred and twenty-five miles north of Base Independence in the District of Nowazad."

Joe turned to the map behind him and pointed to an area circled in bright red.

"A brief history of the area—and try to keep awake while I give it—is that between 2006 and 2009 there were a number of interlocking insurgent compounds spread over the Nowazad area. There was an ongoing stalemate between the International Security Assistance Force—a coalition force of marines, British army, and Gurkhas—until the end of December 2009 when it appeared that the ISAF had gained the upper hand. However, Intel has alerted us to the fact that there has been an increase in insurgent sightings in the area. They poke their nasty little heads up then disappear. It's believed that some kind of major assault is being planned and it needs to be nipped in its ass before it gets out of hand, which is where we come in.

"Six Afghanistan National Army will meet us at the FOB to join us on missions, act as interpreters and liaise between any nationals and us. We'll be joined by the British army at a later date when a search and destroy mission will be planned and we'll get to kick some ass. Over the next forty-eight hours leading up to the mission, we'll be taking part in a number of exercises consisting of IED and mine incidents, medical evacuation, communications, vehicle recovery and lots of vehicle and equipment checks.

"Now, listen up. I need to emphasize that this is not going to be a picnic, so you need to pay attention to what I am about to say. Okay, let's get to it. We'll be traveling in a close column convoy, consisting of two Cougar mine-resistant, ambush protected vehicles or MRAPs, for the uninitiated, plus a light medium tactical vehicle to carry supplies out to the FOB. A Navy Explosive Ordnance Disposal Team will be on standby in case we need them and army and air force along the route will be ready and waiting to protect our asses, if we need them. Timings will vary, depending on variables on each sector of the journey.

"Our primary route will be ten clicks east to the town of Gereshk. We take a lesser route east-northeast for fifty clicks then north by a track road to the FOB. Our primary and lesser routes are pretty well used but there will still be a need for eyes on for hostiles, IEDs, cover, concealment, obstacles etc. The track route is pretty much unknown territory over rough terrain. All routes will be reconned and checked before we set out, but you all know as well as I do that the terries always manage to plant more. The weather for this year is pretty much the norm but the occasional sandstorm can appear from nowhere. We'll deal with that factor when it crops up.

"You should all know by now who your key personnel are and what your responsibilities are from the WARNO. Make sure you know what you are supposed to do in the event of an ambush or IED incident. Corporal Anderson is our CTM and the Aid and Litter Team will report to her in the event of an incident that involves casualties."

Joe glanced at Katie, who nodded, her gaze skittering away from his once she had acknowledged his statement.

"Parts of the vehicles will need to be camouflaged, vehicle bumper markings, headlights and windshields will require toning down using a mixture of oil and sand. When leaving our start point, we'll be moving in a period of darkness so during reduced visibility we will use blackout lights with chemlights on the front and rear of each vehicle.

"The MRAPs and truck will need to be hardened. A vehicle is less vulnerable to the effects of fragmentation and small arms fire by adding sandbags. Its primary purpose is to protect the truck's occupants. The protection afforded is significant and often means the difference between someone getting his nuts or his foot blown off.

"Your own personal safety measures include the wearing of protective equipment and the use of safety belts. Make sure your seat belts are tight, otherwise whiplash may occur during an explosion. Also, fasten the seat belt as low as possible on the stomach. Use correct posture. Keep the backbone straight and supported by a backrest to better absorb shock and place feet flat on the floor."

Katie scribbled down various notes and listened intently to Joe's voice. As hard as she tried, she could not keep her gaze from straying to her husband. She watched the way he handled the briefing, noticing that his voice was firm and calm and that he addressed his comments to all of them, pausing at intervals for notes to be taken then moving on.

On one or two occasions, his gaze had focused on her and their eyes had met. At these glances, Katie tried to keep any reflection of her emotions from showing on her face and quickly glanced back at her notebook, concentrating solely on getting pertinent information down, gritting her teeth and determined not to allow her concentration to waver and allow irritating and painful thoughts of Joe to distract her.

Joe was fully aware of his wife's presence, had observed her quick glances at him, but felt pain at the lack of emotion on her face and in her green eyes, which had none of their usual sparkle. He could see the determination and stubbornness in her face and was almost sure that she was controlling her emotions because of his presence.

He was proud of her ability to maintain her dignity and courage in the face of what must be—for her—a humiliating and uncomfortable situation. She also didn't look well. There was something wrong—he could sense it—but it was too late to show concern for her now. She would reject his queries and his anxiety as just his duty to her, probably give him a mouthful and send him packing. Joe forcefully pushed the thoughts about Katie to the back of his mind and went back to the briefing.

"Radio transmissions will be kept brief. Use low power and maintain signal silence whenever possible. When we reach the last leg of our route, we will need to maintain security elements to the front and rear and, when required, to the flanks of our convoys. The track to the FOB is an unknown quantity and we will also be using the HSTAMIDS diligently.

"The terries seem to have the urge to plant IEDs and mines in the early hours of the morning under cover of darkness, so it's eyes-on and observations for the first few hours even though the primary route is pretty well used. You are all aware that command-detonated mines can precede an ambush. Keep your eyes peeled for mines placed along the shoulder. A booby-trap system is very effective against personnel and equipment. Convoys have now employed guidelines to limit damage from mines. Closely track the vehicle in front, avoid driving on the shoulder of a road and whenever possible, *do not* run over foreign objects. Avoid potholes and fresh earth. Keep a lookout for holes in the road, puddles, boxes, wires on the road surface, evidence of vegetation disturbance, differences in plant growth such as wilting or dead foliage, irregularities in color or texture of the ground and signs warning local populace. Another lovely way for the terries to disguise their handiwork is in the carcasses of dead animals, in soda cans, trash bags and MREs—as long as the poor bastards didn't eat the crap first. Even *I* could feel sorry for them if they do that." There was brief laughter from the marines at this last statement.

"The terries usually like to place mines on frequently used roadways leading to and from construction sites, in brush and other traffic obstructions placed on roadways, bridge bypasses and obvious turnarounds and shoulders. Watch out for local national traffic and the reactions of people on foot because they will often give away the location of any mines or booby traps.

"Designated drivers should watch for suspicious activity on overpasses and never stop under one. Enemy hide positions will usually have line of sight to the kill zone and an easy escape route. They lay IEDs along the side of a road on the shoulder or daisy chained in a decoy attack.

"Okay, now the interesting shit is finished with I'll give you the bad news. I want you all to move accommodations. We have new accommodation in Sector D, our marshaling area. This is where we will carry out our drills and inspections. We have already taken delivery of the Cougars and the truck, and I want you all there with your equipment for 1100 hours this morning. Delivery of supplies will commence tomorrow at 1400 hours. Mission start will be 0400 hours two days from now. Corporal Anderson?"

Joe turned to Katie, who was staring at him in horror.

"Yes, Staff Sergeant," she responded after attempting to clear her throat.

"You need to move your kit as well, and no, you won't be sharing with these numbnuts, you'll be pleased to know. You'll have a tent all to yourself. You'll be solely in charge of checking the medical supplies and ordering anything else that you might need. You'll also have responsibility for storing all the equipment. If you need any help, get one of these ladies to give you a hand."

Joe paused, staring at Katie for long seconds, until she nodded.

"Yes, Staff Sergeant," she responded, and he heard her voice tremble then eventually she looked back down at her notebook.

"Okay." Joe turned back to the marines. "You've got one-and-one-half hours to collect your gear and report to Sector D. Get going."

At Joe's final words, Katie jumped to her feet, sliding her notebook and pen back into the pocket on the sleeve of her combat shirt. Then after quickly grabbing her weapon, she made for the doors of the briefing room. She felt suddenly claustrophobic and needed to get outside.

Hurrying through the crowd of milling men, Katie thrust her way out of the room and almost ran down the corridor, slamming out through the doors. Once outside, she took a deep breath of the sultry air and closed her eyes.

She had stupidly thought she could control her emotions on seeing Joe but it hadn't worked. Being in his presence caused a surge of love and longing so powerful that it was proving to be a difficult internal battle to keep her concentration entirely focused on what she was doing. Now, she felt lonelier than she could have ever imagined herself to be.

A hand landed on her shoulder—interrupting her thoughts—and Dan's voice said, "There you are."

Steeling herself and forcing a smile to her face, Katie turned. "Here I am," she replied.

"I thought you might need some help getting your gear together," Dan asked.

Katie felt relief that she was being accompanied, even though the offer came from a man who obviously had feelings for her and would need to be let down gently.

Her smile more genuine, Katie nodded. "Thanks, Dan. I'd appreciate that."

"Good, let's go then. We don't have much time," Dan urged and the two moved off down the road toward the women's accommodation.

Chapter Seventeen

With her medical pack in one hand and her own personal one in the other, Katie pushed her way through the tent flap and made her way to join Lima squad for their final pre-mission briefing.

It was 0330 hours in the morning and still dark, although on the distant horizon there was a faint lightening to navy blue as a new day prepared to dawn. The moon was still full, even though it was low in the sky and a faint warm breeze lifted wispy curls of hair to tease Katie's warm cheeks.

She paused outside the tent where she had spent the last forty-eight hours alone and she glanced around her. She knew for whom she was searching but after a few minutes, failed to find him.

Taking a deep breath of the early morning air, her senses welcomed the smells of sun-heated earth, oil and aviation fuel and the mumbled grumblings of the ever-present generators. Even through the turmoil of her emotions, she felt a brief twinge of excitement interspersed with sharp pangs of anxiety at the forthcoming mission. She hadn't been able to shake the thought that the next few weeks were going to be the hardest of her life and not just on a personal level.

Members of Lima squad milled restlessly in the area in front of the row of tents, talking quietly and smoking, their large, heavily laden rucksacks piled on the ground ready to be loaded into the convoy vehicles. All the men were dressed in full combat clothing, weapons slung casually over their shoulders and a number of marines — by their jerky gestures — appeared nervous. Occasionally an outburst of raucous laughter shattered the silence as someone cracked a joke — the volume and over-the-top humor proclaiming the pressure of the moment.

Katie's mind went back over the previous two days. She and the rest of the squad had not had a moment to draw a relaxed breath. If they were not receiving supplies, checking same then unloading them, taking part in drills or attending the constant mission briefings for updated Intel, Katie herself was inventorying her own medical supplies and equipment, ordering items that she was short of and thereafter making sure that all of it was stored according to regulations in the MRAPs and the truck. She had only caught six hours of sleep over the last forty-eight, alone in a tent meant for twenty-four people. It had been an uncomfortable, isolating experience and she had wished on numerous occasions that Joe would put in an appearance to speak to her or to see how she was, but there had been no sign of him.

Lying in the dark tent with only a chemlamp to keep her company, she had found it impossible to believe that their marriage was over. After all that they had been through together — the love they had for each other — Joe, without warning, had thrown it all away.

She could only hope that after this mission they could salvage something.

Now, straightening her slumped shoulders, she walked slowly toward the men. Dan, seeing her approach, immediately came to stand beside her.

"Ready?" he asked grinning at her.

Katie nodded. "As ready as I'll ever be, I suppose," she said, giving him a small smile in return.

"You'll do okay, Katie," Dan reassured her gently. "Everything will be fine."

"You think?" Katie responded — unconvinced — trying to quell the butterflies that were quivering agitatedly in the pit of her stomach.

At that moment, a loud familiar voice ordered, "Okay, marines, form up."

Jumping slightly, Katie saw Joe exiting from the operations tent followed by Sergeant Eastman. Trying to remain as composed as possible, heavily burdened with both her packs and weapon, she and the squad quickly formed up into two lines. She took her place in the front row, standing to attention, her personal pack placed neatly in front of her in line with those belonging to the others.

Refusing to turn her head to watch her husband, she stared straight ahead but as he and Louis Eastman took up position in front of them, both wearing full combat gear and carrying weapons and helmets, her gaze darted to his face.

He looked calm and relaxed but alert, his eyes studying his men as they stood silently. His gaze seemed to rest on her for a second before moving on and Katie felt a sharp pang of hurt at his seeming indifference.

Joe, I love you but screw you for doing this to me.

The small, forlorn thought popped unbidden into her mind and brought with it the sting of tears to her eyes.

I miss you and I want you. I don't want to lose you.

Katie bit down hard on her bottom lip, tasting the brief tang of blood as her teeth penetrated the soft flesh, causing a sharp pain that was enough to banish the unhappy thoughts. She once more focused her gaze directly ahead until she suddenly saw, from the corner of her eye, a further person exit the operations tent to join Joe and Sergeant Eastman. Her eyes darting to the new arrival, Katie felt her whole world take a nosedive.

What the fuck is she *doing here?*

She was shocked as she recognized the woman who strode over to stand beside Joe.

She was tall and elegant, even attired in full combat gear, with ash-blonde hair and beautiful, high cheek-boned features. Katie watched the woman smile at her husband and felt the first stirrings of unease. It was the sinking feeling that every woman experiences when she perceives a threat to her marriage and to the love that she always believed was hers.

The newcomer was Sergeant Dana Edwards, the woman who had been involved with Joe before Katie had entered his life. Katie grew rigid with tension and — *yes, let's be honest* — jealousy.

She watched as Joe turned to the woman, say something to her then smiled, and Katie suddenly wanted to scream aloud, run to him and lash out, hurting him as badly as he was hurting her. He looked as though he didn't have a care in the world, as though Katie, along with their baby daughter and unborn child, did not exist. She wanted to run as fast and as far as she could. Instead, she stood stiffly, gritting her teeth, focusing her attention to the front again, hoping and praying that she could maintain her control long enough until she was alone.

"Right, Marines," Joe suddenly announced. "Let's get this show on the road. Designated drivers and crew-served gunners, go to your places. The rest of you load up."

Lima squad broke ranks and moved toward the two huge MRAPs and the truck. Katie went to the open doors at the rear of the first MRAP — the head vehicle of the convoy — and waited at the end of the line for the men to climb aboard. To keep her mind off the unexpected appearance of Dana Edwards in the squad, she studied the heavy vehicle she was about to board with intense concentration.

Over the last two days, she had learned a great deal about the transport that she and her squad were going to be virtually living in for two hundred kilometers, so for her own peace of mind, she went over the statistics.

The sand-colored Cougar mine-resistant, ambush protected vehicle was a powerful machine. A six by six, seven-meter long monster, it could carry ten troops, a crew of two plus equipment and supplies. It had an armored, reinforced base offering added insurance that its occupants would be reasonably protected if a mine or IED was to go off beneath it, with sides that were reinforced with enough armor to stop 7.62-millimeter armor-piercing rounds and rocket-propelled grenades. The semi-circular gun turret, positioned in the center of the roof, was made of reinforced armor plating disguised with sand-colored netting which protected a remotely controlled weapon station with a fifty-millimeter heavy machine gun.

It would never win any beauty contests but Katie was fully aware that she and the rest of the squad were going to be reasonably safe while traveling in the confines of the Cougar MRAP, and she allowed herself to relax slightly.

She became aware that Joe, Louis Eastman and the female sergeant had joined the line behind her, interrupting her assessment of the monster vehicle. Determined not to give any sign that the arrival of Sergeant Edwards had unnerved her, she completely ignored their presence, waiting patiently as the men in front of her moved forward, each one, on reaching the open heavy hydraulic doors, climbed the two metal steps up into the vehicle's dim interior. As Katie herself prepared to take her turn climbing aboard, Dan Reed, who had entered the vehicle immediately before her, reached down to take her personal pack from her.

Handing it up to him and acknowledging his assistance with a small smile, she shrugged out of the rucksack on her back, ready to give it to him, when she heard quite clearly from behind a female voice order, "Get a move on, Corporal. We haven't got all day to stand around waiting for you."

For a brief moment, Katie felt her whole body freeze — at first unable to believe that she had indeed heard those words — the soft but firm voice barely hiding a hint of rudeness. She hesitated, debating on whether to retaliate, then with irritation getting the better of her she turned slowly to face the female sergeant who was standing with her arms folded and an impatient look on her beautiful face.

Katie noticed Joe and Louis Eastman standing behind the sergeant, both showing expressions of surprise. Standing her ground and choosing her opening words carefully, she stared for long seconds at the woman in front of her then responded with a stilted and controlled, "I beg your pardon?"

Sergeant Edwards glared back, and Katie instantly realized with an intuition that only women have, that she and this woman had one important thing in common—a man— and for that reason, Katie felt an immediate personal antagonism.

"You heard me, Corporal," Sergeant Dana Edwards snapped in an unfriendly manner, her dislike of Katie evident in the look of contempt she gave her.

Katie straightened slowly, outwardly calm but seething with anger inside.

"With all due respect, Sergeant," she began, taking a deep breath, her voice sounding icy with fury to her ears, "if you'd kindly have the manners to wait for a few more minutes, I'll be out of your way."

Her green gaze held the sergeant's blue one, knowing that the tone of her words as well as the words themselves had been bordering on the insubordinate and Katie didn't care in the least. She waited for the resultant explosion.

It was her husband's voice she heard instead when he ordered, "Move on, Corporal."

Turning her gaze away from her adversary, Katie glanced briefly at her husband, glared dismissively back at Sergeant Edwards then finally dismissing all three, turned her back on them. Trying to keep her hand from trembling, she handed her equipment up to Dan, who was leaning out of the back of the MRAP studying the confrontation with an amused look, and she climbed up the two steps into the interior of the vehicle, taking the last seat on the left, closest to the doors.

Hastily she strapped herself in, using her legs to push her personal pack beneath her, then, straddling her medical pack, she rested her weapon across her thighs. She could feel the double layer of sandbags and rubber matting beneath her boots, the depth of the reinforcing material already making her limbs feel uncomfortably cramped, but she would have to deal with it.

"Nice one, honey," Dan said quietly, tilting his head toward hers. "I'm impressed."

Turning to the young corporal, Katie grimaced. "Dan, that was nothing to be proud of," she replied quietly and distastefully. "I just don't like being spoken to like that for no reason, even if she is a sergeant."

Not wanting to discuss the confrontation any further, she leaned back against the side of the vehicle and, closing her eyes, heard what must have been the two sergeants getting into the vehicle, knowing that Joe would take position up front in the cab.

She listened to the hydraulic doors hissing shut, the heavy locking mechanism engaging then the engine starting with a low rumble. Radios, both personal and from the MRAP cab, crackled harshly, then Joe's voice sounded, giving the order to move out. There was a jolt as the heavy vehicle began to roll forward, then they were increasing speed and pulling out onto the main road leading to the first checkpoint at the base entrance.

Once they were on the move, Katie opened her eyes and gazed around the interior of the enormous vehicle. It was almost dark inside with the exception of dim light seeping in through the partial partition of bulletproof glass separating the cab from the rest of the MRAP. Apart from the dull rumbling growl of the engine, it was quiet. Some of the marines dozed, their helmeted heads swaying to the rocking movements created by the powerful suspension and some gazed into space, possibly thinking about the upcoming mission or dwelling on their own personal thoughts.

Turning to look out of the back window, Katie could see the lights of the airfield and motor pool receding into the distance, comforting halos of luminescence with flitting firefly pinpoints of torchlight and twin cones of headlights from the vehicles driving along the road.

In the direction they were traveling to leave the base, there was a slight golden glow in the sky as dawn began to break, tendrils of lemon and citrus and orange beginning to spread out to silhouette the distant peaks of the mountains. If Katie had been feeling in a better frame of mind and not so depressed and lonely, she would have admired the beautiful sight. Previous sunrises had always given her a sense of freedom, made her feel refreshed and ready to start the day, but not today and probably not for a number of days to come.

She sighed and shifted uncomfortably on the metal and canvas seat. Seething with barely concealed anger and experiencing a sharp pang of jealousy at what had occurred back at the base, Katie turned again to stare unseeingly out of the back window, wondering whether her husband was deliberately antagonizing her and playing on her love for him. If that was the case then he was not the man she had known and loved.

Despite feeling hot and claustrophobic in the confines of the vehicle, Katie eventually closed her eyes again. She just wanted to sleep, blank her mind and slip into a dreamless oblivion. She wondered drowsily what, if anything, Joe was thinking.

Does he still care about me? Does he really want to end our marriage? Did he ever love me at all or has he finally reached the conclusion that he made a mistake?

The thought that it might be over between them made Katie realize how much she still loved him and what it would do to her if he left. She was not about to let him go. The presence of Dana Edwards had triggered her woman's instinct to fight to keep her man. If she had to she would tell the other woman the exact nature of hers and Joe's relationship and advise her in no uncertain terms that she was not about to hand the father of her children over to another woman without an all-out battle.

The slight rocking from the reinforced suspension of the MRAP and the rolling tidal-like movement over the road began to soothe her and Katie's body slowly began to relax. As it did so, her head slipped sideways and came to rest on Dan Reed's shoulder.

Joe, seated in the front of the MRAP, glanced in the oversized windshield mirror and had a clear view of Katie's pretty face and her head resting all too comfortably on the young corporal's shoulder. He was not amused by the sight at all. In fact, jealousy had begun to eat at his insides, gnawing away like a tenacious rat. Part of him thought with an element of rationality that she had not rested her head on the man's shoulder intentionally but that did not make it any easier for him to have to watch.

He was confused. What had been so clear to him back in the U.S. — before this most recent deployment — was now a mixture of indecisiveness and fear. Anger and revenge had been his primary all-consuming thought, the only real emotions remaining after his capture and the death of his men which had prompted him to volunteer for another tour of duty.

He had had every intention of getting to Afghanistan, biding his time then somehow hunting down the insurgents and taking them out. Up until he had told Katie that night at the PX that he wanted her out of his hair — and let's face it that was exactly how it had come across no matter how he had tried to pretty it up — all he had wanted was to regain his commitment to the

Marine Corps and get back what dignity and values he had been gradually losing over the last few months.

Now, something had changed. Instead of his anger and revenge feeding from the tension in the atmosphere, the obsessive urge for resolution had slowly begun to dissipate, leaving him empty of direction.

Katie's arrival, proving that she was willing to put herself in danger purely to be by his side, had brought him up short. His priority should always have been Katie and his daughter back home in the States but instead, due to his own stupidity, he had screwed up his career and his marriage big time. With startling clarity, he had come to realize that there was nothing more important than Katie and his baby daughter.

He'd made the decision that once this mission was over, he would see a psych doctor at the CTH and get his deployment cut short. He'd hoped that Katie would help him but after what he had done to her, an empty gut-wrenching feeling told him that he might already have lost her.

A sudden violent jolt of the vehicle startled Katie awake, bleary-eyed and dry-mouthed, and after feeling disoriented for a few seconds she discovered with mortification that her head was resting comfortably on Dan's shoulder. Uttering a small moan of discomfiture, she bolted upright, noticing that it was now broad daylight, and that her comfortable sleep on the corporal's shoulder was blatantly on show for all to see, including Joe. Heat suffused her face as she turned to Dan, who was smiling at her.

"I'm so sorry," she murmured with embarrassment.

Dan shook his head. "No worries," he answered, a smile on his face.

Taking note of the warm expression that Dan was directing at her, Katie shifted uncomfortably, feeling uneasy and sad that this young marine appeared to have fallen for her and knowing that in the not-too-distant future he was going to be hurt. Eventually, she would have to tell him gently that she was not interested, that her heart was already committed to someone else and she was not looking forward to that future appointment.

She turned away from him and glanced out of the back window of the vehicle, hoping that her non-committal demeanor would give him the message.

Chapter Eighteen

Katie immediately noticed that the scenery had changed. Bending forward slightly to look out of the dirty, reinforced glass set in one of the back doors, she frowned and turned to Dan.

"Where are we?" she asked curiously.

Dan leaned forward, his shoulder brushing against hers, his face a few inches from her own.

"Just coming up on Gereshk," he answered.

Sliding farther forward, almost to the edge of her seat and as much as the belt allowed her to, Katie studied their surroundings.

From what she could see through the dust and grime of the small window, it looked as though they were passing through an agricultural area consisting of small fields of different crops. There was rice, wheat and several vegetables. Men of all ages worked among them, tilling the land, and an occasional woman and young girls assisted with the work and carried water. Dressed in brightly colored Afghan dresses worn over pants, they wore *chadors*, or large scarves, over their heads, which Katie knew was a sign of modesty and respect.

As the convoy entered the outskirts of the town with its speed greatly reduced, evidence of twenty years of war immediately became visible.

The road they traveled was full of craters and holes from landmines, haphazardly filled with sand, gravel, and rubbish. Lining the road were bombed-out shops and homes and Katie was horrified to see that people still lived and worked in the ruins. Brightly colored lengths of material hung from wrecked ceilings and rafters or from glassless windows, obviously shielding the inhabitants from inclement weather. Cardboard blocked empty doorways and holes, and hammered roughly across ragged apertures in roofs and walls was splintered and broken scavenged wood. She could even see that on the crowded streets, there were people — families — living on the littered pavements in makeshift shelters.

"How many people live here?" Katie asked, feeling a sense of dismay at the living conditions and the mass destruction wrought on the Afghan people.

"At least forty-three thousand Pashtuns," Dan answered. "About three men to every woman."

Katie glanced at him, feeling horrified.

How could so many people survive in what is obviously a ruin, their livelihood and their lives virtually destroyed?

"You're kidding me," she replied at last, shocked. "And they're still here? Look at the place. It's a ruin."

"Where would they go?" Dan asked her. "They're not nomads. Each Pashtun has a home or place of business that has been in their family or clan for decades. These people would die before giving them up and moving on."

Katie turned back to look out of the window again. "How do you know so much about these people?"

Dan laughed quietly. "What? You think someone like me can't be interested in culture?"

Katie glanced over her shoulder at him. "Not at all," she said. "I'm just curious."

"I've always been interested in the culture of other countries," Dan explained. "It's like looking through windows into other people's lives, maybe even their souls. Makes you appreciate the things you have in your own life."

Small wooden stalls lined the single dirt road and Katie wondered whether it was a market. The most basic of goods were on display, with several fruit stalls and one butcher shop with slabs of meat hanging in the open air. Kate shuddered at the thought of people buying and eating what was, without doubt, contaminated food. The poverty-stricken people likely didn't have fridges or freezers or fresh water. How they survived, she had no idea.

Children, thin and dirty, clad in ragged clothes, thronged the streets and Katie was horrified that most of them were below the age of approximately ten years and were completely alone without an adult in sight. Men and women walked past the young ones — completely ignoring them — going about their business as though the children did not exist.

Refuse littered the narrow road and Katie fervently hoped that what looked like pools of sludge filling the shallow drainage trenches on each side was run-off from rain and not something more horrendous.

Most of the people ignored the convoy moving slowly through the street, going about their daily business of trying to survive, as though they were used to seeing heavily-armored vehicles, but Katie noticed that some — mostly men — had stopped and were staring at the intrusion, their gazes intent, bearded faces expressionless.

"Do you think the Taliban are here?" she asked, once more addressing the question to Dan.

"Probably," Dan answered. "The bastards move among ordinary people, take them as hostages and use intimidation to gain information about us. They take their possessions and control them through fear, get them to trail and track us by blackmail. They always seem to know when we're around."

"Doesn't our presence create more trouble for the people?" Katie asked worriedly, turning to stare at Dan once more.

From the corner of her eye, she noticed Joe's reflection in the cab mirror, and saw that he was watching her. She could not see the expression on his face but wondered if he could hear every word of the conversation. His gaze was intense, hypnotic and for a few short moments, she fell silent, forgetting what she had been thinking or the question she had asked of Dan. At last, not reacting to Joe's stare, she turned back to the other man.

"We build roads for them, schools for the children. We help them with power and water drainage systems, and we protect them," Dan answered. "Hearts and minds, Katie."

"Fuck! All vehicles stop! *Stop! Stop!*"

Joe's words were loud and abrupt as a man darted out from the crowd, congregating on the ruined pavement, almost falling to the ground in front of the huge front tires, but careening instead against the reinforced grill of the MRAP, rebounding off it and only saving himself by slamming the palms of his hands down onto the hood. He came to a stop, dead center of the road, staring through the windshield at Joe, shoulders heaving with his efforts, his almost black eyes seeming to pin Joe into his seat.

The driver obeyed Joe's command, instantly bringing the MRAP to a sharp stop, suspension bouncing with the abrupt cessation of forward motion, brakes hissing in protest.

For a few seconds, Joe sat frozen in his seat, his breath locked in his throat as he waited for an explosive of some kind to be unearthed from the man's voluminous robes and thrown at the vehicle.

Shit! He hadn't been concentrating. His gaze and thoughts had been focused solely on Katie in the back, straining to listen to the conversation she had been having with the corporal – again.

His gaze held that of the Afghan man through the reinforced dirty glass and silence fell within the vehicle, broken only when the driver exclaimed, "What the fuck?"

Joe raised a hand to stop the marine from saying anything further. Moving slowly and carefully, he thumbed his PRR then hesitated. Giving one last glare at the man impeding the convoy's movement, his eyes eventually moved away from him to the left then to the right side of the road, his eyes searching the Pashtuns lining the street. Even though he did not see anyone acting remotely suspiciously, he couldn't be sure that the man was alone and he remained uneasy.

He finally thumbed his PRR. "Okay, Lima squad. Listen up. A single individual has run in front of this vehicle and doesn't appear to want to let us pass. He seems to be alone, but I want crews on the guns, surveillance of all rooftops for hostiles. Security teams of two get ready to dismount and take up positions around the convoy. This could be an ambush so I want all weapons to go live. I am going to have to dismount to speak to the man. Does anyone speak Pashto?"

In the back of the MRAP, everyone glanced at each other. It was unthinkable for the convoy to stop in an urban location. Normally, any convoy traveling through a built-up area where hostiles could so easily use diversionary tactics or take hostages as cover to enable an ambush to take place, did not stop, no matter what occurred. The Taliban, as a general rule, tended to disregard the fact that innocent victims often fell foul of their strategies, and they either ignored or simply did not care about how much carnage and destruction on a massive scale their mercenary actions caused.

Katie, Joe's words ringing in her ears and unable to believe what was happening, stiffened as tension mounted. She was fully aware that the convoy was now a sitting duck, the vehicles hemmed in as they were by people, neither able to go forward or in reverse and were effectively trapped in a kill zone. She jumped as Dan spoke up beside her, his words shattering the silence.

"I speak a bit, Staff Sergeant."

"Good," Katie heard Joe acknowledge. "Join me outside, Corporal Reed and you too, Corporal Anderson. I want one security team to dismount. That individual needs searching before we can approach him. On my order…go."

Katie heard the sound of the heavy passenger door opening then closing. She stood up, thrusting her arms through the webbing of her medical pack, and waited while Dan unlocked the back doors, swung them open and jumped down. Two more marines, buddying up to form a security team followed behind him and Katie dismounted last, closing the doors behind her.

She landed heavily on the rutted, uneven road, staggering slightly, and quickly looked around her. The first thing to hit her was the smell then the heat. The air reeked of refuse, sewage and rotten meat. The odors seemed to form an almost tangible cloud about her face — viscid and moist — making her feel instantly sick. She briefly put a hand to her mouth and swallowed hard, gritting her teeth.

The crowd lined the ruined street, staring at the scene unfolding before them. There was heavy silence. There was no murmur of conversation or of children making a noise. The crowd stood unmoving and she felt as though she were on display in a zoo. The direct, unblinking dark stares of the Pashtuns caused fear to bloom in her stomach.

The security team walked around Dan, taking the lead from him, raising their weapons slightly and moving around to the right flank of the MRAP. Dan followed and Katie moved into position behind him. She kept her eyes on the crowd, her breathing slightly rapid. She fully expected gunfire to shatter the silence, an explosion to rip apart the buildings in front of her or see heavily-armed Taliban come running toward them. If that happened, Lima squad would have nowhere to run or hide.

Katie saw Joe standing by the passenger door. The Afghan man had joined him and her gaze fell on the stranger, immediately noticing that he looked young, guessing his age to be nearer her own. He sported a beard, had dark piercing eyes, but was very thin, as though he hadn't had a good meal in some considerable time. As she drew closer to him, she heard the sound of rapidly spoken Pashto and noticed the man gesturing at Joe in what Katie thought was an agitated manner.

He did not appear to be either angry or hostile, only desperate to make himself understood.

The security team slowly approached Joe and the newcomer. They took up positions close to the Afghan, still facing toward the crowd, their body language showing tension, evident by their erect posture and the lift of their shoulders. Although they had not raised their weapons into firing positions, they were semi-aimed at the man and, by definition, at the crowd beyond him.

Joe beckoned to Dan and she came to a stop a meter or two behind them, turning to face the noiseless crowd. Their silence and stillness was unnerving and she wondered how so many people could remain so quiet and unmoving. It set her nerves on edge and she licked dry lips and clenched her weapon more tightly.

At a gesture from Joe, one member of the security team approached the Afghan man slowly and proceeded to pat him down while the other marine stood close by, his weapon now aimed solely in the stranger's direction. They paid particular attention to searching the stranger's loose robes and when the marine was finally satisfied that there was nothing concealed about his person, he ordered the man, with a twirl of one finger, to turn a full circle while he checked for wires or any bulkiness that might denote explosives tied around his waist or anywhere else about his body. After a tense few minutes, they completed the search and the marine who had completed the body frisk turned to Joe.

"He's clean, Staff Sergeant."

With his rifle raised slightly, also aimed at the man, Joe nodded. "Okay. Reed, ask him why the fuck he tried to kill himself in front of my MRAP then ask him what his fucking problem is?"

"Yes, Staff Sergeant."

Keeping his distance, Dan repeated Joe's questions in slow Pashto. Even before he had finished speaking, the distraught-appearing Afghan blurted out a virtually incomprehensible sentence and Dan—frowning—lifted his hands and with palms down gestured him to slow down his speech. The man took a deep breath and appeared to repeat his previous statement.

Dan turned to Joe. "He says he's sorry for stopping us in the way that he did. He felt that this was the only way of getting our attention. He says that his wife is in labor and has been for a long time but there is no sign of the child coming. He thinks there is something wrong and asks if we have a doctor, as he needs our help."

Joe nodded his head and glanced over his shoulder at Katie. He saw that she was watching them, saw the alert tilt of her head as she listened to the conversation and the way she had straightened at the mention of someone in trouble.

Shit, he thought to himself. *She'll be off to search for the woman any minute.*

He turned back to Dan. "Ask him where he lives."

Dan obeyed, and they all waited while the Afghan turned and pointed to a small, almost hidden, side street opposite to where the convoy had stopped and he said something back to Dan.

"He says he lives halfway down that side street. He also promises that there is no danger. He only wants help for his wife," said Dan, once the man had finished speaking.

Joe, following the man's pointing finger, saw the narrowness of the street—almost an alleyway—and felt a sinking sensation in his stomach. Lined with bombed-out buildings on either side, he suspected that there were going to be plenty of places where the Taliban could hide and spring an ambush, or even bomb them out of existence if they wanted to.

"Oh, fucking perfect," he exclaimed, gritting his teeth. He remained silent for a few moments—thinking—then said to Dan, "Tell the man that we will help him but first we have to set up security. Tell him to wait." He thumbed his PRR and said, "Louis?"

Sergeant Eastman's response came back immediately. "Yeah, Joe. What's happening?"

Joe briefly explained what he knew so far and what he wanted. "Offload three teams and send them down to me. Take the MRAP and drive down that side street as far as you can and seal it off. I want you to set up the rest of your security teams in a perimeter facing east. Keep your engine running, gun crew watching those rooftops. Is that understood?"

"Roger that, Joe. Moving out."

Katie heard the loud growl of an engine starting up and watched as the trail MRAP moved slowly past, turning right into the street pointed out by the Afghan. It disappeared from sight and cringed, expecting to hear the loud eruption of gunfire or the ripping roar of explosions from IEDs. Nothing happened and she sighed inwardly with relief. She moved to stand beside Joe, listening to his continuing radio conversation.

"All on this net…security teams from the lead MRAP, dismount. Two teams secure the rig, the rest of you form up into three fire teams. Driver, once we are in position, seal the entrance to the street. Dana?"

When Sergeant Edwards responded, Joe continued, "Take your truck down the street a couple of meters and stop, keep your engine running."

The truck drove past and turned into the street and the remaining marines formed into their fire teams.

They positioned themselves in a staggered formation with fire team one offset to the left from fire team two, fire team three offset to the right of fire team two.

Once everyone was in position, Joe held up a hand signaling for everyone to wait then gestured with one finger and pointed at the side street. Fire team one jogged across the main road, with the two remaining fire teams covering them, and disappeared into the street. Joe waited then repeated the gesture, ordering fire team two to follow. Again, he waited then ordered fire team three to proceed. He then turned to Katie and Dan. "You're with me. Let's go."

He gestured to the Afghan man to follow and he and Katie ran across the road, into the side street where the teams were waiting.

Joe led the way through the waiting marines to take the lead, then halted, turning to watch as the lead MRAP pulled into position behind them, effectively sealing off the street. He then raised a hand and gestured for the teams to move off, each man concentrating on empty doors, glassless windows and parts of roofs that had not collapsed from bomb damage.

Every now and again, Joe would lift up one, two or three fingers and the fire team allocated that number would disappear through a doorless ruin, carry out a hasty sweep then exit, confirming all was clear.

Eventually the Afghan man stopped at a small house that still appeared reasonably intact, halfway down the deserted street. He spoke to Dan who turned to Joe. "This is his house, Staff Sergeant."

Joe ordered two members of fire team one to wait outside the building, either side of the doorway. Fire teams two and three continued on down the street, spreading out and then stopping on either side, taking up positions equidistant from each other. The remaining members of fire team one carried out an internal sweep of the man's house while Joe, Katie and the Afghan waited outside for confirmation that the interior was clear. Joe carried out a final visual check on the MRAP in place down at the far end then gestured for Katie and Dan to follow him into the building.

On entering, Katie was appalled at her surroundings. Someone had obviously tried to patch up holes and cracks in the walls with bits of cardboard and lengths of material and although the house was in a much better condition than others she had seen, it was still not a fit habitation for humans. There was a dank smell in the air, which was laden with dust, and because the sun could not reach through the glassless windows due to the narrowness of the street, it was cold. The furnishings were pitiful, the combined kitchen and lounge littered with a scattering of rubble and debris.

The man gestured frantically for them to move through the small lounge into a tiny back room and having followed him, Katie was horrified to find a young woman of no more than seventeen or eighteen lying on a pile of rugs and blankets on a dirty floor. She instantly assessed her patient, noting that the woman appeared to be in a great deal of pain and there was a look of exhaustion on her pretty face. Her skin glistened with sweat and her long black hair hung soaking about her shoulders. Although she lay very still, low moans escaped from her now and again.

Her mind now totally focused on the patient, Katie hurried toward the makeshift bed, shrugging out of her pack. Throwing it to the floor, she knelt beside the woman and gently touched her arm, carefully alerting her to her presence. The woman slowly opened her eyes and as she caught her first glimpse of Katie, a look of terror crossed her face.

Murmuring soft words of reassurance, guessing that the woman might not understand but hoping that the soothing tone of her voice might convey her intent, Katie pulled on a pair of nitrile gloves, which she took from the front of her body armor, and turned to Dan.

"Can you tell the husband to come and sit on the bed? We're going to lift her shoulders and he's going to support her. Staff Sergeant, can you help me lift her?"

Speaking to the Afghan man again and after what appeared to be a brief explanation of what they needed him to do, the man complied, seating himself on the makeshift bed and moving to sit behind his wife. Joe moved around to the woman's side opposite to Katie and they both gently lifted her into a semi-upright position so that her husband could move close enough to her to support her shoulders. Katie took his hands, brought them under the woman's arms, and joined them together across his wife's upper stomach. This elicited a moan of panic from the young woman and Katie spoke softly to her, stroking her forehead.

The woman went quiet, and Katie turned to Joe and Dan. "I need to examine her, so you both need to move away to give her some privacy."

Once the men had moved, Katie took a combat casualty blanket from her pack and, unfolding it, spread it across the woman's slightly raised knees. Making reassuring noises, Katie gently pushed the woman's knees into a more bent position and farther apart.

Speaking aloud, she said, "Dan? Can you please tell the husband to tell his wife that I am here to deliver her baby? Tell her that I need to examine her and that I will not hurt her. I have to know how the baby is lying and whether there is room for it to be born."

Dan relayed the message to the man and he in turn explained it to his wife. The woman stared at Katie, wide-eyed, and made a small pitiful noise but then nodded.

"Okay. Let's do this," she murmured to herself. She positioned herself between the woman's legs and carefully and gently examined her. After making her assessment, she said, "She is fully dilated and the baby is crowning. She is very narrow so there might not be enough room but she needs to push. Dan, can you please tell her husband to tell her that she needs to push as hard as she can at the next pain."

While Dan was relaying the request to the husband, Katie glanced quickly at Joe. He was staring at her and as he saw her gaze on him, he winked slightly and said, "You can do this, Corporal."

Katie nodded and turned back to her patient. Placing a gentle hand on the woman's stomach, she felt the abdominal muscles begin to tighten and saw a grimace on the woman's face, confirming that a contraction was on its way. She said in a commanding voice, "Push!"

The husband relayed the word and the woman uttered a wail of fear and frantically shook her head.

"Push," Katie ordered again and glared at the husband. "She has to push, otherwise the baby will start to suffer. Dan, tell him she needs to push."

Dan, his voice sounding nervous, spoke at length to the woman's husband who in turn spoke to the woman. Katie held the young woman's eyes and nodded.

Gritting her teeth, her face turning bright red with the effort, the woman raised her head and began to push hard. Katie raised a hand and lifted first one finger, then two and so on until she had alternately raised ten fingers, then she gestured with the palm of her hand to stop. The woman's head slumped back against her husband and she closed her eyes, whimpering with the effort.

"That's excellent," Katie praised, giving the laboring woman a minute or two to regain her breath then, "Again. Push!"

For about five minutes, with Dan then the woman's husband relaying Katie's requests, she cajoled, ordered, then bullied until at last she delivered the child's head and could finally see what the problem was.

Trying to keep the alarm out of her voice, she ordered sharply, "Stop pushing." She looked up at Dan. "Dan. Don't repeat this but the baby has the cord wrapped around its neck. I have to unwind it. Tell her under no circumstances must she push."

As the room fell silent, Katie hooked a finger beneath a tight loop of umbilical cord around the infant's neck, tugged gently, then firmly unwound it. Once the baby was free, she stared intently at the woman and said, "Okay, push. Push as hard as you can."

The woman, at last seeming to understand, obeyed, her face contorting, every muscle straining in her frail body, a wail of pain coming from her mouth, which spiraled up into the air in a scream and finally, the baby slithered out into Katie's waiting hands. She quickly turned it on its side and using her little finger, scooped out the mucus from inside its mouth. The child spluttered, choked then let out a lusty cry.

The Afghan man suddenly laughed and gently stroked his wife's forehead. The young woman opened her eyes at the sound of her baby's cry and offered a weak, tired smile of her own.

Katie, cuddling the newborn, carried out a visual assessment then said to Dan, "Tell them it's a boy, small but he's fine with ten fingers and ten toes. He looks surprisingly healthy. We have to wait for the placenta to deliver. Can you ask if they have something to wrap the baby in?"

As if he understood, the man got up from the blankets and hurried from the room. In a few minutes, he returned, carrying a brightly colored, beautifully crafted afghan blanket that he handed almost reverently to Katie, who was cleaning the baby with some gauze and bottled water.

Once she had dried the now-sleeping infant, she wrapped him gently in the elaborate cover then, standing up, went to the woman and laid him gently in her waiting arms. The man gently touched his son's thick black hair then stood up and proceeded to approach Dan, Joe and Katie. With the palms of his hands placed together as though in prayer, he bowed to each of them in turn, murmuring, *"As-salamu alaykum."*

Katie inclined her head, thanking the new father, then went back to the bed. She massaged the woman's abdomen, waiting for the next stage of the baby's birth then once this had taken place, gave the placenta to the husband to dispose of. After cleaning the woman, making her more comfortable then washing her own hands in bottled water, she turned to Joe.

"Can I speak to you, Staff Sergeant?" she asked.

"Yeah, sure," Joe replied and drew her to one side. "What's up?"

"They can't stay here," she began. "This is no place for a newborn."

Joe put his hands on his hips. "What do you want me to do?" he asked.

Katie heard the note of impatience in his voice but continued, "We need to medevac them out of here. The dust alone could cause the baby to become sick and the woman could contract an infection. We need to get them extracted to the CTH."

"Sorry, Corporal. That's going to have to be a no."

Katie glared at him. "Why?" she asked, her tone barely civil.

Joe straightened. "Because, Corporal, these people are proud and will not leave their homes. It probably took a helluva lot for that guy to jump out in front of the convoy like that. Besides, we have a mission to complete and we need to get out of here before anything else gets fucked up beyond all recognition."

"Oh, yes, right, your precious mission. I forgot how important it was to you," Katie snapped, her voice still low. She saw Joe stiffen at her tone and frown, his brows lowering over his eyes.

"You're stepping over the line on this one, Corporal," he replied.

"I'll step over the line anytime where a patient is concerned," Katie protested stubbornly, knowing that she was pushing her luck. "The baby will suffer if we leave him and the mother in this godforsaken place."

Joe pointed a finger at her. "Enough of this shit, Corporal. *Don't* fucking push me on this. It's a no." With that, he turned his back on her and thumbed his PRR.

Katie stood glaring at his back then strode to her pack, bent and slammed it closed. Picking it up, she shrugged into its straps, and turned back to Joe.

"I'm ready to leave, Staff Sergeant," she announced coldly and with a last look at the new family, she left the tiny disheveled room, wondering whether the newborn would live and feeling a terrible sadness that she could not help the pathetically proud family.

Chapter Nineteen

Once everyone was safely back inside the vehicles and with no further hindrance — the crowd having gone about their business — the convoy crawled through the single street for another hour until eventually it reached the outskirts of the town. The tumbled buildings and blatantly poor lifestyle of the Afghan people began to turn once more back to the dun-colored flatlands of the desert.

Katie — exhausted — slumped back in her seat, feeling sadness at the poverty she had seen, particularly the lost and lonely children wandering the streets, thin and hungry.

She wondered if their presence in Afghanistan had done any good for these people at all, whether the ISAF's offered protection from the Taliban was worth all the deaths and the destruction of their homes.

The Taliban took hostages from small villages and towns as they moved through them and onward, using them as a shield to prevent themselves being set on by security forces. Whichever way you looked at it, the

Afghanistan people couldn't win. On the one hand, the constant infiltration of the Taliban into their lives, on the other, the security forces plaguing them in their attempts to protect them and help them, ended up causing as much damage as the enemy.

"Okay, Marines," Joe suddenly announced, startling Katie from her thoughts. "In a few minutes we'll be stopping at a building where we'll have an hour's downtime. Before we dismount, I want two HSTAMIDS teams out — you know who you are — and a sweep done of the perimeter, walls and doors."

He thumbed his PRR, repeated the order to the occupants of the truck and second MRAP, then said. "Corporal Anderson, dismount and stay with me until the sweep is done."

"Yes, Staff Sergeant," Katie acknowledged the order.

Still feeling angry with her husband, she was unable to stop herself from feeling a small thrill of internal excitement when she realized that in a few minutes she would be able to be with him, then immediately felt annoyed at herself for feeling as she did.

Girl, she thought, *you need to get a grip. Make up your mind what you want, Joe or your own personal feeling of worth.*

She was tired of her mind warring with her heart. One minute she wanted to hurt him as he had hurt her, the next she wanted them back as they were, melted when he looked at her, and desperately wanted him.

In the front of the MRAP, Joe's face reflected in the over-sized windshield mirror. As if they were telepathically connected, Joe's gaze caught hers and held it.

Joe saw her green eyes looking into his and with a painful jolt in his stomach, realized that she still loved him. She drove him mad sometimes with her stubbornness and her refusal to back down, particularly on a mission. He tried to tell her with his own gaze how he still felt about her and watched as a flush of color mounted in her cheeks. As he saw her response, a small smile twitched at his mouth.

Reluctantly withdrawing his gaze from hers and forcefully turning his mind to the present, Joe thumbed his PRR and ordered, "All on this net…let's move it. I want the guns manned in both MRAPs and two two-man security teams wait out until everything is clear. Let's move. Go."

A few minutes later, the MRAP halted, the heavy back doors of the vehicle hissed open and Katie, struggling with a pack on each shoulder, her weapon held across her forearms, climbed slowly down the steps.

She winced as heat from the harsh sun hit her like a slap in the face. Squinting against the glaring light, she studied her surroundings—endless flat, desolate landscape with a heat-haze shimmering and rippling in the distance, distorting an unending vista of brown and ochre cracked desert dotted here and there with scorched, stunted vegetation, which clung to what little life it could eke out in the barren harshness. There was not a breath of wind to dissipate the clouds of dust stirred up by their passage along the road that hung almost motionless in the stagnant air. The surrounding desert was silent now that the vehicle engines were quiet.

She moved around to the left flank of the vehicle, joining Joe who was now standing by the driver's door. She struggled to draw the heavy, burning air into her lungs and sweat broke out on her face, beginning to trickle down between her breasts and along her spine.

Trying to ignore the suffocating temperature, she turned in a slow circle, trying to pierce the distant haze in an effort to see if the squad was alone. She could see nothing beyond a few hundred meters because of the dust clouds. Glancing to her right, her gaze finally rested on the long, low, partially ruined, sand-colored building toward which four men were moving very slowly and carefully.

Two men in a line abreast of each other carried a mine detector each, which they swept slowly from side to side. The second row of two men walked precisely behind and in the footsteps of the men in front, weapons pointing out to the left and right, scrutinizing the landscape on either side.

Katie watched as they reached the building and split into two teams, one going to the left, the other to the right, both swiftly sweeping the perimeter, window frames, and doors. Tension mounted as the four men disappeared out of sight around each end of the building, finally appearing back at the front before entering through the doorless entrance. Time dragged interminably before both teams re-emerged from the interior and Katie breathed an audible sigh of relief as a radio transmission confirmed that all was clear.

"All on this net...stand down. Sergeant Eastman, detail one security team to patrol the perimeter. Rotate teams every fifteen minutes." Joe spoke into his radio then silently gestured for Katie to follow him.

Following the flattened areas in the sand and dust made by the mine detectors and the slight indentations of footprints created by the men, they paced the exact same newly-cleared route to the building.

Avidly scanning the ground for anything that could possibly resemble a mine or an IED, Katie followed Joe, keeping precisely behind him as she had seen the others do.

She heaved a sigh of relief when they eventually reached safety and heard the rumble of engines as both MRAPs moved location to take up position at either end of the building, one vehicle facing their approach route, the other pointing in the direction they had yet to take. The supply truck parked parallel to the building between both MRAPs.

On entering the building, Katie was relieved to be out of the hot sun. Although the temperature remained high, inside it was tolerable. Shafts of sunlight speared through the glassless windows lining the front and sides of the structure, motes spinning and dancing in the light as her boots stirred up the dust lying thickly on the cracked mud floor. As she looked around, from what she could see of the interior, it was distinctly unwelcoming with dirty bare walls, rotten woodwork and with part of the flat roof open to the elements. Katie wrinkled her nose when she detected the odor of rot and decay.

The rest of the squad came almost tumbling through the open doorway, uttering groans of satisfaction, throwing equipment down onto the ground, propping weapons against the mud walls, weary bodies slumping down beside them.

Katie found her own space on the floor some distance away from the rest of the men, most of whom were gulping water from bottles, ravenously eating MREs or simply using their rucksacks as pillows as they lay down and closed their eyes. Dropping both of hers to the floor with relief, Katie seated herself beside them and immediately extracted her own bottle of water, drinking long blissful swallows from it. Leaning her head back against the wall behind her, she closed her eyes and tried to relax for what little downtime they had left. A few minutes later, she heard movement beside her and on opening her eyes was surprised to see that Joe had joined her, seating himself on the floor.

"You okay?" he asked quietly, glancing sideways at her as he removed his gloves and helmet.

Katie nodded, giving him a small smile. "I'm fine," she answered equally quietly.

Turning to prop his M4 against the wall, Joe ordered gently, "Make sure you rehydrate and eat something. I don't want you passing out." He turned back to stare at her.

Katie nodded and as she continued to look at him, their brief argument back where she had delivered the baby seemingly forgotten, he winked at her. She felt her emotions soar to a new level as she realized that there *was* something left of her marriage after all, but before she could assimilate this much-needed revelation, her fragile peace was shattered as Sergeant Dana Edwards entered the building and moving with a purpose, approached her and Joe and sat down on his opposite side. She began to speak to him in a voice that was low and private.

Almost hissing aloud at the interruption, Katie grabbed her helmet, thumped it on her head, slung her weapon over her shoulder and with a bottle of water in her hand, rose to her feet and strode outside.

Watching her go, Joe heard Dana remark, "That little lady sure has an attitude problem."

Joe, glancing at his sergeant, found himself almost snapping back at her, "*That little lady happens to be my wife*," but stopped himself just in time.

Dana wanted them back on their old romantic footing, wanted something he was not prepared to give — in fact, did not want to give but if he told her this, it would create awkward questions about his and Katie's relationship and he did not want Katie subjected to any further hurt or humiliation. Instead, keeping silent, he leaned back against the wall with the intention of relaxing for a few minutes before checking on his men.

Dana placed a hand on his arm and brushed herself against him. "So, what is it between you and Corporal Anderson?"

Joe's eyes flew open and he gazed straight at the beautiful face, inches away from his own. "What makes you think there's anything between me and Corporal Anderson?" he asked carefully.

"Well, there was on your last tour," Dana answered. "I believe you mentioned that it was possibly *the love affair of the century*. And now she's in your squad. A pretty big coincidence, don't you think?"

"Yeah, a pretty big coincidence, Dana. And that's all it is. By the way, sarcasm doesn't become you," Joe answered, gritting his teeth, anger beginning to flare in his stomach, feeling threatened at the encroaching questions about his personal life. "It's none of your goddamn business anyway."

"Whoa," Dana responded. "It was a simple question, Joe. There was no need to bite my head off." She rose gracefully to her feet. "I'll leave you to your thoughts then."

Joe watched with narrowed eyes as the woman moved away from him, heading to exit from the building. He had the feeling that Dana was on a non-stop course to speak to Katie and he wondered with a sense of irritation what she was going to say. Amusement followed on the steps of the irritation as he mused what Katie's reaction was going to be and wished he was a fly on the wall and able to watch.

Outside, Katie moved along the side of the building until she found a shady spot thrown by the roof and sat down. Taking off her helmet, she slammed it down on the ground beside her, shoved her weapon out of the way with some irritation and unscrewed the cap of the water bottle, taking a large swallow of the lukewarm water. Absentmindedly, she put the top back on and rested her head back against the wall behind her, closing her eyes.

"So, here's the little corporal," came a voice from beside her.

Katie opened and lifting her head, she shielded her eyes with a hand and saw Dana Edwards standing beside her.

"What do you want?" she asked dismissively and sighed with irritation.

"Oh, just a little chat," Dana answered. "You do realize that whatever went on between you and Staff Sergeant Anderson is over. He doesn't want you anymore, if he ever did. You know marines... They're all for picking up stray fledglings then throwing them over for the real thing."

Katie glared at the sergeant. Biting her lip, she attempted to force back the angry words that Dana Edwards had provoked but finally, unable to keep from retaliating, she snapped, "Oh really?" Her tone was cold and sharp. "What would you know about it?"

"I've known Joe a long time," Dana replied. "We go back a long way, have things in common, including our ranks. Don't fool yourself into thinking that your little war romance was anything more than that."

Katie rose to her feet, putting on her helmet and turned to face the sergeant. She knew that she should walk away, turn her back on the other woman to avoid a confrontation, but it wasn't in her nature to do so.

"Who are you trying to convince, me or you?" she exclaimed, stung with anger. "But I guess you're the type of woman who always thinks she's cleverer than she really is."

She was perfectly aware that the discussion was quickly moving toward a juvenile squabble between two adult women over a man but could not bite her tongue. An angry expression settled on the other woman's face.

"My, you are so full of yourself, aren't you?" Dana responded, her voice rising. "Don't forget who has the rank around here."

"Oh please, this has nothing to do with rank," Katie retorted bitterly. "This has to do with wanting a man you know you can't have, and…who doesn't appear to want you as I'm sure you've found out at your cost."

If we were anything other than humans we would be hissing and spitting at each other, Katie thought, but the image did not amuse her in the slightest.

"You think?" Dana responded. "Oh. Joe wants me all right but he has integrity and he feels responsible for you."

"Why would he feel responsible for me if he doesn't want me?" Katie asked, feeling herself bristle at the inference that Joe might want another woman. "Get your facts straight, sergeant, before you start throwing accusations around."

Katie watched the sergeant, feeling combative and furious at the fact that another woman obviously wanted her husband. She had no intention of giving him up — no matter what the cost. Joe was her man, the father of her children — one yet to be born — but apart from that, she loved him. Still, she could say nothing to get this predatory woman off her husband's scent. She folded her arms.

"Let me give you a piece of advice, from one woman to another," Dana said slowly. "No man likes a woman to throw herself at him, offer herself as easy meat so to speak. We all know what marines are like and Joe is no exception."

Furious now, Katie glared at the woman standing in front of her. "Let me reciprocate the advice," she said quietly and evenly. "Stop putting yourself about. It's not becoming for a woman of your…intelligence."

With a last stony glare, Katie spun on her heel and began to walk unhurriedly along the wall of the building toward its end. As nonchalant as she hoped she looked, inside Katie was boiling with fury.

How dare that woman speak to me like that? Who the hell does she think she is?

Deep inside her, the sergeant's words had stirred up some vague doubts.

Does Joe want Dana Edwards? Does he really love me — want me as his wife, even after all the hostility and fighting that has gone on between us?

Katie was about to turn the corner when an angry voice shouted from behind her, "Corporal Anderson! Where the fuck do you think you're going?"

Katie spun round to see Joe jogging toward her, a look of annoyance on his face. As he approached her, he asked forcefully, "Corporal, what the fuck do you think you're doing? This location is dangerous. We've only swept the immediate area for mines and IEDs. You could get your ass blown to Hell and back or get shot by an insurgent."

Realizing that he had every right to be angry, Katie nodded. Glancing over her shoulder at the marine manning the gun in the MRAP to see if he was listening in on their conversation, she finally answered quietly, "I needed to…go to the bathroom."

Tipping his helmet back on his head and nodding, Joe said, "Okay, be that as it may. You always take someone with you. You should know that. Never wander around out here alone. For Christ's sake, you don't even have your weapon off your shoulder. This is not the goddamn English countryside."

Realizing again that his anger was fully justified, Katie pushed her helmet back from her forehead and nodded.

"I'm sorry, Staff Sergeant," she said meekly. "I had a run-in with your…Sergeant Edwards and got distracted. I won't do it again."

Putting his hands on his hips, Joe gazed off into the distance, shook his head, then glanced back at Katie. He sighed and rubbed at his stubble-lined chin.

"I thought as much. She followed you out and when I saw her come back into the building it looked like she'd swallowed a piece of lemon."

Katie tried not to smile at the image his words had conjured up and said, "That's an awful thing to say."

"What was the run-in about?" Joe asked.

Hearing the curiosity in his voice, Katie hesitated. "You," she finally answered. "She tried to tell me in no uncertain terms that I was to stop throwing myself at you."

A grin spread across Joe's face. "She did, huh? Hell, I think I can picture what your reaction to that was."

Katie looked down at the ground and intently toed a pile of dust into a small mound with her boot.

"I told her that my advice to her was to stop putting herself about. That it wasn't becoming for an... intelligent woman," she eventually replied, gazing back at her husband to see his reaction. She could see his face was working and that he appeared to be struggling to prevent himself from laughing.

"You did, huh?"

Feeling a warm shiver run up and down her spine at the look on his face and wanting suddenly to be in his arms and have him kiss her hard and passionately, Katie nodded, feeling breathless.

The silence stretched between them, suddenly full of sexual tension and Joe moved uncomfortably.

"Look," he began, his voice husky, "I'll take you somewhere private where you won't be disturbed then I'll escort you back here. But, don't do this again, Katie. Make sure you always take a buddy with you. If you don't want one of the other guys to escort you then come and get me. By rights I should haul you over the coals but under the circumstances..."

Katie nodded and together they continued around the corner of the building, almost bumping into the security team patrolling the perimeter.

"Anything to report?" Joe asked them as they passed. Both marines answered in the negative and moved on.

Joe and Katie left the shadowed safety of the building and headed in the direction of a tall, broken mud wall — all that was left of an outbuilding — a few meters distant.

"I'll wait here," Joe said, indicating the outer side of the wall. "You go in there."

Katie did as she was told, carried out her business undisturbed, and was just going to join Joe when he appeared at her side.

"Wait one, Katie," he said. "I need to talk to you while we have time, before we move out."

Noting that he looked uncharacteristically nervous, Katie stepped back into the shelter of the ruined wall and waited, wary at what he had to say to her, hoping that it wasn't going to be anything that would hurt her any more than she already had been.

Joe hesitated. He folded his arms, glanced off into the distance then said, "First off, I wanted to say that you did a good job with that pregnant woman under difficult circumstances. I'm sorry we couldn't medevac them out like you wanted. I didn't like saying no. I understood where you were coming from, but, time is tight and we need to get to the FOB before nightfall."

Katie nodded, was about to speak but Joe interrupted her quickly.

"Let me finish, Katie. This is hard enough for me as it is. This is really not the right moment, I know. The place is all wrong, and the timing definitely is but I have to say this to you now because I haven't been able to say it before." He took a deep breath.

"I never meant to hurt you, Katie. I wouldn't have hurt you for the world. I've been thinking a lot since I've been back out here. I don't know why but everything has become much clearer." Joe paused again, struggling to find the words.

Katie waited patiently, realizing that he was actually talking to her for the first time in months.

"You've always been right. My thinking back in the States and in the early days here was pretty wacko. In fact, sometimes I think I was nearly off my rocker. All I wanted was revenge for the murder of my men and for what those fuckers did to me. I thought coming back here would give me that chance. I was going to hunt them down and...kill them. One. By. Fucking. One."

Katie, watching Joe's face, saw a familiar cold blankness come over it and for a moment her breath caught in her throat as she wondered if the words he was speaking would dry up as they had so many times before, but he seemed to shake himself, cleared his throat and the cold expression disappeared.

"But then you arrived and I realized that you'd put yourself in danger to be here with me, presumably to keep me from doing something I might regret, and that knocked me back on my ass. I am so sorry, Katie, for everything I've done to you. It all got out of control. *I* got out of control and it took coming back here to set me straight.

"At the PX that night, I thought that if I committed myself to the marines again, got that bit straight then I would be getting rid of the guilt at the death of my men, but it hasn't worked out like that. I'm not saying that everything is...okay with me. I still have some...issues so when we get this mission over and done with, I'm going to hand myself over to the psych guys at the CTH and I want you to be with me. I want us to get out of here and go home, and I want to do what I should have done before it got bad and get some help. I know I'm asking a lot of you. You could just tell me to fuck off and I would deserve it. I need my ass kicked for what I've done to you and Josie."

Katie, on hearing the words that she had been praying to hear for so long, stepped toward her husband, wanting to ease his struggle to find the words to explain the torment he had been under and his attempt at making amends to her for his actions. Placing the palms of her hands on his chest, she rubbed her hands over his body armor.

"Joe," she began gently. "Who accused you of murdering your men?"

Watching his face settle into a stony expression, Katie wondered if she had said the wrong thing, but her husband's face relaxed and he cleared his throat.

"Nobody has ever accused me," he answered at last.

"Well then, you have your answer," Katie continued softly. "You're the one accusing yourself, punishing yourself for something that was a tragedy and something that you couldn't prevent. The sooner you come to accept it — come to terms with it — the sooner you can find peace."

Nodding, Joe put his hands on her waist and pulled her toward him. "I love you, Katie. You and our marriage have never been a nuisance. You and Josie have been the best things in my life and always will be."

Katie raised a finger and gently placed it on his lips. "I love you too," she said gently. "I've never stopped loving you."

She smiled slightly at the bemused expression on his face. "Shall we start again, even if the time and place is totally wrong and the terries are probably having a field day watching us?"

Instead of answering her question, Joe pulled her closer to him, his arms tightening around her waist. Their body armor separated them but Katie could still feel the warmth of him against her and experience the flare of passion that was always present between them burn intensely the instant that his mouth touched hers. She put her arms about his neck and returned the kiss with all the love she had for him. The heat from the sun and the dusty, burned-smelling air faded and all that remained was the feel of a warm body, hot breath against skin and warm moistness of lips.

After a few minutes, Joe drew back. "God, I've missed you, Katie. I've been such a fucking asswipe."

Katie shook her head then laughed. "Not a fucking asswipe, just a misguided asswipe," she answered. "No more talk about the past until we need to, Joe. I have something I have to tell you. Like what you've just said, I may be making a big mistake by telling you—wrong time, wrong place and putting you under more pressure what with one thing and another—but I think you deserve to know."

Pulling her closer, Joe tilted his head to one side and said, "Okay, shoot."

Katie hesitated, wondering if she was doing the right thing and he shook her gently and frowned. "What's up?" he asked.

"I'm pregnant," Katie suddenly blurted, wanting to get it out in the open as quickly as possible. She held her breath and watched his face closely, noting the stunned expression that crossed it followed almost immediately by concern.

"Christ, Katie. What the fuck are you doing out here?" he asked. "You should be at home."

"Hey," Katie said soothingly. "I didn't know I was pregnant until I was already out here. I don't want to go home without you. I don't intend going home without you. I want you with me when our baby is born, not thousands of miles away as it was with Josie. You deserve that and so do I. Everything is okay with me and the baby, I promise."

"Oh, yeah, right, everything is okay," Joe responded, and Katie detected annoyance in his voice. "My wife is pregnant in the middle of a desert, heading out on a mission with every chance of getting her head blown off and she says everything is fine." He looked down at her. "How far along are you anyway?"

"Almost three months," Katie replied then, reaching back, she took one of his hands from around her waist and gently laid it flat on her stomach. "I think it was the night of the Marine ball."

"Oh yeah, I remember the Marine ball," Joe answered, his voice deepening as he remembered their lovemaking in the grounds of the hotel. He felt the warmth of her body through her combat shirt and also a faint curve to her lower abdomen, below the bottom of her body armor, where there had been no roundness before. He felt a powerful emotion soar inside him at the thought that the woman he loved beyond anything in the world – the woman that he had nearly lost – was carrying his child. He felt a new and emotional responsibility toward her, to protect her at all costs and get her back home in one piece.

"Okay," he said softly. Removing his hand from her stomach, he pulled her against him again. "I am never going to let you out of my sight again, you hear me? You do everything I say without argument. I'll try to give you light duties but you *will* take it easy, Katie. We need to get through this together with no heroics."

Smiling slightly at her big, not-so-tough marine acting so protectively toward her, Katie said teasingly, "Yes, Staff Sergeant."

"Now, I suggest we get moving."

"Just one more minute, Joe," Katie said softly and put her arms about his neck. Pressing herself against him she continued, "We might not have a minute to ourselves for a long time so, I just wanted to say I love you — we love you — and I am so proud of you."

She gently kissed his lips, relishing being back in his arms, then he was holding her so tightly that she could barely breathe and kissing her hard and hungrily.

"Love you back," Joe said after pulling his mouth away from hers. He placed a warm hand on the side of her face and rubbed a thumb across her moist lips. His gaze roamed her face intently, his expression serious, then he smiled. "Now, we have to get back."

Releasing her, he slipped his M4 from his shoulder. "And get that rifle off your shoulder and ready to use, Corporal."

Without waiting for her answer, Joe moved to the edge of the wall facing the building and hesitated, scanning the land surrounding them before moving out beyond its confines. Instantaneously, a loud crack sounded with a horrifying loudness, reverberating across the desert with frightening intensity.

Chapter Twenty

A puff of sand and concrete-hard shards of mud splintered away from the wall beside Joe's head and with lightning fast reflexes, he jumped backward, grabbing Katie's shoulder, and shoving her to the ground to join him in a crouch.

Katie held up her rifle, unsure in which direction she was to aim it, her breath suddenly coming fast with panic. She stared at Joe, eyes wide, watching him as he bent low, crossing to the edge of the wall again. Peering around it, he aimed his M4 and immediately ducked backward when a fusillade of gunshots came at him from the same direction as the first, projectiles thudding into the wall causing chunks of mud to break away leaving gouges and cracks in the surface.

"Fuck!" he exclaimed.

Katie watched him turn, stare at her then he scrambled back to her side. "The bastards have a bead on us. They must have been watching us all the time. Are you okay?"

Katie nodded silently, unable to find her voice as terror attempted to strangle her vocal chords.

Joe pressed his PRR. "All on this net...Sergeant Eastman?"

Releasing the button, he waited and received an immediate response. "Copying you, Staff Sergeant."

"We have contact from the north-west," Joe continued his voice calm. "We are taking fire. I repeat, taking fire and are pinned down behind a wall approximately three-meters from the building. Can you get a fix on the terries?"

"Negative on that at this time, Joe," Louis Eastman responded. "Who's with you?"

"Corporal Anderson," Joe answered. "We need to get those co-ordinates as a starter, Louis. My plan is that I'm going to try to draw their fire so someone in there with you can get a bead on them. I want two teams of four outside the building in case they're planning an ambush. Get them to take up positions both sides of the building facing northwest. Keep them out of sight unless I say otherwise. Gun crews?"

He received two acknowledgments from the marines operating the guns in the MRAPs.

"Keep those guns manned. Eyes on for the exact location those shots came from," he ordered. "Do not fire, I repeat, do not fire until I give the order. I don't want them getting a location on the vehicles. Is that clear?"

He received confirmations from both gun crews then spoke to Louis Eastman again. "You there, Sergeant Eastman?"

"Roger that, Joe. What's your plan?"

"Same plan as before," Joe repeated. "Once they start firing, eyes on, pal."

"Roger that, Joe. Watch your ass," Sergeant Eastman returned.

"I aim to do just that, Sergeant," Joe replied.

Once the transmission had ended, he turned to Katie, who was still staring at him, eyes wide, breathing fast and panicky.

"Hey," he soothed gently, placing a hand on her arm. "Relax. You'll be fine."

Katie whispered, "Be careful."

Joe nodded his mind already on the task at hand. He moved slowly in a crouch toward the edge of the wall, raised his weapon and sidled out from its protection. He had only moved a foot or so when the sound of gunfire shattered the silence. Bullets struck a few inches from his boots and two more bullets hit the wall. Joe dove backward, landing with a thud on his back, his weapon clasped to his chest. The back of his helmet hit the ground and he grunted with the impact.

Katie dropped to her knees and crawled toward him. Placing a hand on his body armor, she shook him roughly. "Are you all right, Joe?" she asked.

Joe sat up and nodded. "Yeah," he answered, trying to inhale a breath through his winded lungs. Thumbing his PRR he barked, "Anyone get the co-ordinates? That was my ass out in the wind."

Sergeant Eastman responded immediately, "Got them. Now get back here."

"Copy that. Everyone in place?"

Sergeant Eastman acknowledged in the affirmative and Joe turned to Katie. "Okay, honey," he said quietly. "This is what's going to happen. See that broken wall about two-meters from us?"

He pointed a finger off to the right toward a low, broken wall about one-meter in height. It was barely long enough to hide an average-sized person.

Following the direction in which he was pointing, Katie nodded.

"We're going to make a run for it and use it for cover before heading toward the building. As soon as we leave concealment, they're going to open fire. The terries are normally crap shots but we can't rely on that. You'll go first and I'll follow. Do you understand me?" Joe stared at her.

Katie turned to look at the low wall only a short distance from where they were crouched. Taking a deep breath, she turned back to Joe.

"Okay," she said, "I'm ready."

"Good girl," Joe answered. "Okay, let's go. Move to my right. Keep your cool. Don't panic. You'll be fine." He gave her a small smile of reassurance then gestured for her to move to crouch by his right side.

Katie moved to the edge of the wall beside him and waited for his signal. Joe thumbed his PRR again. "We're about to move," he stated.

He turned to Katie. "Okay, sweetheart, on three, run like hell. Do not wait for me." He placed a gentle hand on her shoulder. "One. Two. Three!"

Immediately on three, Katie was up onto her feet and leaping into a sprint, keeping her body low so as to present as small a target as possible.

Joe watched her run, his heart in his mouth. Short as the distance was to the next wall, he thought that she looked so vulnerable and exposed. Gunfire erupted in her direction as soon as she moved and Joe opened fire in retaliation.

He checked that Katie was safe then with a final volley of shots, began to run to join his wife. He made it easily, slithering to a halt beside her, immediately noticing with some anxiety that she was rubbing her stomach.

"What's wrong?" he asked. "Is everything okay?"

Katie nodded. "I landed on my weapon," she replied. "It's okay. We're okay."

Nodding, Joe glanced at the distance remaining to the building. He saw four marines lined up at the far corner of the wall as he had ordered, facing northwest, one behind the other, in the direction that the gunfire had come from.

"Ready?" he asked Katie.

Katie nodded, rose to a crouch, grasped her weapon across her chest and waited for Joe's order.

"Go!" he yelled, and Katie ran again, reaching the end of the building on a few strides and pressing herself up against the wall. There was no further gunfire as Joe joined her.

"Let's get inside," he ordered and urged her in front of him, past the MRAP with its marine on the gun, rounding the corner and jogging to the entrance to the building.

Once inside, Katie saw marines manning the windows facing out toward where the insurgents were located. Two of the squad had binoculars aimed in that direction and there was a tense, deathly hush from them all until Sergeant Eastman approached them both.

Nodding at Katie he said quietly, "Hey, Joe. Glad you both made it. What's your call?"

"Call in an air strike," Joe announced. "We're not gonna be able to move out of here until we wipe them out. The road and surrounding area are under enemy control so we can't send out the men to do a recon and make contact. Call in the co-ordinates, Louis. Let's wipe those bastards off the face of the earth."

Louis Eastman nodded, "Roger that," he replied and spoke into his PRR, uttering a string of numbers that would inevitably result in an air strike on the distant enemy hotspot.

Joe moved to stand at one of the windows and raised binoculars to his eyes, focusing them on the distant horizon. He panned them from left to right and finally said, "I can't see any movement. I bet the dickwads have crawled away into their holes. Time to strike, Louis?" He turned to Sergeant Eastman, and waited for a response.

"Ten minutes," Louis answered.

Turning back, Joe raised his binoculars again, trying to discern any movement that would signify that the enemy were still in position and unaware of the fate that was on its way to them. His body remained motionless except for the slow movement of his eyes from left to right as he gazed intently ahead.

Katie joined the squad lining the windows, her body still jittering from the incident outside the building. The room remained silent and the atmosphere gradually filled with tension and anticipation. She strained to hear the sound of the approaching aircraft and she felt the first stirrings of excitement and fear of the unknown trail cold fingers up and down her spine. She was breathing slightly faster than normal and she kept her gaze on the almost limitless terrain out of the windows.

What are the insurgents doing? Are they aware that they are about to die? Do they honestly think that the people they shoot at are going to go quietly on their way without retaliatory action?

As she thought these thoughts, she heard a muffled sound in the distance, like the muted rumbling of thunder. The noise grew as two aircraft approached their location, the thunderous scream of their engines proclaiming that they were flying low level for their mission. Once they were overhead, the noise was deafening. The flimsy building shook, dust and particles of debris showering down onto the squad, Katie clamping hands to her ears as the aircraft passed over them.

The marines began to cheer, their noise rising to compete with the ear-splitting shrieks of the two sleek, charcoal-gray British GR4 Tornado aircraft that screamed into view, outlined against the vast, pale blue canopy of the sky, the harsh sunlight striking in scintillating shards off the cockpits and the ASRAAM missiles slung beneath their torpedo-shaped bodies.

"Oh, you fucking beauties," a marine crowed with almost child-like delight and the men gave each other high fives and chortled like children.

Katie felt as though she were watching a dream unfold before her eyes. She found herself holding her breath as the aircraft flew straight and true for their target, neither Tornado deviating from their low flight path.

Then, the distant horizon exploded. The muted crump of high explosive ordnance roared back to them across the flat desert, the building foundations shuddered slightly and again, small showers of dust drifted down from the rickety beams as the shock wave hit them.

A dense wall of leaping flame, clouds of sand, soil and dust shot up into the air, coiling and swirling in on itself to form a miniature mushroom cloud before spreading out dense black-gray tendrils of debris across the skyline, which plunged back down to be eaten hungrily by the quickly diminishing flames.

Cheers erupted from the squad and even Katie felt a thrill of excitement as she watched the Tornados soar upward to a higher flight level, one banking to the left the other to the right, the one on the right rolling over to complete a graceful victory role, both aircraft then disappearing into the blue sky, their mission accomplished.

Katie turned to glance at Joe and heard him speak into his radio.

"Eagle One to Strike One. Thanks for the help, you guys."

There was the crackle of static then a British voice came back through the electrical ether. "No problem, friend. Any time. Over and out."

Joe moved to stand by Katie's side, his gaze roaming over the now murky horizon. The flames had vanished, beaten low by the heavier debris filtering slowly back to ground level but dark clouds still hung in the air, unmoving.

"Do you think we got them all?" she asked in a low voice.

Joe glanced at her. "Nope, probably not all of them," he answered. "But if we didn't, the shockwave will have given them a hell of a headache." He noticed that she looked pale and uneasy. Concern eased its way into his mind.

"Are you okay?" he asked.

Katie returned his gaze. "I'm fine," she murmured, "but it's been a crazy few hours."

Joe sighed. "Yeah, you got that right," he agreed. His voice remaining low, he continued, "Listen, I'm going to have to sit up front of the MRAP for the rest of the route. There could be more hostiles around. Will you be okay?"

Katie nodded. "Do your job, Joe, and stop worrying about me. Just keep us safe, okay?"

Giving her a last lingering glance, he winked. "Roger that."

He turned regretfully away from her and yelled, "Okay, kiddies, listen up." He waited for the squad to turn and face him before continuing. "The air show is over, and we need to move out. The situation has changed. We need to focus on our surroundings. I want Sergeant Eastman to ride shotgun with binoculars in the trail MRAP, Sergeant Edwards in the truck. I will take the head MRAP. Keep the binoculars to your eyes as if they were part of your face. I want the guns manned at all times. I don't care how you do it, what shift system you use, just make it happen. I want the vehicle sensor systems activated and on at all times in both MRAPs. I want five, two-man teams, each team with a HSTAMIDS on standby in the lead vehicle, no clusterfucks. There's to be a team on each flank of both MRAPs and one team in front of the lead. One hour outside then rotate. We're gonna be tracked, guys and girls, for the rest of our route and one small slip up could have us dead. My guess is that we're gonna have to watch out for IEDs, both primary and secondary. The first one we come across we call in the EOD guys. You all know the drill, what to look out for. These SOBs hide and wait for some poor sons of bitches to appear then ambush or remote detonate the IEDs. They may be crap shots but they have the balls to take us out and to give us a fucking hard time. We have a long way to go and it's going to be damned hot, uncomfortable and slow."

Joe glanced around at his men, all of whom were listening intently. "I don't have to tell you how dangerous this is going to be. Stay focused, stay frosty and stay alert. Any questions?"

The squad remained silent, shaking their heads unanimously.

"Outstanding," Joe said. "Let's get out of here."

The squad and Katie moved away with a purpose, collecting their equipment, putting on helmets and picking up their weapons, forming up at the doorway of the building.

Joe moved to the door ahead of the squad. Before exiting the building, he glanced back over his shoulder, eyes searching for Katie. He found her standing motionless, watching him, green eyes wide and a fearful expression on her face. Their eyes met then he turned and stepped outside, raising his M4 and aiming it ahead of him. Speaking into his radio, he raised four fingers, and beckoned to the first four men standing in the doorway.

He surveyed the surrounding area while they ran from the building and formed a security perimeter a few meters distant, weapons raised, each man focused on his own individual line of sight.

Waiting until the security team was in place, Joe beckoned to the remaining squad members still inside the building, who jogged out toward their respective vehicles.

Katie was nervous as she made her way to the lead MRAP. She studied her surroundings, expecting to see the hazy figures of hostiles sneaking toward them, exposed as they were to an ambush or sniper out to make a killing.

On reaching the MRAP, she waited in line behind Dan, who looked over his shoulder at her and winked reassuringly. She found herself shifting from one foot to the other, nervously glancing over her shoulder out to the surrounding land, feeling as if somebody was staring intently at her. The hair rose on the nape of her neck and she swallowed, her mouth suddenly devoid of all moisture.

It'll get to be my turn and I won't make it, she thought. *Someone will put a bullet in my back just as I put my foot on the first step.*

She knew stress had created the morbid thoughts popping erratically into her mind but she also knew that fate enjoyed stepping in, destroying hope and complacency in all manner of ways and was never discriminating.

Finally, it was her turn to climb aboard. Once Katie found herself in the dim interior, she took the same seat as before, sat down and allowed her body to go limp with relief. After she had regained her equilibrium, she kicked her personal pack beneath her seat and rested her medical one between her legs. As she fastened the buckle of the seat harness across her lap, Dan nudged her.

"What happened to you out there?" he asked. "Are you okay?"

"I'm fine," she answered pretending to fiddle with her weapon. "I got myself into trouble with the Staff Sergeant and he saved my life."

She turned to watch as a marine rose from his seat, stood up on a small platform in the center of the vehicle, unlocked a hatch in the roof and slid it open, thrusting his head up and through into the turret of the remote controlled weapon station.

With everyone on board and the back doors closed and locked, the engine roared into life. Katie heard Joe speak from the cab.

"Nice and easy does it. Gun crews, three hundred and sixty degree surveillance."

On hearing his words, Katie shifted nervously in her seat, suddenly aware that this mission had become all too real and much more like a living nightmare.

Chapter Twenty-One

The convoy moved slowly away from the building and out onto the rough, two-lane road. When all three elements were in position — one behind the other — Joe called a halt.

"First three security teams dismount and take up your positions. All convoy elements maintain a speed of ten kilometers per hour, twenty-five meters safe distance between each vehicle," he said over the PRRs.

Inside the back of the MRAP, Katie felt stifled. The temperature inside was intolerable and before she passed out from the heat, she knew that she needed to shed some of her clothing, particularly as she had made up her mind that she was going to be in one of the first teams to dismount.

Quickly pinning her weapon between her knees, she undid the chinstrap of her helmet and took it off. Unfastening the Velcro fastenings of her body armor and slipping it over her head, she shrugged off her combat shirt, relishing the immediate coolness as she did so. She was about to stow the item of clothing when she heard a low wolf whistle and looked up to see who had made the noise. Her eyes fell on the marine who she knew by the nickname of Mattie, and frowned as he smiled at her.

The man winked and said aloud, "Hey, Staff Sergeant. We have a strip tease going on back here. A...very nice one it is too. Hey, Andy. Nice form, lady."

All eyes immediately fell on Katie, who felt her face burn ferociously at the flirtatious and almost ribald comment. One marine simply stared at her as though he couldn't take his eyes from her.

Katie glared at him. "Why don't you take a photo, Marine?" she asked, her voice falling into the silence. "It might last longer."

Joe suddenly choked violently, then coughed and spluttered before he attempted to clear his throat and snapped, "What the fuck is going on back there?"

Nobody answered his question and he continued angrily, "That's enough of the bull shitting. Get your asses outside."

Face continuing to flush with embarrassment at the attention she was receiving, Katie put on her body armor and helmet, heaved her medical pack on and grabbing her weapon stood up.

Dan joined her. "My team?" he asked.

Katie noticed that he also seemed a little put out at the remark made at her expense and he turned and glared at Mattie and at the marine who had been staring at her.

Katie nodded in answer to Dan's question and turned as the rear doors swung open, squinting as harsh sunlight flooded into the vehicle interior. She swallowed with a sudden onset of nerves and speaking into her PRR, said, "Dismounting," and jumped down. She waited for Dan to join her and watched as he unfolded the HSTAMIDS before letting him lead the way round to the right flank of the MRAP.

Waiting for Dan to take up his position approximately a meter back from the cab, Katie took her place another meter behind him. She thumbed her PRR. "Team one in position," she stated.

"Copy that," Joe said his voice still hoarse from the coughing fit and retaining a note of irritation.

While waiting for the other two teams to confirm that they were also ready, Katie stared around her, weapon at rest across her forearms but ready to use if she saw any enemy approaching.

The road was unpaved, its surface rock-hard, full of ruts and buried rocks, nothing but a worn track. On the topographical map at the mission briefing, it had shown up as two lanes. If it was, Katie thought, then they're bloody narrow. The width of each vehicle easily took up one complete lane, the huge tires resting on what would be the center line separating both if Afghanistan had had proper, well-marked roads.

There was a risk for anyone traveling on the less-than-ideal tracks. The chances of encountering IEDs or mines on one not frequently used and therefore not regularly checked and cleared was high, with convoy elements needing to follow directly behind a head vehicle, keeping to the exact same tracks, with no deviation and certainly not drive on the shoulder or swerve over the centerline. This made for slow going and security teams, such as Katie and Dan, in position on the right flank, did not have much room to maneuver.

Shallow ditches on either side, full of stones and rubbish, posed just as much of a threat. The detritus could also conceal IEDs — usually secondary — attached to detonator cables trailing from the primary IEDs buried in the road.

The landscape stretched for miles on either side in an unending vista of softly undulating sand and dust, scattered here and there with boulders and piles of rocks. The inevitable heat-haze rippled in the distance, distorting the horizon and merging into a pale blue cloudless sky. It was searingly hot, the air dusty and sultry.

At last, teams two and three acknowledged that they were in position.

"All on this net...move out," Joe announced.

Katie heard the harsh hissing of brakes, the suspension of the MRAP beside her dipped forward slightly and it began to slowly move.

She began to walk, keeping her distance from Dan, pacing beside the vehicle, alert and watchful of her surroundings. She had no doubt that it was going to be a fraught but tedious journey with endless patrolling on a dangerous and unknown road.

They moved passed the area of the air strike. Katie, being on the right flank, was unable to see the incinerated area but after tilting her head back, noted that the roiling dark clouds were still in evidence even though it was some sixty minutes after the attack.

Time passed slowly. As mid-day grew closer and the sun reached its zenith, it became hotter, the heat more intense with the dust thrown up by the wheels becoming more suffocating.

Katie quickly grew tired and was grateful that after an hour, the vehicles again drew to a brief stop. The security teams on patrol climbed back aboard the MRAP, replaced by new ones.

Katie slumped down in a seat and immediately pulled a water bottle from her pack, gratefully easing her thirst. She then rested with her eyes closed until one hour later she dismounted again and resumed her patrol.

Sometime later, Katie was carrying out her meticulous and methodical sweep—twelve o' clock down to three o'clock then from three o' clock to six o' clock—never keeping to the same line of sight—alternating from three to six back to twelve and so on, varying it each time.

The glaring sunlight was torture on her eyes, the brightness causing her to squint. It was hot—unbelievably so—and Katie felt perspiration begin to trickle down from beneath her helmet. She was glad that she had removed her combat shirt inside the MRAP but it wasn't too long before her T-shirt beneath her body armor, became damp at the front and back and moisture trickled down her spine, gathering at the waistband of her combat trousers. It made the thin material cling in places likely to cause more remarks from the men if it didn't dry before she needed to get back into the MRAP.

The desert was silent with the exception of the dull rumbling of the three heavy vehicles. The MRAP's huge tires—even going as slow as it was—churned up the dust and sand into motionless clouds, which rose to head height and stayed there, the dust clinging to their moist arms and faces.

Katie wished that she had thought to bring a scarf to tie around her mouth. It would have gone some way to preventing her from having to spit out gritty saliva every now and again.

Shifting her weapon in her gloved hands, the palms of which were sweating beneath the heavy-duty material, Katie freed one hand and extracted a water bottle from one of her utility pouches. She deftly unscrewed the lid and took a big gulp of the liquid. It was warm but regardless, Katie sighed as it slipped down her throat like silk, soothing the dryness there. As she put the bottle back in its carrier, she did a further sweep then glanced up toward the passenger side of the MRAP.

She was startled to see that Joe had — at some point — wound down the window of the vehicle and had adjusted the huge wing mirror so that she could see his face reflected in it.

He was watching her intently, gaze unblinking, and she wondered what he was thinking. She stared back, waiting for a response, but his face remained impassive. His elbow rested casually half out of the window and he looked relaxed and unworried.

Even from her position some three-meters away, Katie could see the cobalt blue of her husband's eyes and suddenly — for no apparent reason — felt a surge of desire.

Here we are, out in the middle of the desert, probably with dickers and terries watching us, and I want to make love with my husband.

Images began to fill her mind and she felt her face grow warmer and not just from the heat of the sun. Something else was becoming hot as well and the seams of her combat trousers began to chafe more than usual.

Katie glanced once more at Joe's reflection and felt an ache of sexual excitement spread outward to the pit of her stomach. She needed to get her mind off the idea of being naked in her husband's arms and suddenly, surreptitiously glancing behind her to see if there was anyone in view and checking that Dan in front of her was preoccupied with the HSTAMIDS, she turned her attention back to her husband's face, and making sure that he was still watching her, poked her tongue out at him.

Katie had to bite her lip to prevent herself from bursting out laughing when she saw Joe's reaction, which was instantaneous. His right eyebrow quirked upward, his eyes widened slightly then a smile twitched his mouth, almost widening into a full-blown grin before he quickly moved his elbow and his gloved hand covered his mouth as though to prevent himself from laughing aloud. She could hear him coughing above the grumbling noise of the MRAP engine and as she allowed a wide smile to cross her face, she saw him wink.

Knowing that she was distracting him from his job and that it was dangerous to do so, she turned her attention back to her own slow progress.

Letting her eyes drift from left to right and out to the horizon, eyes focused for any sign of human intrusion, she suddenly heard the violent hissing of air brakes, the MRAP dipped forward sharply on its suspension, its forward momentum was arrested and it came to a dead stop.

Joe's voice came over the radios, the tone sharp and harsh. "Stop! Stop! Stop!"

Dan stopped instantly in front of her, and Katie followed suit, her body suddenly rigid with tension.

.

Chapter Twenty-Two

"All on this net...suspected IED ahead. Stay in your positions and wait out."

In the cab of the head MRAP, Joe brought the binoculars up to his eyes and focused them on the road ahead, adjusting the lenses until the object of his interest was crystal-clear in his sight.

Twenty-five meters ahead, in the exact center of the road, he saw a rough pile of disturbed soil and sand creating a low ridge about one-half meter wide.

Millimeter by millimeter he slowly moved the binoculars, first to his right to check whether the mound of soil stretched into the second lane but could see nothing then to his left, backtracking across the road surface and onward. He stopped all movement when the height of the mound diminish to a faint line of disturbed soil leading to the edge of the ditch and disappeared down into it. He saw another mound, almost indistinguishable from the rubbish and stones already there.

He let his eyesight rest on this new anomaly, his eyes barely moving behind the lenses of the binoculars until he froze, his heart sinking a little as he saw the barely discernible wires jutting out from the sides of the mound in the ditch.

"Gun crews." Joe thumbed his PRR. "Head MRAP, eyes left. Shout out if you see anyone around. Rear MRAP, eyes on right. Louis?"

"Yeah, Joe." Sergeant Eastman's voice crackled over the PRR.

"There are signs of primary and secondary IEDs approximately twenty-five meters ahead of us. There's a disturbance of the road surface leading down into the ditch with wires in evidence."

"Copy that, Joe. Are you calling in the EOD guys?"

"Roger that, Louis. All on this net...wait out. Nobody move from your positions."

Joe picked up the handset in the cab and spoke the Navy Explosive Ordnance Disposal Team's call sign. When he received a response to his transmission, he explained the situation, gave the team the convoy's co-ordinates, and received confirmation that they were on their way. Once he had terminated the conversation, he used his PRR.

"EOD are on their way with an estimated time of arrival — thirty — three-zero minutes."

Katie turned to look out at the landscape, nervously aware that there could be someone out there, hiding in wait, ready to detonate the suspected IEDs.

It was common knowledge that the Taliban used mobile phones and satellite radios to multi-detonate explosives or planted command wires then lay in wait for unsuspecting traffic, such as their own convoy, before detonating it.

On the other hand, the IEDs could be dummies, placed there to distract an approaching convoy so that an ambush could take place, or to delay them to watch how an EOD team took care of incidents while dickers made notes of equipment and procedures.

Katie squinted against the bright sunlight, eyes watering, and carefully surveyed her immediate surroundings. The heat-haze distorted her perception of distances and what she thought on one or two occasions were the shimmering outlines of figures were — in fact — distortions of her own wavering vision. Repeatedly she swiped at her eyes to clear them of moisture, blinking frantically.

It was as she was wiping her eyes for perhaps the sixth time that she thought she saw movement at her two o'clock. She stiffened, blinked, and slowly brought up her weapon. Holding her breath, she watched the area of land, her sixth sense buzzing with alarm.

Again, the rippling of the horizon disturbed her eyesight and she almost dismissed the movement as her imagination when quite clearly she saw it again. Perhaps one hundred meters from the convoy's location, she saw a dark shape half rise from behind a slight incline in the terrain. It stayed in one position for a few seconds before disappearing back behind the slope again.

Tensing and releasing a hiss between her teeth, she took a deep breath before thumbing her PRR.

"All on this net. Staff Sergeant, I see movement at my two o'clock. Distance — approximately one hundred meters behind the rise in the land in that direction. One person sighted."

Dan immediately rested the HSTAMIDS against the side of the MRAP and, raising his weapon, swung round to face in the direction that Katie had indicated.

"Copy that," Joe answered. "Gun crews, weapons."

Katie continued to study the place where she had seen the figure. For long minutes, there was no further movement, then her heart leaped as she saw two dark figures appear in the same location as the first.

"Two figures sighted," came a radio transmission from the marine operating the gun in the head MRAP. "Confirmed eyes on, Staff Sergeant."

Katie raised her weapon, heart thundering almost painfully in her chest, mouth dry and not just from thirst. It was the waiting that caused the most anxiety. *How many are there? Just the two I saw or are there more? Are they waiting to ambush the stationary convoy? We're sitting ducks out here. We can't go forward because of the suspected IEDs and we can't reverse.*

Some twenty minutes passed. The trail MRAP now had its own security teams dismounted and surrounding it with two more teams on either flank of the LMTV, all facing outward, alert and tense for any sign that the convoy was about to be ambushed. The silence was heavy and almost tangible until the head MRAP radio crackled harshly with static, causing Katie to jump at the sudden noise.

A voice, sounding almost light-hearted, erupted loudly into the quiet.

"Mama Bear to Eagle One. We are five minutes from your location. Get the kettle on."

Joe quickly grabbed the handset to stop the static.

"Eagle One to Mama Bear. Good to have you join the party. No kettle but beer is on ice. Be advised, confirmed sighting of hostiles in the kill zone, two possibly more. Security perimeter of convoy is in position. Please advise instructions."

"Mama Bear to Eagle One. Thanks for Intel. Be fifty-meters back from the big bang and we would appreciate it if you could keep our asses covered for this one."

"Roger that. Out."

Katie heard Joe's voice when he spoke on the PRRs.

"All on this net…fall back twenty-five meters. Guests for the big bang are nearing our location and need room to work."

The three vehicles immediately started their engines and slowly began to back up, each keeping meticulously to the faint tire tracks already outlined in the dust of the road. After reversing the required distance, the convoy came to a stop and again, heavy silence reigned.

A few minutes later, the muted sound of engines from the rear alerted Katie and the rest of Lima squad to the approach of two vehicles and the Navy EOD Team began to drive slowly into sight. They pulled up behind the convoy and stopped.

Katie shifted her feet nervously, fumbling with her weapon. She felt exposed on the right flank of the MRAP, the vast vista of desert in front of her offering concealment to any insurgent out to make a killing that day. Although her skin burned from the heat of the sun, her insides felt chilled and trembled with fear. She longed to be somewhere safe with Joe, away from the desolation and death hiding behind every rock or lurking in every crevice.

Joe spoke to the Chief Petty Officer in charge of the four-man EOD Team very near Katie, and she could hear them discussing the strategy for assessment and, if confirmed IEDs, either dismantling or detonating them.

"First off, I'll do a walk round," Chief Petty Officer Bond announced to Joe. "We need to see if there is a pressure plate or two. Then we'll send in the Talon to check around the area. We'll decide the plan after that."

"Copy that," Katie heard Joe agree.

From beside the MRAP, Katie heard the EOD vehicle engines start up then watched as a small, low-slung vehicle slowly passed by in the second lane. She recognized a Husky, a vehicle mounted mine detection system and vaguely remembered that it had a detection array mounted beneath the vehicle deployed during route-clearance operations. On detecting a suspected explosive device, the system marked the spot on the ground for follow-up interrogation by a JERRV.

Following it was an enormous vehicle, similar in design to an MRAP, known as a Joint EOD Rapid Response Vehicle. It carried the team, state-of-the-art equipment, two small Talon robots to handle high explosive packages and charges for detonating same, and had adequate armor protection to repel thirty-pounds of TNT under each wheel.

Both vehicles moved to the front of the convoy, the Husky stopping approximately ten-meters from the suspected IED, the JERRV stopping a few meters behind it.

In the cab of the MRAP, Joe watched the vehicles come to a stop and the radio immediately crackled with an incoming transmission.

"Mama Bear to Eagle One. We are in position and all clear so far. I am dismounting to do a walkabout. Care to join me, Staff Sergeant?"

"Copy that, Mama Bear. Give me five."

Joe thumbed his PRR. "Eyes on for any hostiles in the area."

He opened the heavy door of the MRAP, said, "Dismounting," into his PRR and jumped down. Closing the door behind him — about to walk away — he glanced over his shoulder and saw Katie staring at him, eyes wide. He gave her a small smile then walked slowly toward the EOD vehicles.

Joe and Chief Petty Officer Bond paced slowly and carefully toward the suspicious mound of earth in the center of the lane. Joe, alert but relaxed, kept his M4 in a semi-raised position, ready to act in defense of the EOD man beside him.

He knew that his squad would obey his orders to the letter, could trust them to remain focused and alert to any sign of intruders in the kill zone. Nevertheless, he still felt anxious for Katie, left exposed on the right flank of the MRAP. He was fully aware that he needed to concentrate completely on the task at hand and after a slight struggle managed to push the thoughts of his wife to the back of his mind.

As they drew closer to the suspected IED, the Navy man, who had been studying the pile of earth intently as they approached, spoke quietly to Joe.

"You may be right on this one, Staff Sergeant. Looks like a primary and a secondary as you suspected. I only need to find a pressure plate to confirm."

At a distance of approximately one-meter, the Chief Petty Officer held up a hand to Joe, halting him.

"Wait here," he ordered.

Joe watched as Chief Petty Officer Bond completed the distance to the pile of soil, walking almost delicately on the uneven surface of the road. Reaching the pile of dust and earth, he crouched down and Joe heard the joints of his knees cracking like gunshots in the silence.

To Joe, he appeared to survey the disturbed surface carefully, then he reached out, rested the tips of his heavily-gloved fingers on the road and walked them toward the debris until they came up against the slightly raised side. Gently, he began to scrape away the hard soil in long, smooth strokes.

Joe watched as, for about ten minutes, the navy man carefully made a shallow trench then stopped. Straightening up, he turned to Joe.

"Okay, we have a pressure plate. The plan is to get the Talon out with an explosive package. We'll plant one here and one as close to the secondary device in the ditch as we can get it. I want all your teams back in the MRAP, gun hatch sealed."

Nodding, Joe followed the Chief Petty Officer back to the JERRV, waited until the navy man boarded his vehicle then went on back to the MRAP, climbing back in.

"Everyone back onboard and seal the gun hatches. Any sign of the intruders?"

Receiving various responses from each vehicle that there had been no further sightings of any hostiles, the security teams climbed back aboard and settled down for the long wait.

Climbing inside herself, Katie wished she could visit Joe and snatch a brief moment alone with him, but this was most definitely not the time or the place. He needed to focus on the incident. It was frustrating to have her time curtailed so severely where he was concerned. What was happening at this time was the sort of adrenaline-fueled situation that made her want to be close to him.

"Louis, Dana. Keep your eyes out for those two intruders. If you see anything at all, sing out," she heard Joe's voice continue and felt the nervous butterflies in her stomach become even more agitated.

Inside the JERRV, the atmosphere was relaxed, belying the intensity and thoroughness of the EOD Team's preparation of two explosive packages consisting of four blocks of C4, each package having a trailing detonating wire inserted. Already lifted out of the back of the JERRV, one of the small Talon robots had maneuvered around to the passenger side of the vehicle and the first explosive package gingerly laid across the extended arm, the detonating cord held by the gripper. A standard Talon robot consisted of a removable, double-jointed, sixty-four-inch arm and gripper mounted on two miniature versions of a tank track. It was controlled through a two-way fiber optic link from an attaché-sized operator control unit from inside the JERRV.

The little robot trundled off to lay the first of the charges next to the primary IED. Once it had delicately placed the explosives, it came back by remote control, trailing the detonating cord, which Chief Petty Officer Bond took from the gripper. The second charge was then taken to the ditch and laid as close to the second suspected IED as was possible.

Once the Talon had returned safely to the JERRV, the Chief Petty Officer again retrieved the end of the second detonation cord and attached both to the remote control detonation mechanism. Once he was satisfied that the cords were securely in place, he placed a single finger on the detonator switch and said quickly over an open radio, "Fire in the hole. Fire in the hole. Fire in the hole."

From the MRAP cab, Joe had a bird's eye view of the detonation. He heard the double explosion as if it was just outside the vehicle and knew, by the double thud, that there had indeed been two IEDs. He was awed that two such relatively small charges combined with the hidden IEDs could cause the miniature mushroom cloud. He flinched reflexively as the ground trembled beneath the heavy vehicle, then he heard debris rain down on the roof, the pattering of sand and soil, the heavier impact from stones and the distinct crash of larger rocks. It went on for some time and Joe exclaimed, "Fuck me!"

He watched through his binoculars, peering through a mist of dust and dirt, at the debris raining down over ground zero and the convoy then picked up the radio handset as it crackled with an incoming transmission.

"Mama Bear to Eagle One. Over".

"Yeah, Mama Bear. Very impressive."

"Two for the price of one, Eagle One. We have some spare time. Fancy some company for the rest of your trip? Could be that you might need us again, sometime soon."

"That's mighty nice of you, Mama Bear. You'd be very welcome."

"No problem. Out."

Joe watched the Talon robot again trundle off to confirm that final detonation of both IEDs had taken place even though the resultant explosion could not dispute this and the EOD gave final confirmation that the route was clear for the time being.

The convoy, Joe and the rest of its occupants, feeling relieved that the operation was over, moved off.

* * * *

The convoy had to halt three more times for the Navy EOD Team to clear IEDs from the route and for clearance investigations by the Talon.

Lima squad eventually arrived at the FOB at 2000 hours, just as it was getting dark. The EOD Team had left, ordered to another incident, but had volunteered to roam ahead to check the remaining route and clear whatever IEDs or explosives they found. Once the EOD had left the convoy, the security teams had again dismounted, so by the time Katie could see the walls of the FOB, she was exhausted.

Forward Operating Base Nowazad nestled against a backdrop of tall, rugged mountains, their peaks like the pointed, serrated edge of a knife, outlined by the setting sun in a blaze of red and gold. The cream color of the FOB's Hesco walls stood out incongruously — limned with bright orange from the sun's rays — on the flat, dun-colored landscape. A gentle wind had risen and the temperature had lessened considerably.

The convoy approached the huge double steel gates, which Katie guessed were about three-meters in height. All four walls were comprised of square blocks of Hesco, stacked to the same height as the gates, each wall about one hundred-meters in length with four guard towers at each corner, shrouded in green camouflage netting.

As they drew closer, the gates opened outward, and two Afghanistan National Army soldiers appeared, taking up positions either side of the open gates and keeping their eyes on the surrounding landscape.

Feeling relieved, Katie walked the last few meters to safety, the teams stepping aside to allow the two MRAPs and the truck to drive inside before following them in. The sound of the gates closing behind her at that moment was the best sound she had ever heard.

Chapter Twenty-Three

The two MRAPs and the LMTV parked — one behind the other — along the wall with the gates set into it, and the remainder of Lima squad dismounted.

Katie noted the accommodation tents, a covered area that looked like a makeshift kitchen and mess area and finally settled on what looked to be the medical tent. When she saw it, her heart sank.

It was long and low, set on a raised wooden platform covered in khaki-green, anti-slip tiles. Some enterprising person had drawn a white cross on the dingy canvas and beneath it the words, *medical center.*

At least someone has a sense of humor, Katie thought wryly.

She turned to look back at the gates and saw black writing scrawled on the steel — *welcome to Hell* — which did nothing to raise her spirits. There was a soldier, in Afghan uniform, in each tower and this brought home to her that they were in a desolate region where insurgents were at their most prolific. The thought shoved a shiver down her spine. Her new home was a place where lack of concentration and complacency could get you killed.

Around her, the squad was unloading their personal equipment, piling it on the ground. They then started on the truck. Katie retrieved her own equipment and made her way slowly toward the medical tent that was to be her home for an indefinite period of time.

Stepping up onto the raised platform, she walked wearily to the entrance and, lifting aside the canvas flap, pushed her way through the mosquito netting. She found herself in a long tent, which stretched off to her right.

Katie dropped her packs on the floor and gazed around her. To her left were shelves crammed with medical supplies, to her right six low beds with blankets stacked on top of each. Directly in front of her was a small entrance to another tent, which she suspected was her sleeping accommodation. Apart from the shelves and the beds, the only other furniture was a rickety metal table and an equally battered filing cabinet, a chemlamp and fan placed strategically on each one.

Sighing, Katie walked toward the smaller tent. Lifting aside a second curtain of mosquito netting, she found a camp bed, more shelves and a small bedside locker with a second chemlamp situated on it. Another even smaller tent led off from the one she stood in and, poking her head through the closed tent flap, she saw with relief that it was a chemical toilet with tent shower.

At least I won't have to shower with the men.

She turned to go back into the main tent itself to collect her packs to begin unpacking and jumped when Joe entered. A smile crossed her face when she saw him.

He came toward her, grinning, and he looked tired.

"Hey, how are you?"

He stopped immediately in front of her but didn't take her in his arms as she wanted him to.

"Tired," Katie replied. "That was some journey."

"Yeah," Joe answered. "Listen, some of the guys are unloading your medical supplies from the truck and will bring them in here. Once everything has been unloaded someone's going to cook up some chow, so come out and get something to eat. You'll need it. Not sure if it's going to be edible though."

Katie nodded, staring at him, her eyes devouring his face. They both jumped as voices approached the tent.

"I'm sorry. I have to go," Joe announced. "Everything will grind to a halt if I'm not out there to kick some butt. I'll try to see you later. Love you, honey. You take care."

"Love you too," Katie whispered and watched him turn then leave.

* * * *

Twenty-four hours later, Katie was finishing the last of the cleaning of the medical tent and was pleased with the results. Getting rid of a covering of fine dust from all the equipment and bed linen on the camp beds had been the hardest task. Making everything hygienically clean for use was almost an obsession with her. Now she straightened and put her hands in the small of her back, then rested one hand on her stomach.

"Sorry, baby," she murmured.

She looked around her, again satisfied with what she saw then glanced at her watch. It was 2000 hours and she wondered where Joe was. She hadn't seen any sign of him since their brief meeting after they had arrived and she missed him, even though he had important things to do such as organizing the FOB.

Sighing, she reached for a water bottle standing on the metal table and took a mouthful. She needed a shower and could kill for a cup of coffee.

She heard a rustling sound behind her and turned to see Dan standing at the tent entrance watching her. There was a serious look on his face and he only gave her a small smile when he saw that she had noticed him.

"Dan," Katie greeted. "What's the problem?"

Hesitating slightly, Dan came toward her. When he was close to her, he replied, "I need to talk to you."

Katie frowned. "Okay," she said, "Are you ill? Do you need medical treatment?"

Dan shook his head and glanced almost nervously around him. "No, nothing like that."

Katie waited patiently, a vague idea surfacing that she knew why he was here and it made her feel both sad and uneasy at the same time.

Dan coughed. "I have to get this off my chest, Katie," he began. "I've fallen in love with you. I tried not to, so help me. I kept telling myself that it wouldn't do any good. Rules and all that—no dating other members of the squad etcetera—but I was kidding myself. You really are the most beautiful woman I have ever met."

For a moment, Katie stared at him in silence, stunned at his admission. His dark eyes were watching her intently, a hopeful look in them. He shifted from one foot to another waiting for her response.

"Oh, Dan," she answered at last. "I really wish you hadn't said that."

Her voice was gentle, knowing that she was going have to hurt the young corporal.

"I'm very flattered, and thank you for…loving me but I don't…have that kind of feeling for you."

She winced inwardly at the hurt expression that crossed his face at her rejection.

"I wish you didn't love me," she continued sadly. "I really appreciate your friendship but… I love someone else and have for a long time."

Dan looked down at his boots. "I see," he said, his voice husky with emotion. "Is he out here?"

Katie nodded hesitantly. "Yes," she answered carefully, "but I can't say anything more. You know the rules."

There was a small silence. "Well, he's a lucky guy," Dan stated and straightened. "I had to tell you, Katie. On the off chance…"

Katie nodded. "I'm so sorry, Dan. You are a lovely man. Any woman would be so fortunate to have you."

Outside the medical tent, Joe stood stock-still. He had heard every word of the conversation. He knew the saying that eavesdroppers never heard anything good and to hear another man declaring love for his wife was not.

Detecting a small silence within the tent and deciding now was the time to interrupt whatever was going on, he coughed and pulled aside the netting.

Katie jumped almost guiltily and felt a sinking feeling when Joe entered. Although his eyes had darkened in color and there was no sign of his usual easy grin, he did not look angry.

Dan almost jumped backward away from her.

"I'll be going then," he announced.

"Feeling ill, Reed?" Joe asked and Katie detected the slight tinge of annoyance in his voice.

"No, Staff Sergeant," Dan answered quickly. "I'm on my way."

With this last remark, the marine turned and hurriedly left the tent.

Joe stood and stared at Katie. "So?" he queried and waited for her response.

"So?" Katie responded in kind. She suspected that Joe had heard the conversation between herself and Dan and wondered what he was thinking.

"So, you have an admirer," Joe stated, his tone neutral.

Katie shrugged. "If you heard the whole conversation, Joe — which I suspect you did — then you would know I don't reciprocate his feelings. I had to let him down gently. He deserved that much."

She set her water bottle down on the table and walked slowly toward him.

"I happen to love — adore, actually — a big, tough, jealous marine Staff Sergeant."

Joe folded his arms, watching her.

"Jealous? Me? Nope."

Reaching him, Katie stopped about six inches away.

"Jealous? You? Yes," she teased, a small smile on her face.

"Never been jealous in my life."

Joe tried again to dismiss Katie's light-hearted accusation then grinned at last. "Okay. I lie. I'd never been jealous until I met you."

Katie moved close to him, her gaze holding his. Still not touching him, she said softly, "There's no need for you to be jealous."

"I know," Joe replied. "Still, not every guy wants another man being in love with his wife."

"No, I suppose not," Katie replied. "Did you want something, Staff Sergeant?"

Joe unfolded his arms. "Yeah," he answered, "you," and he reached for her and pulled her into his arms. "I want you."

Katie moved her hips against his. "I want you too," she whispered then, taking his face between the palms of her hands, she stood slightly on tiptoe and gently kissed his mouth.

Pulling away she said, "I've missed you, Joe. I hate this situation."

She put her arms about him and pulled him closer, feeling his grip tighten around her waist and the hardness of his arousal against her.

He nuzzled the top of her head. "I've missed you too."

Resting her face against his shoulder Katie murmured, her voice muffled against his T-shirt, "Can you stay for a bit?"

Joe sighed. "I'm sorry, honey. I can't. I wish I could. I have a radio call with my squad leader."

Katie felt herself wilt against him.

"That's okay," she responded in a small voice. "Maybe later?" She raised her face and managed a smile.

Joe lowered his head and kissed her hungrily and at length, pulling her in even tighter against his body.

Katie moaned softly as his tongue touched her own and she reached up a hand behind his head to pull it toward her so that his mouth crushed against hers.

Eventually, he pulled away, his breathing sounding harsh and irregular and she put her head on his shoulder again, trying to stop the trembling of her body.

"Joe," she murmured.

"I have to go," Joe announced and lifted her chin so that she was gazing directly at him. "You and the baby will be okay?"

Katie nodded, not trusting herself to speak, then finally managed, "Be careful."

"I will," Joe said, "You look after yourself. One more thing. There's an ANA medic here. A Corporal Afzaal Bakht. He's going to be giving you a hand. He seems a good enough guy."

"All right." Katie replied, "I'll watch out for him."

Joe stepped back, lifted a hand and touched her face. "I love you."

"I love you too," Katie whispered and again, watched him turn then leave the tent.

Chapter Twenty-Four

It was midnight as Joe walked tiredly into the medical center tent, slowly removing his helmet and body armor. He stopped just inside the entrance and glanced about him, eyes searching the far corners of the long, shadowed tent to see if there was anybody else present.

A chemlamp burned on the rickety metal table — barely illuminating its surroundings — dim white rays throwing a pool of light onto the green, slip-resistant rubberized floor. A fan whirred almost silently from its perch on top of the dilapidated metal cabinet, its blades barely stirring the hot air.

The six camp beds — neatly made — stood ready for casualties. Equipment gleamed — for now — free of dust and sand and Joe was impressed at the way Katie had cleaned, tidied and reorganized supplies so that they were readily available. The examination table had a layer of pristine white paper along its length, a medical rucksack laying open beneath it, its contents ready for use and easily accessible in case of emergency.

Joe could see no sign of his wife anywhere and he quietly set down his equipment on the floor, leaning his weapon against a canvas wall. Straightening up, he stretched the stiffness from shoulder and neck muscles and felt a sense of lightness at having removed his body armor and helmet.

Looking around again, he finally observed Katie through the mosquito netting hanging across the entrance to a small tent adjoining the one in which he was presently standing. She had her back to him, doing something to her hair.

Smiling slightly, Joe stood studying her for a minute or two, feeling a warm sense of anticipation that he would be near her once he made the short journey across into the adjoining tent.

Joe had been trying to get to see Katie since arriving at the FOB two days ago but each time he completed one task, be it a briefing with the six members of the ANA in the compound, radio conference meetings with the USMC Command back at Base Independence or attending planning and strategy mission meetings, he found that there was always something else that needed to be done, taking up his time. In addition, he had also pulled guard duties in the towers and had only been able to catch a few hours' sleep over the last forty-eight. Finally annoyed and frustrated at the lack of opportunity to see Katie, he had scheduled further meetings for a later time and now had four hours free to spend with his wife before he had to report for more guard duty. He was hoping that his absence would go unnoticed and that nobody would come searching for him.

Joe moved quietly toward the small tent and on reaching the entrance, gently pulled back the netting so he wouldn't startle Katie, who hadn't noticed he was there. He stepped inside the small sleeping quarters, letting the netting drop behind him and stood still, folding his arms, admiring the tall, slim figure of the woman in front of him. She had obviously just come from a shower because her hair was wet and she was drying it with a towel.

In the dim light from a second chemlamp that stood on a locker, Joe's eyes feasted on her long, slim but muscular legs and tanned arms and shoulders. She was wearing tight cycle shorts and a white strappy T-shirt and also the pink fluffy elephant slippers he recognized from her last deployment, now a little worse for wear. She was swaying and shimmying to some hidden music and with his grin widening, he saw that she had the earphones of her iPod inserted in her ears and was completely oblivious to his presence and his hungry stare.

Joe, watching the way her hips moved and the way she swayed with a natural sexiness, felt a pleasurable ache start in his groin. An image of their night at the Marine ball, when they had left early to sneak out into the grounds of the hotel to make passionate love in a grove of trees, entered his mind and he wondered at Katie's power to turn him on so quickly whenever he was in her presence. He had an almost insane urge to grab her, kiss her hard and hungrily, then make love to her on the camp bed.

That had not been his intention when he'd decided to visit her. He'd just wanted to make sure that she and the baby were all right because he'd made up his mind that at the first sign that she or their unborn child were suffering any ill effects from her deployment then—

even if it was against her will—he would send her home.

Katie vigorously dried her curly hair with a towel, music blaring in her ears, for the first time in months feeling a sense of calm happiness, feelings that she thought she would never feel again. Now, even though it was late, midnight tipping over into the early hours of the morning and she should be feeling exhausted from the work she had been doing over the last two days, she felt energized. The music filled her ears. She couldn't help but move to it, loving the heavy beat— and the fact that she wasn't feeling nauseous and she felt loved and wanted by Joe.

Having finished taking most of the moisture out of her hair, she fluffed up the curls and then turned to throw the damp towel onto the end of her bed. It was then she saw the man standing inside her tent and for a split second her heart jumped in her chest and she felt a sick feeling of fear. In the next instance she recognized Joe and sagged with relief.

"What are you doing here?" she asked in a soft voice, mindful that in the silence of the desert and the FOB, sound carried. "You nearly scared the living daylights out of me."

"Admiring my sexy wife," Joe replied.

Katie raised her eyebrows, "Oh?" she queried in a teasing tone.

"Yeah, oh," Joe continued. "C'mere, wife."

Katie hesitated, the prospect of being in his arms in a few short seconds making her tingle with anticipation. She sauntered slowly toward him, feeling her heart beating unsteadily, her eyes on his face, recognizing the expression on it.

She took in his stubble-lined jaw, his tanned face and arms, and the way his khaki T-shirt outlined the muscles of his chest and stomach and she shivered inwardly with sexual excitement. Aware of the electrically charged atmosphere building between them, she stopped just out of his reach.

"You're teasing me," Joe announced and, reaching out for her, he grabbed her by the waist and pulled her toward him. When she was close enough, he put his arms fully around her.

"I've missed you," he announced. "I'm sorry I haven't been able to get to see you sooner."

"You're here now," Katie said gently. "That's what counts."

"How have you been?" Joe asked. "You and the baby?"

Katie rubbed the palms of her hands up and down his arms. "We're fine," she replied, "but you look tired."

"Briefings, planning and guard duties," Joe answered briefly. "The mission coming up is going to be hell."

"That bad?" Katie asked frowning. "Are you worried about it? Because if you are, then it must be a bad one."

Joe sighed. "You can never trust in anything out here," he replied. "No matter how well you plan things, something can always go wrong. Anyway, I didn't come here to talk about the damn mission."

Katie tilted her head back. "So what did you come here for, Staff Sergeant?" she asked.

Joe grinned, remaining silent.

Katie laughed. "Are you flirting with a lower rank?"

She snuggled closer to him, pressing her body against his, the palms of her hands flat against his back, feeling the play of his muscles as he moved and gently rubbing her hands across them, wishing she could feel the warmth of his skin.

Joe withdrew his arms from around her and slowly ran his hands down each side of her body, ending at her hips before drawing them inward to rest on her stomach. She shivered and her stomach muscles quivered as Joe gently began to knead her lower stomach, moving them downward, lower and lower.

She sagged, feeling hypnotized at the slow, exquisite circling motion of his thumbs, moving tantalizingly millimeter by millimeter to the place that was crying out to be satisfied.

"Nope," Joe responded at last, keeping up the movement. "I'm just flirting with my beautiful woman."

With this last remark, he lowered his head and gently kissed her.

At the touch of his mouth, Katie parted her lips and closed her eyes. The kiss was gentle at first and she sank into the sensual searching contact, then the kiss deepened and she put her arms up around Joe's neck. She pressed herself closer to his warm body, sandwiching his hands between them, the touch of their bodies increasing the pressure of his thumbs against her abdomen. He kissed her harder and with increasing passion, Katie moaning softly, grinding her hips against his, feeling his hardness and relishing the way it pushed against her lower extremities.

At last, Joe pulled his mouth away from hers and withdrawing his hands from between them, cupped her face. "Christ, you turn me on so much," he said.

"Are you going to stay with me for a bit?" Katie asked hopefully, her voice breathless, running her fingers through his short hair.

"I go back on guard duty at 0400 hours," he answered then glanced at his watch. "You have me for three and one half hours. What do you have in mind?"

Katie offered him a smile, stepped back, and took his hand. Turning, she led him to her camp bed and gestured to it.

"Make yourself comfortable," she said.

Joe sat down on the bed, swung his legs up and moved to the far side, lying down and resting his head on his hand, watching her as she too sat, then lay, down beside him.

There was a small silence as they stared at each other, not yet touching.

"You are such a bad influence on me, Katie Anderson," Joe suddenly said with a hint of seriousness in his voice.

"Really?" Katie asked teasingly, "How's that?" She put the palm of her hand on his chest, resting it there.

Joe glanced down at it then back up at her.

"I should be setting an example," he replied. "Not seducing a female on the FOB."

"Aaahhh, but I'm not just *any* female," Katie murmured. "I'm your wife and, as my husband, you are well within your rights to demand your conjugal rights, any time and any place, and who am I to argue?"

She began to rub his chest in slow circular motions.

"Conjugal rights?" Joe responded, grinning. "Is that what it's called?"

Katie slid across the bed, closer to him.

"You can call it what you like," she said, a gurgle of laughter in her voice. "I have a few names for it and not all of them are polite."

Joe raised an eyebrow. "Enlighten me," he urged.

Katie turned onto her side facing him, propping her head on her hand. For a moment, she stared at him, licking her lips.

Leaning forward and stopping with her face inches from his, she murmured, "What would you say…if I told you that I love you so very much?"

She continued to move her face slowly toward his then closer still until their lips were touching. As he moved to deepen the kiss, she drew back away from him.

"Go on," he said, his eyes staring intently into hers.

Katie moved her body even closer. "What would you say if I told you that I can't wait for you to kiss me again and that your kisses turn me on?"

Her voice sounded husky and low and she moved her mouth back to his and this time parted her lips, making the kiss longer and deeper.

Joe put a hand on her waist, preparing to pull her toward him, but for a third time, Katie drew back.

She stared silently into his blue eyes—which had grown darker—and for a few minutes studied his face, at the twisted line of the scar marring his tanned cheek and the small smile playing about his mouth.

Licking her lips again with the tip of her tongue she asked, "What would you say if I told you that I wanted you to…fuck me?" and this time, when her mouth met his, it was hot and eager.

Joe groaned slightly and tugged her body toward his, pressing his groin against hers so that she could feel the hardness of his cock.

Katie fell back onto the bed, her hands going up behind his head to pull it down so that his mouth pressed forcefully against hers. He ran his hands up and down her body, his touch sending electric shocks up to her nipples and down to the cleft between her legs.

She felt his warm, rough palm run up the smoothness of her leg and on to the hem of her T-shirt, where he pushed it almost roughly above her breasts. She watched as he stared at them, then, bending forward, he kissed her stomach with a feather-light touch, before licking a swirling trail teasingly and slowly to the valley between her breasts. He paused there before his mouth moved to her right breast, his tongue creating slow circles around her nipple until he almost savagely took the hard bud in his mouth.

Katie clutched his hair and arched her back, tossing her head from side to side at the exquisite sensations coursing through her body. The almost teasing touch of the tip of his tongue on her nipple made her want to savagely grasp his cock and guide it to the place that was wet and aching for his penetration.

She eventually wrenched her mouth away from his and said almost pleadingly, "Make love to me, Joe."

Gazing down at her, his breathing rapid and uneven, Joe asked, "Are you sure? Won't I hurt the baby?"

Katie shook her head, slightly amused. "No, you won't hurt the baby. Just don't get carried away. Okay?"

Pressing his rock-hard penis against her leg so that she could feel it, he smiled, "I'll try not to," he said.

"In that case…" Katie gently ran her hand down his chest, over the waistband of his combat trousers and rubbed the palm of her hand against his cock. "Don't wait on my account."

Moaning, Joe began kissing her again. He gently teased her nipple with the tips of his fingers and Katie arched her back and moaned as the feelings inside her body soared to a new intensity.

"Joe," Katie whispered, "Please."

She moved her hands down to his combats then quickly unzipped him, pulling the cloth away to release him. She grasped the hot length of his dick to gently rub it, alternating the pressure of her hand from light to firm. She lifted her own hips so he could pull down her shorts and when they were almost down, she kicked them off.

Joe was instantly between her legs, resting on his elbows so that his full weight was off her body. Staring into his eyes, Katie reached a hand down between them to grasp the hard, hot length of him, then guided him close to her until he glided smoothly and silkily inside her.

Sensing intuitively that he was on the verge of losing control, she began to move her hips slowly and gently, wanting him to orgasm deep inside her, to feel the power and strength of him.

"Katie, I can't…" Joe began.

"Love me, Joe," Katie whispered, "Fuck me hard. Please."

As he moved inside her, Katie immediately felt the exquisite sensation of her orgasm soar outward and upward. She arched her back and her neck, biting her lip to stop the moans that wanted to spill from her lips. She dug her nails into Joe's back through his T-shirt, her internal muscles tightened on his cock with the spasms of her climax and she felt Joe let his control go as, with a final thrust, he came, his body shuddering with the force of it.

Katie closed her eyes and clutched Joe's body as though he was a lifeline that if she let go of she would float away. Her heart was thundering in her chest and Joe's body trembled with reaction to their lovemaking.

It hit her with the force of a hammer that this man was her world and if something happened to him and she lost him then life would not be worth living. She opened her eyes and found Joe staring down at her.

He brushed the damp curls from her forehead and smiled. "I didn't hurt you, did I?" he asked gently.

Katie shook her head. "No," she answered. "Joe, I love you so much."

Joe gently kissed her mouth. "I love you too. You, Josie and the little one are my life. All I want to do is protect you, get this mission over and done with and take you home."

"Just promise me you'll be careful," Katie announced, "I couldn't bear it if anything happened to you, if you were taken away from me."

She suddenly felt filled with sudden panic. "Please promise me that you'll stay safe, that nothing will happen to you."

Rolling off her, Joe pulled the crumpled sleeping bag up over their nakedness then took her in his arms, running his hand gently across her hair.

"Katie, I can't promise you that. You know I can't."

Pressing her face against his shoulder, Katie shuddered with the force of the fear that was gripping her for no apparent reason.

"You have to promise me, Joe. I need you to tell me so that I can get through each day."

Joe tried to lift her face up to his but she resisted and eventually he said firmly, "Look at me, Katie."

Reluctantly, Katie raised her face.

"I promise you that I will do my utmost to stay safe," he said softly. "That's about the best I can promise."

Katie nodded, "That will have to do," she murmured.

"What's wrong?" he asked, "What brought all this on?"

Katie shrugged. "I don't know," she replied. "I think I'm just tired or maybe it's hormones." She managed a small smile.

"C'mere," Joe said and pulled her toward him so he could hold her tight. "Nothing is going to happen to me. Fate wouldn't be so cruel as to get rid of an old marine like me. There's too much shit left to deal with."

Katie relaxed against him, loving the warmth of his body against hers. She nuzzled his chest and sighed in contentment.

"I want to go home," she whispered, "so we can have a life together with Josie and this baby."

"I know, honey. A few more weeks and we can kick this place in the teeth and leave. I will promise you that."

For the remainder of his time with her, Joe held his wife, talking to her quietly, attempting to reassure her and allay her fears that he thought were unfounded until eventually he glanced at his watch.

"I need to get going," he announced.

He felt Katie stiffen and heard her sigh.

"Okay," she agreed in a small voice.

As Joe rose from the camp bed, Katie pulled on her shorts then sat and waited for him to do up his combat trousers. Once he had finished, he stood and stared down at her. Reluctantly he said, "I'm sorry to do this to you, honey, but I'm out on patrol tomorrow, a coupla days."

He watched as Katie raised her eyes to his, anxiety materializing on her face again. "Patrol?" she queried.

"Yeah, but I'll be fine. Come here."

Katie rose from the bed and moved toward him, walking straight into his arms.

"Be careful," she murmured, eyes roaming over his face.

Joe kissed her mouth. "I will," he answered.

He stepped away from her and walked backward a few paces, his gaze still on her. On reaching the exit to her sleeping quarters, disappeared out into the medical tent.

Katie stood staring at the empty place where he had been standing, then sat down on the edge of her camp bed and bowed her head, knowing that the next forty-eight hours were going to be hell.

Chapter Twenty-Five

As he waited in the searing sunlight for the giant steel gates of the FOB to open just wide enough to allow himself and his men to file through, Joe had never felt so tired.

The rucksack on his back felt like it was loaded with cement, the webbing straps tugging on the aching muscles of his neck and shoulders. His feet were blistered and sore inside his dusty combat boots, his T-shirt and combat shirt soaked with sweat. The bullet graze on the upper part of his left arm throbbed like a rotten tooth. Dust and sand clung to his sweat-dampened face, the stubble along his jaw itched and he stank.

He was relieved to be back at the FOB – the last five days had been hell – and he knew that Katie would be frantic. Desperate though he was to see her, he needed to shower first before reporting to the medical tent, primarily to see her but also to get his wound tended to.

He turned to his weary squad, watching as they halted in ragged formation before him—shoulders sagging and exhaustion evident on their haggard and dirty faces.

"Okay, guys," he said. "Debriefing is at 1700 hours. That gives you enough time to get some chow inside you and have some downtime. You did a good job out there. I know it was tough but we came out on top. Take advantage of the next few hours. Dismissed."

With murmurs of relief, the men moved off, some to the mess area for food while others went slowly toward their accommodation tent.

Joe began to head toward his own tent, ready to dump his equipment and head for a shower. He had only gone a few paces, head bowed beneath the weight of his helmet, when a female voice hailed him. Looking up and squinting, his eyes half shut to shield them from the sunlight, he saw Dana Edwards hurrying toward him, a bright welcoming smile on her beautiful face.

"Hey, Joe," she greeted happily. "Glad you're back safely."

Stopping in his tracks, Joe grimaced inwardly. He knew a confrontation was inevitable between himself and the sergeant. Although feeling exhausted at the moment, he realized that this was an ideal opportunity for him and Dana to talk and for him to explain to her where she stood in relation to him.

"Dana," he greeted politely. "It's good to be back."

Dana reached his side. "I hear you had a tough time out there."

"Yeah, you could say that," Joe answered coolly. "What do you want, Dana? I am shit-canned tired. I stink like a skunk and I need to report to the medical center." He folded his arms.

Dana hesitated. "I've been worried about you, Joe, and...I missed you."

Joe glanced down at his boots then back at her. As he did so, she reached out a hand and placed it on his arm.

He shrugged it off, feeling embarrassed at what he perceived as the woman's forwardness, particularly as Katie could come walking out of the medical tent at any moment and also because they were standing in the center of the FOB—very conspicuous—exposed to any onlookers who might be taking an interest in them.

"Look, Dana," he began but she interrupted him.

"I had to discipline your medic while you were away," she announced.

Joe felt his body stiffen and a surge of annoyance rise up inside him.

"You did what?" he queried, glaring at her.

"She was playing around with some of your squad. I told her twice to get back to her duties but she was pretty damned insubordinate so I gave her some extra duties," Dana explained.

"Really?" Joe's voice was now dangerously quiet. "What extra duties were those?"

"Guard duty in one of the towers," Dana answered, failing to see the warning signs of impending anger in Joe's voice.

Joe tried to control his temper. "Corporal Anderson is a fucking medic, Dana, not an infantry grunt. You had no fucking right to discipline one of my squad. When I'm out in the field and if there's trouble, you make a note and let me know when I return. You don't take it into your own hands to eke out punishment off your own back."

At his words, Joe saw a shocked expression cross Dana's face.

"I didn't expect that reaction from you, Joe. You really surprise me."

"Yeah? Well, there you go," Joe replied, "and while we're on the subject, let's get one thing straight between us. I'm sorry you feel as you do about me, Dana, but it's over between us and has been for a long time. There's no chance in hell that there can be anything between us again so get over it."

He paused then took the plunge. "I'm in love with someone else and have been for a long time. It's over between us. I'm sorry."

With that parting shot, he started to walk away from her.

Dana hurried after him and grasped his arm, stopping him.

"Are you sure it's over between us?" she asked softly.

Joe took a step back from her. "Leave it, Dana," he snapped, gritting his teeth. "You're making a fool of yourself. What we had was nice but it was no fireworks display. As I said, I love someone else."

Dana folded her arms.

"Who's the lucky lady?" she asked.

"That's my business," Joe answered. "Butt out, Dana!"

Dana's eyes narrowed. "Really? It wouldn't happen to be the little medic, would it? What's her name— Anderson? You do realize that you'd be breaking every marine code going, if it is?"

Joe straightened up at her words. "Are you threatening me, Dana?" he asked, ice coating his words. "If you are, you'd be making a big mistake."

With that last remark, he turned and strode off in the direction of his tent.

Once inside his accommodation, Joe angrily threw his rucksack on the floor, kicked it for good measure and began to shed his body armor and combat clothing. Naked, he began to relax, trying to dismiss the uncomfortable confrontation with Dana.

Damn her. Well, if she goes to the CO and blows her mouth off, I'll deal with it. Until then…

Joe stretched, relishing the cool air blowing on his hot skin from the fan on his desk. He grabbed for a towel, wrapped it about his waist, slid his feet into flip-flops and grabbed his toilet bag. Hastily, he exited the tent and made his way behind it to a row of four wooden makeshift showers, three already occupied by members of his squad.

He let himself into the fourth one, threw off his towel, and turned on the shower. He cringed as icy water poured down onto his hot skin but started to enjoy the way it quickly cooled him. As it warmed up, he vigorously soaped himself, now eager to see his wife. He peeled the bandage and dressing from his arm and winced as the water pounded the long, deep bullet graze. He definitely needed it looked at.

Ten minutes later, Joe was back in his tent toweling the rest of the moisture from his tanned body and dressing himself quickly in clean combat trousers and a fresh T-shirt. Some of the tiredness had left him and as he laced himself back into his worn combat boots, he felt better than he had on his arrival back at the FOB.

Joe quickly left his tent and with his gaze focused on the medical center, almost jogged toward it, his mind full of the tantalizing images of the woman inside.

Lifting the mosquito netting at the entrance, he went quietly in, glancing around as he did. He saw Katie almost instantly, standing halfway down the tent by an empty bed making a notation on a clipboard.

Joe stood watching her in silence, drinking in the way she looked and realizing that he had missed her more than he could ever explain in words.

Sensing movement in the tent, Katie glanced up to see Joe standing at the end of the row of beds watching her, a grin playing about his mouth. For a moment, she stared at him in disbelief, then her beautiful smile greeted him and she threw the clipboard on the bed and hurried toward him.

"Joe!" she exclaimed, joy profoundly evident in her tone. She almost flung herself into his arms and felt him clasp her body close, pulling her in tight against him as she rested her head on his shoulder.

"Where have you been? You said two days."

"God. It's so good to hold you," Joe said. "I've missed you so much."

Tilting her head back, Katie gazed into his face. "What happened? I couldn't get any information out of anyone."

"Before I answer your questions, I need to give you this," Joe announced and he proceeded to kiss her mouth then her face and hair before returning to her mouth and kissing her with a deep and passionate hunger.

Katie relished the sensations coursing through her body at her husband's kisses and the strength of his arms around her. She pressed herself as close as she could and her own kisses were just as hot and intense.

Joe drew back from her. Studying her face then her body he asked, "So, how have you been?"

"Good," Katie replied. "Tired. I missed you. I was worried sick. Are you going to tell me what happened or do I need to beat an answer out of you?"

Joe laughed then grew serious. "It was tough. We walked right into a hot spot and a two-day patrol turned into a five-day firefight. The terries were waiting for us. How they knew we were gonna be there I have no idea. Dickers must have seen us leave the FOB and followed us all the way to Check Point Eleven, then the fuckers ambushed us. If it hadn't been for some British infantry guys nearby, we'd have had our asses kicked."

"Oh, Joe," breathed Katie, powerful images of him caught in a firefight infiltrating her mind. "Are you okay?"

"Well," Joe began, "I got shot a little bit."

Katie abruptly stepped back from him. "Shot?" she echoed, horrified "Where?"

"Hey, it's okay. It's just a bullet graze but it needs looking at."

Joe pushed up the sleeve of his T-shirt and flinched when she saw the long, livid wound across the upper muscle of his arm.

"Ouch," she exclaimed and took the limb gently in her hands. She studied it closely, looking for signs of infection. It was weeping clear fluid and the area around the wound was red but there was no sign that the redness was spreading outward.

"How long ago did it happen?" she asked, delicately pressing the muscle around the area of the wound.

Joe hissed slightly at the pain as she manipulated it.

"Coupla days ago," he finally answered.

Katie's bent over him as she continued to probe the wound. "Well, you've been lucky," she eventually responded. "You've escaped infection but your eagle tattoo has lost some of its feathers—poor thing. I'll bathe it, dress it and give you a couple of antibiotic pills to take. It should be okay if we keep an eye on it."

She glanced back at Joe to see that he was staring at her.

"What?" she asked, her attention captured by his gaze.

"What would I do without you?" he asked softly, lifting his hand and gently cupping her chin.

Katie smiled. "Oh, I think you'd survive," she answered teasingly. "You're a big boy. Now, are you going to let me get on with this? Behave yourself, Staff Sergeant. I'm in charge in here. This is my territory."

Joe laughed aloud. "Yes, ma'am," he responded.

She walked away to collect a bowl of antiseptic liquid, scissors, gauze and dressings. As she turned to come back, she ordered, "Sit up on the examination table."

Shaking his head, Joe hopped up onto the table and Katie placed the liquid-filled bowl down beside him and laid the rest of what she needed alongside it.

Firstly soaking the gauze in the warm solution, Katie glanced sideways at Joe and said, "This might sting a little."

She proceeded to wipe the moist material across the bullet graze, cleaning the wound competently but gently. Joe winced at her touch and Katie laughed.

"You big baby," she teased tenderly.

She dried the edges of the wound with more gauze, then laid a dressing across it and swiftly fastened the edges down with surgical tape then bandaged it to keep the dressing in place.

"There you go. You're done."

She walked to a small locked cabinet situated on the metal table, produced a small key and unlocked it. Opening the door, she extracted a small bottle of tetracycline, unscrewed the lid then tipped two tablets into the palm of her hand. She filled a small plastic cup with water from the water cooler beside the cabinet then walked back to join Joe.

"Here," she said. "Take these."

She watched as Joe threw the two antibiotic tablets into his mouth, chasing them down with the water.

"Thanks, honey."

He gazed at her then parting his knees, he put his hands on her hips and pulled her in between them.

Katie put her arms around his neck and leaned in against him.

"I wish I could spend more time with you," he said, "but I need to go talk to the CO and get some shut eye."

Leaning forward, Katie rested her forehead against his. "Me too," she replied softly.

"Are you sure you're okay?" Joe asked. "You look more than tired."

"I'm fine," Katie answered, "now that you're back."

"What happened between you and Dana?" Joe asked.

Katie jerked away from him slightly, raised her head and frowned. "How did you find that out?" she asked.

"She stopped me as soon as I walked through the gates," Joe went on. "She couldn't wait to tell me. She said something about you mucking around with the squad members that stayed behind."

Brief anger showed on Katie's face. "Not exactly the truth. I went over to the mess area for lunch. The lads were horsing around. They made me laugh and she pulled me up about it. I suppose there must be some rule in Standing Orders that says, *thou shalt not laugh or joke when Sergeant Edwards is around.*"

"Meow, hiss, scratch," Joe teased, grinning. "It sounds like there might be a feline or two on this here FOB."

Katie studied his face, smiling only slightly. "You do know that she's keen on you, don't you, Joe?"

"Honey, I've put her straight about that," Joe responded. "I told her in no uncertain terms that I loved someone else and that there was no chance."

"Joe!" Katie exclaimed. "That was a risky thing to do. Do you think she suspects anything?"

"I don't give a damn if she does," Joe replied. "Anyway, what if she does? What the hell can she do about it?"

Kate hesitated. "It won't look good on our records," she finally responded. She took Joe's hand in hers, smoothing her thumb over the palm.

"No, I guess it won't." Joe agreed. "Then again—I don't think it much matters anymore."

Katie glanced at her husband's face and cocked her head to one side.

"You know something?" she said. "You've changed. A few months ago, you would never have allowed this sort of thing to happen. I think you've always been an *'everything by the book'* man."

Joe pulled his hand from hers and put his arms around her, pulling her body close to his.

"That's down to you, honey. My priorities have changed. My career is no longer top of my list. I never thought I'd hear myself say it, so you're right on that score. I have changed." He lowered his head and gently kissed her then drew back.

Katie saw an expression of regret on his face. "I really have to go," he announced. "I'll come back tonight if you want me to."

Katie put her arms up about his neck, fingers playing with his hair, feeling him shiver at her touch.

"I want," she agreed softly. "Just make sure you do turn up. And if I'm asleep, you'd better wake me up otherwise I'll come and hunt you down."

Joe smiled. "Yes, ma'am."

There was a teasing note in his voice and he kissed her again before lowering himself from the examination table. He took her hand again and raised it to his mouth to kiss it, all the while with his eyes on hers.

"I hate to leave you all the time," he said, "You take care, all right?"

"You're not that far away—the next tent over," Katie said softly, "If I need…seeing to, I'll give you a call."

She pressed herself against him—making her meaning clear—feeling his tongue against the knuckles of her hand, the touch of it sending shivers through her body.

Joe raised an eyebrow, showing he understood her meaning clearly.

"You're a tease, ma'am."

He released her hand and placed the palm of his against her swelling abdomen. "Look after the little one."

To Katie's puzzlement, he suddenly crouched and, putting his face close to her stomach, said, "Hey, kid. This is your dad. Take care of your mom for me."

As he straightened, Katie burst out laughing. "You're nuts," she said, but her heart swelled with love for him.

Joe stood and stared at her for a long moment then sighed. "I need to be gone. Love you." With this last statement, he turned then walked away.

Katie watched him go and as he reached the tent entrance and turned, she smiled at him and called softly, "Love you. See you later."

"You will," and Joe swept aside the mosquito netting and was gone, leaving Katie alone, wishing that they could spend more time together.

Chapter Twenty-Six

Katie glanced at her watch for what must have been the umpteenth time and sighed. It was after midnight and there was still no sign of Joe. Her spirits sank as she wondered whether he was going to turn up at all, then she berated herself for being selfish. He had so much to do and she had seen him much more then she was really entitled to.

The FOB was silent. Katie couldn't believe how quiet it was. She could even hear faint bursts of static from the PRRs belonging to the guards on duty in the towers. Sound carried much farther in the desert and she smiled as she realized that if she and Joe made love that night, they would have to wear gags.

She tried to relax on her camp bed. She was tired but refused to close her eyes. Knowing Joe, if he found her asleep, he wouldn't wake her up.

The chemlamp stood on her bedside locker, its dim glow pushing back the shadows and making the atmosphere a little less lonely, and she gazed around at her small sleeping quarters.

She had showered, washed her hair and dressed herself in clean combat trousers and a strappy T-shirt. Feeling ridiculous, she had dabbed some perfume behind her ears and between her breasts. The bottle was the only luxury she had brought with her.

Now, she felt restless. She wanted Joe here, yearned to be in his arms and have him kiss her with the reckless abandon that was a part of their passion for each other.

She rested a hand on the small curve of her stomach and wondered whether she was carrying a boy or girl. She hoped it was a boy who would resemble Joe. She prayed that it would be healthy and felt guilt that her escapade in Afghanistan might have gone some way to harming her baby. She would never forgive herself if it had.

Katie suddenly tensed as she heard a sound from out in the medical tent then soft footfalls walking toward her sleeping quarters. Even though she was expecting Joe, it could also be someone else coming to her for medical treatment and she was just about to get up when the mosquito netting was swept aside and Joe thrust his head through, a grin on his face.

"Anyone waiting for me?" he asked.

Katie bounced up from the bed and hurried toward him, almost throwing herself into his arms.

"Whoa," he said, staggering backward slightly, then Katie covered his mouth and face with kisses, effectively stopping his words, hugging him tightly. Eventually she stopped and leaned back to look up at him.

"Wow," he announced, "That was some welcome."

"I thought you weren't coming," Katie said, defending her actions with a little embarrassment.

"Well, damn, I'm not complaining," Joe responded. "Could we try that again?"

Katie laughed softly. "I think that could be arranged," she teased, "if you're interested of course."

She backed away, took his hand, and began to lead him deeper into the tiny tent.

"Oh, I'm interested all right," he replied, complying with the direction his wife was leading him in.

Katie suddenly stopped and turned back toward him. "Have you been okay?" she asked.

Joe put his arms around her. "I've been good," he replied.

"I should look at your arm," Katie announced, laughing inwardly at the impatient look appearing on her husband's face.

"Are you wasting time deliberately?" he asked.

"Me?" Katie asked, "Now why on earth would I try to waste time?"

"Because you're a tease," Joe growled, "and you know what I want."

"And what would that be?" Katie responded, her breath catching in her throat.

Lowering his head, Joe gently kissed her ear then whispered, repeating. "You know what I want."

"Well, this is cozy!"

Katie jumped and turned her head in the direction of the unexpected voice and as she did, she felt Joe's body grow rigid against hers. When she saw who had appeared inside her tent, Katie froze.

Sergeant Dana Edwards was standing with her arms folded, glaring at them both, a look of anger and jealousy twisting her beautiful features.

Joe, with his arms still around Katie, snapped, "What the fuck are you doing here?"

"Just checking on what you're up to, Joe," Dana answered. She turned her attention to Katie, who noticed that the other woman's eyes gleamed balefully at her and her ire began to rise.

"You followed me here?" Joe asked, speaking as though he was gritting his teeth.

Dana had the audacity to say, without any embarrassment, "Of course. How else was I going to find out about this little...*fling*."

Joe's body give the slightest of twitches and Katie knew that an explosion was imminent. What he would do to the smirking woman, she had no idea, but whatever it turned out to be, it wouldn't be good.

With quick reflexes and before he could move anymore, she grabbed his hand and clenched it. She winced as his hand squeezed hers hard enough to grind the fragile bones together. His features looked grim, as though carved from stone.

She turned back to Dana. "Get out of here," she ordered rudely. "This is none of your business."

"Remember our little talk?" Dana asked. "Looks like you decided to ignore my advice. Then again, I suppose Joe needed a fuck buddy and you were readily available."

Katie felt her own temper begin to fray at the edges. "If he was my *fuck buddy*, as you so delicately put it, then it would be your loss," she snapped.

"You really have lowered your worth, Dana," Joe suddenly stated angrily. "Didn't you get my fucking message when you stopped me the other day? Not clear enough for you?"

Dana's face flushed and some of her smugness began to dissipate. "I think you don't know what you want, Joe," she replied.

"Well, fuck you, Dana," Joe exclaimed, his tone steely with fury. "I get it. You want it put in layman's terms. Okay. Here you go. Fuck off!"

Katie saw an expression of disbelief cross Dana's face.

"Joe! We used to have something so good. We could have it again."

"Enough, Dana!" Joe began, his voice rising. "You're living in a dream world."

Katie, feeling Joe struggling to free his hand, used her other hand to grab his arm.

"Joe," she said quietly, attempting to get his attention. When he ignored her, she spoke his name louder and finally, he glanced down at her.

"What?" he snapped sharply.

"It's okay," Katie murmured. "Calm down."

Joe continued to stare at her with eyes that were almost black in color and she thought uneasily that he was going to refuse to listen to her. Suddenly, he relaxed completely and squeezed her hand gently.

"Yeah," he agreed and took a deep breath.

Katie turned to Dana. She almost felt sorry for the sergeant. Dana Edwards was obviously deeply in love with her husband—that she could understand—but she was making a fool of herself and Katie thought that it was about time that she imparted a few facts.

It didn't matter anymore. Whether she told the sergeant about her marriage to Joe or anything else of a personal nature, she and Joe would be out of Afghanistan in a few weeks and she didn't think that, at this moment in time, the brass would kick them both out of the country while they were on a mission.

"Sergeant Edwards," she began. "I think it's about time you learned a few facts. It might change your view of matters."

Dana almost sneered at her. "What could you possibly tell me that would change my feelings?" she asked.

"Joe is my husband," Katie explained as gently as she could. "We were married a few months ago and we have a baby daughter."

Katie watched the mixture of emotions cross the sergeant's face—anger, hurt, disbelief and jealousy—before her face finally began to crumple with grief.

Then all hell broke loose.

Chapter Twenty-Seven

The horrifying sound of an explosion—almost directly outside the medical tent—ripped apart the silence of the FOB, followed almost immediately by a second and a third.

The ground shook beneath their feet, the canvas material of the roof and walls of the tent first billowing upward then inward with the sound of a strained crackling, as though a gale-force wind had materialized from nowhere.

There was a strange tearing sound from the medical tent and a muffled thud as something landed on the floor, followed by a thunderous pattering on the roof and against the sides, as though the heavens had unleashed a monsoon. Almost at the same time as the explosions, there was a rending screech of metal, which seemed to go on unendingly. In the background was the continuous and unrelenting sound of gunfire.

For a split second, everyone in Katie's sleeping quarters froze, expressions of horror showing on each face, then Joe ran, shoving Dana out of the way. Then she also turned to head outside.

Katie grabbed for her equipment, quickly pulling the body armor over her head then fumbling with suddenly nerveless fingers to fasten the Velcro. After slamming her helmet on, she quickly picked up her weapon, slung the strap over her shoulder then ran into the medical tent to pick up the medical pack. Sealing it shut, preparing to leave the tent, she stopped dead in her tracks as an unearthly scream suddenly rent the air. It went on and on for what seemed like an eternity before it tapered off, then the yelling started.

"Medic, men down. Medic!"

"RPG attack!"

Katie ran, her mind now totally focused on getting to the casualty or however many there were and helping them. Once outside the tent she stopped, gasping in horror at the scene unfolding before her.

It was pitch dark, and this made the scene seem even more like Dante's Inferno. Flickering flames lit up the FOB with a red-gold, strobe-like effect from a burning MRAP, its hulk twisted and warped from tremendous percussive forces, completely unrecognizable as a vehicle. Whatever fuel that was in the tank burned with a fierce hissing roar. Two marines were attempting to put the conflagration out but the fire extinguishers they were using seemed pitiful.

Beyond the burning vehicle and lit by the flames—at a guess—at least twenty-five meters of the FOB wall had been obliterated, chunks of Hesco lying in piles, some of it still burning. Greasy smoke from the burning tires of the MRAP and thick clouds of dust hung unmoving in the air. Katie's nostrils burned and her eyes stung from the pungent odors of burning rubber, oil, fuel, and smoke.

Coughing as the smoke congealed in her throat and feeling sick, Katie glanced hastily around for casualties and eventually saw, through the shimmering firelight, a figure lying on the ground with another dark outline crouching beside it. Katie jogged over to them and as she grew closer, an ANA medic who had been tending the marine glanced up at her.

Recognizing a member of the Afghanistan National Army, Katie crouched down beside him and nodded at him. "And you are?" she asked.

"*As-salamu alaykum*. I am Corporal Afzaal Bakht. I am ANA and a medic. You will need my help."

Katie wasted no time in general chit chat. Getting straight to the point she asked, "What have we got?" She wished that there was more light to see by but started a full body assessment to see if she could find any obvious injuries.

"He has no injuries," Corporal Bakht began. "I have already carried out an assessment. I believe the concussion of explosions has rendered him unconscious."

Confirming that indeed there was no bleeding or any apparent injuries, Katie glanced at the medic.

"I'm sorry, Corporal Bakht. It's automatic for me to carry out a full assessment. I meant no offense or to undermine your experience. We can't do anything more out here in the dark. We need more light."

She looked around them to see if there was any help available, but there were too many people running around through the smoke haze with more important things to do such as holding off enemy forces, and Katie realized that she and the ANA medic were on their own.

"It looks like we'll need to get him inside the medical tent ourselves," she continued. "I'll take his head if you'll take his feet."

Katie crouched and lifted the unconscious marine's head and shoulders while Corporal Bakht took his feet. Slowly, and with a great degree of effort, they managed to carry the injured man across to the medical tent and inside, where they laid him on the examination table.

"You are able to deal with this casualty alone?" Corporal Bakht asked. "I will go to find more casualties and bring them back here."

Dragging her gaze away from her patient, Katie stared at the corporal and nodded. As he hurriedly left, she turned back to the unconscious casualty and quickly and thoroughly checked out his face and neck.

There were small but deep scratches on his young face, which appeared to have bled very little but needed to be cleaned. She gently ran her hands over his skull, trying to gauge by feeling alone whether there were any concavities which could indicate fractures or contusions, but found none which could have caused him to remain unconscious.

Katie raised each eyelid to check the pupils and found them slightly dilated. She realized that this symptom went some way to confirming her unskilled assessment that the young marine lying in front of her had sustained some sort of brain injury.

Without any visible injuries to his skull, she guessed that it was more than likely that he was the victim of a tertiary blast injury from the concussive wind caused by the explosions. He had probably been at ground zero when the three explosions had occurred and the combined force might have thrown him some distance. Without the patient being conscious, she was unable to carry out the most basic of tests and so therefore had no idea how severe the damage to his brain was.

Katie quickly cleaned the scratches on the man's face then stood staring at him, biting the knuckle of a finger anxiously, her mind turning over treatment possibilities.

The primary treatment was for shock. There was no visible bleeding unless it was inside the cranium. He had dilated pupils, so there was obviously some swelling of the brain. She couldn't give him too much intravenous fluid in case of internal injuries.

Discarding various ideas, she was left with setting up a simple IV infusion of plasma volume expander that would keep shock to a minimum and keep his body hydrated.

Katie quickly collected together the plasma cannula and a chart on which she could record the patient's vital signs. She finally wheeled an IV stand over to the examination table.

Quickly, she began to check pulse, respiration and blood pressure. She wasn't happy with the BP reading but the other results appeared to be within normal parameters and after noting them meticulously on the chart, she proceeded to insert the cannula into the back of the man's hand and set up the IV. As she was doing this, Corporal Bakht appeared in the tent, assisting a second casualty.

Katie hooked the clear bag onto the IV stand, made sure that the tubing into the cannula was free of kinks and that the fluid was dripping at the appropriate rate. She looked up and with a quick glance, assessed the outward appearance of the new patient. She pointed to a bed.

"Sit him there, please," she said, "then could you come and help me put this one to bed."

Corporal Bakht did as he was told then joined Katie at the examination table.

"He is still unconscious?" he asked.

Katie nodded. "I think he has a traumatic brain injury, which isn't good. I haven't been able to do a proper assessment of him because he's out of it. He really needs to be medevacked out of here urgently."

Katie and Corporal Bakht managed to lift the first patient off the examination table and, awkwardly maneuvering the IV stand, they carried the comatose man to the closest camp bed. After laying him down, Katie left the ANA medic undressing the marine and covering him up while she assisted the second patient to the examination table.

Again, she carried out a quick body assessment before asking, "Any dizziness, double vision or nausea?"

She was relieved when the marine answered in the negative to each symptom. She noted the answers on another chart, checked his pupils and found them normal, then studied the presenting head wound.

The gash on the man's temple was deep, long and ragged and had bled profusely. There were also a number of grazes on his face and these she cleaned before proceeding to the main wound. She used steri-strips to close the gash, put a dressing on it and gave the man two painkillers to take with a plastic cup of water.

Corporal Bakht left again to search for more casualties, arriving back with a third. Katie had the second patient moved to a bed where she advised him, much to his irritation, that he would need to remain in the medical tent under twenty-four-hour observation.

The third patient had sustained a shrapnel wound to the upper arm. A piece of flying metal had gouged out a triangular wedge of skin and muscle approximately three-inches in diameter.

After carrying out a body assessment, Katie also discovered a very large severe bruise on the right side of his body in the location of his ribs and wondered whether it was just bruising or cracked ribs.

She cleaned the shrapnel wound then packed it with hemostatic gauze and dressed and bandaged it before ordering him to bed. She gave both the conscious patients their antibiotics then a sleeping tablet each to allow them the opportunity to rest.

With the three patients settled and asleep, Katie sank down onto one of the vacant beds and began to fill out the requisite casualty reports. Once finished, she left Corporal Bakht completing twenty-minute observations on all three and went wearily through to her sleeping quarters, where she perched on the edge of her bed.

She rubbed her face tiredly. It was after 0200 hours and she felt exhausted. She could still hear gunfire and shouting. The air inside the medical tent smelled of smoke and burning rubber and it was beginning to turn her stomach. All she wanted to do was curl up on her bed and go to sleep but even though she had the assistance of the ANA medic, she knew that she could not leave him to handle the casualties or anyone else that might come in for treatment.

She wondered where Joe was and tried not to picture him out there with the gunfire. She hoped fervently that he was all right. If anything happened to him… She didn't want to even entertain the remotest idea that he could be shot and injured. She needed him with her desperately and had the feeling that the next twenty-four hours was going to be hell for everyone, including herself.

* * * *

It was 0400 hours in the morning and Katie had sent Corporal Bakht to get a couple of hours' sleep. She was carrying out observations on her three patients, two of whom were sleeping comfortably, the third still worryingly unconscious. She was engrossed in writing up her notes on the respective charts when she heard movement at the entrance to the tent. Expecting to see another casualty for treatment, she saw Joe standing watching her.

"Joe!" she exclaimed then was running toward him. His presence had triggered all the repressed fears in her for his safety that she had been trying to dismiss. To try and stop herself from launching at him was impossible.

She cannoned into him, almost knocking him off balance, flinging her arms around him. Joe's arms went around her and held her tightly in a bear-like hug. For long moments she clung to him, so relieved that he was safe that her legs felt weak. At last, she looked up into his face.

She noticed immediately that he looked exhausted. His eyes were red-rimmed, probably from the variety of dirty emissions in the smoke in the atmosphere, his face covered in black streaks and his T-shirt was equally dirty, dotted here and there with smears of blood. She could smell smoke and oil on him.

"Are you all right?" she asked quietly and fearfully.

Joe kissed her mouth before answering. "I'm fine. It's hell out there. I can only stay a few minutes. I just wanted to see how you were."

He glanced around the tent. "What's the status of the men?"

"Come and take a look for yourself," she said.

She led him between the two rows of beds to where the unconscious patient lay. "This man has been unconscious since we brought him in. I haven't been able to assess him properly because some of the tests I need to carry out can only be completed when conscious.

"It's my opinion—basic though it is—that he's sustained a brain injury of some kind caused by the percussive effects either of the blasts or as a result of having been thrown. He really needs to get to the CTH as an urgent case."

She turned away and went to stand beside the second head injury case.

"This man is here for observation because of a head wound. He's fine, just needs some rest for twenty-four hours and painkillers. The third patient has a shrapnel wound in the upper part of his arm and some abrasions and cuts. I think he might have cracked a few ribs as well. I need to keep an eye on the wound for infection and twenty-four observations as well."

Katie sighed and led the way back down the tent. Turning to face Joe she said, "The unconscious patient needs to be medevacked out of here, Joe, because I can't treat him. When can we have it? What's going on out there?"

Joe reached for her and pulled her against him. Holding her tightly and resting his chin on the top of her head he said, "From the Intel we've received, the

Taliban pretty much has the FOB surrounded. We have no idea how big their force is but they have some pretty heavy duty firepower. They used RPGs to blow up the wall, so we have added security issues.

The plan is to drop two lots of reinforcements about five clicks from here then outflank them from their rear. Once we beat the shit out of them, we can have a medevac in. Twenty-four hours, not until then. There's too much of a risk of any bird being shot down."

"What about an air strike?" Katie asked.

Joe sighed and rubbed his eyes, as though tired. "We received some Intel from a drone a while ago. The hostiles are too close to the FOB for comfort. The amount of explosive needed to get them all or even most of them would take them out but probably blow us all to Hell and back. They won't risk it."

Katie remained still and the stress of the situation brought tears to her eyes.

"Twenty-four hours until we can have a medevac?" she echoed. "Joe, I'm not sure the unconscious patient will last that long."

Joe could feel her trembling. "You can only do your best, honey," he said. "I'm sorry but I need to get back out there. Stay in here. Get Corporal Bakht to get you chow."

"I'll be fine," Katie said, loathe to let him go. "But you be careful, you hear me. Please."

Joe lowered his head to kiss her once, hard, then slowly releasing her, he backed away, turned, then was gone.

Chapter Twenty-Eight

Joe stood outside the operations tent and wiped a gloved hand across his stubble-covered chin. His eyes ached from exhaustion—no sleep in forty-eight hours—and they felt irritated by the thick dust in the air. The temperature had soared late that afternoon and his combat shirt was soaked with sweat. He needed a drink of water and a shower in that order but could not see himself getting either any time soon.

He gazed around him, checking on each pair of marines on duty in the guard towers and the two-meter high sandbag wall built to partially seal the gap in the FOB. He noted that his men's postures looked alert, all pairs of eyes focused directly out onto the terrain surrounding them.

He glanced casually over his shoulder toward the medical tent, hoping he would catch a glimpse of Katie, but he was out of luck. He had not seen her since the previous day and wondered how she was and how she was coping with having to deal with multiple casualties. He remembered the unshed tears that had glimmered in her eyes when he had briefly visited her in the tent the day before and the desperation he had heard in her voice when she had flung herself into his arms and asked pleadingly when help would be there so that her badly injured patients could be extracted to the safety of the CTH.

Joe remembered the courageous tilt to her chin — such an inherent part of his wife's character and one that brought on a surge of pride in her abilities — when he had explained that they were on their own for twenty-four hours.

Now, smelling the stinging odor of smoke and coughing when it irritated his throat, he wished he could sneak off to see her again — purely for his own selfish reasons — but knew that that was impossible.

Shrugging to ease the weight of his body armor and taking a firmer grip on his M4, Joe moved off to join his men at the sandbags. He noticed Louis Eastman standing with binoculars held up to his eyes, leaning on the top row of bags, and walked to join him, unhooking his own from his webbing.

"Problem?" he asked.

"Might be. The bastards are back again," Louis answered, turning to Joe. "They popped their greasy heads up a few minutes ago. I think they might be regrouping."

"Fuck!" Joe exclaimed wearily.

Slowly, he moved away from Louis, raising his binoculars to his own eyes and looking out onto the heat-hazed land in front of the FOB.

"Will you get the fuck down, Joe," Louis snapped.

"We need…" Joe began.

There was a sudden sharp retort from a weapon and Joe felt as though something enormously hard and heavy had hit the left side of his chest. His breath exploded out of his lungs and his mind reeled with the physical impact. He glanced down at himself — wondering dazedly what had happened — and felt his legs begin to give out beneath him while simultaneously feeling as though a jackhammer was vibrating through his ribs.

Before he could figure out what was wrong, everything seemed to happen in slow motion. He literally felt himself picked up and thrown through the air before he landed with a thud on the ground, what little oxygen he had left in his lungs leaving through his wide-open mouth. The back of his head smacked the hard surface and he tried to curl into fetal position but found his body paralyzed.

He felt an agonizing burning begin in his chest — gaining in intensity, taking over his body — the nerve synapses in his brain and spine spasming and sizzling with shock and the effects of the trauma to his central nervous system. The pain was like a knife and he found that his vision was beginning to fade until he could see nothing but white. Panic gripped him.

The agony became all-encompassing and he felt his consciousness beginning to slip away. He heard shouts around him — his name called — boots thudding on the hard ground — screams.

"Man down! Man down!"

"Medic! Medic! We need the medic!"

Joe began to feel a coldness growing in the depths of his body — spreading outward — gripping his limbs until he began to shiver. Noises around him began to diminish and he felt his eyes close as he plummeted into blackness.

* * * *

"Medic! Medic! We need the Medic! Man down!"

Katie—inside the medical tent—heard the muffled, desperate-sounding shouts for her assistance and for a brief moment, the thought popped into her mind that she should stay within the reasonably safe confines of the tent using the excuse that she needed to keep an eye on her patients. She even glanced around her at the three men lying on the low beds, two asleep under the protection of their sedatives, one remaining unconscious, each hooked up to their IVs, their chests rising and falling comfortingly.

Corporal Bakht, who had been working with her so tirelessly over the past twenty-four hours and who was now checking the unconscious patient's vital signs, was staring at her, with what Katie could see was a puzzled expression on his face.

Again, from outside came the almost desperate scream, "Man down! Where's the fucking medic?"

At this second prompting, Katie's mind kick started itself into combat mode and she hurried toward the examination table and grabbed for the medical pack lying beneath it. Shrugging into the webbing, she slammed her helmet onto her head and ran for the tent entrance.

Once outside, Katie barely noticed the wide, ragged hole in the wall, now partially sealed by a two-meter high sandbag barrier. Clouds of dust from gunfire, RPG and IED explosions still hung heavily in the hot air, making visibility and breathing difficult. Wisps of smoke still curled upward in to the late afternoon sky from the twisted wreckage of the MRAP.

There were now two marines in each guard tower and lined up in front of the sandbag wall, more marines crouched, resting their weapons on the topmost row of the barrier. As she looked around her, trying to discover where the casualty lay, she spied a small group of marines standing around a figure lying on the ground. Her heart leaped into her mouth and she suddenly experienced a strong surge of nausea in her stomach.

Louis Eastman—standing on the outskirts of the group—saw Katie appear from the tent, look wildly around, then begin to run toward him. His heart felt like a lead weight in his chest as he waited for her. As she drew closer, he saw the expression of fear on her face and held up a hand as if to stop her from approaching any closer.

"Katie," he began and stopped, unable to say anything else.

His up-flung hand stopped Katie in her tracks a few meters from him and he watched as she stared at him, her green eyes wide, face pale. Their gazes locked, then her eyes darted away to focus on the figure lying on the ground.

Katie's legs threatened to collapse beneath her. At first, her mind refused to acknowledge the fact that the man on the ground looked familiar. She shook her head as though physical movement would dismiss the sight then with sudden horror she ran forward, pushing her way past Louis Eastman—who attempted to stop her— shoving her way through the other marines and reaching Joe's side.

"Oh, no, no" she whimpered, her gaze flicking from his white face to the dark blood saturating his body armor and combat shirt and finally focusing on the trembling, blood-stained hand which clutched high up on his left side.

"Oh, Joe, no!"

Katie dropped to her knees beside him and forgetting her role as a CTM and that he was a casualty of war, took his hand in hers.

"Joe," she called, hearing her voice catch on sobs that were threatening to overwhelm her and break free.

A faint popping of gunfire from outside the FOB drifted to her ears but Katie immediately dismissed the sound as unimportant, her mind focused solely on her husband. His hand trembled faintly in hers and his skin was cold, almost clammy. She wanted to touch his face, take him in her arms, but realized that, for the moment, she needed to forget that he was her husband.

Her combat role suddenly kicking in, Katie rested Joe's hand beside him, shrugged out of her pack and threw it on the ground, pulling apart the Velcro fastenings as she did so. Struggling to control her emotions and the trembling that threatened to take control of her hands, she quickly and thoroughly ran them from the top of his head, down his torso and along each leg, performing a full body assessment in an attempt to discover if there were other less obvious injuries, which might be causing hidden bleeding.

Finding none, Katie quickly unfastened Joe's body armor, pulled it roughly over his head then pushed up his combat shirt and T-shirt beneath it. She discovered the neat bullet hole through the left side of his chest immediately and groaned.

Dark arterial blood bubbled out of the small wound and she knew that the projectile had probably penetrated the parietal pleura, possibly piercing his lung, probably collapsing it and rupturing the surrounding outer membrane. The tear in the fragile sac was almost certainly allowing blood and fluids to leak into his chest cavity.

She moved closer to him, bowing her head so that she could listen to his breathing to confirm her diagnosis. She heard his attempts to draw air into a lung that was no longer working and the distinct wheezing and bubbling sound as oxygen leaked from the ruptured organ.

"Joe."

She shook him roughly. When he failed to respond to her voice, she shook him a second time — rougher still — and he groaned and opened his eyes, which immediately focused on hers.

"Stay with me, Joe," Katie begged. Then she said, "I'm sorry, but this is going to hurt."

Grasping his left side, she rolled him forcefully toward her and, delving beneath his combat shirt and T-shirt with her hand, found a large exit wound, the blood slowly oozing out of him onto the sandy ground.

Katie felt as if her own life was ending. The man she loved more than anything in the world appeared to be dying before her eyes and there was nothing she could do for him except the most basic of combat field medicine. She gently allowed him to roll onto his back and blindly reached for dressings.

"We need a medevac," she screamed, hearing panic in her voice. "Cat A — status urgent."

Not waiting for a response, she began to slap dressings on both the entrance and exit wounds. She could do nothing for the type of wound Joe had sustained. It was beyond her medical knowledge and the scope of the equipment she had with her. He urgently needed the CTH's resources and the skills of the medical personnel there. Katie could only make him comfortable by hooking him up to an IV with the usual solutions to replace blood loss and to prevent the onset of shock—and pray that the CTT would reach them in time—if it managed to avoid being shot down by the enemy.

She felt a terrible feeling of helplessness and a deep sense of how futile her place was in the field of war when her expertise, called on so many times—in this instance to aid the most special person in her life—was so inadequate.

Having taped the dressings firmly in place, Katie reached for a cannula and a bag of volume blood expander, necessary to replace blood loss.

Joe—suddenly animated—grabbed her hand.

Her actions arrested, Katie clasped it, not even feeling the claw-like crushing grip he had on her fingers.

Tears filling her eyes, she leaned closer to him. "What, Joe?" she asked.

She watched as he struggled to speak. He coughed hoarsely and thick, glutinous blood trickled slowly from the corner of his mouth and down his neck. He began to choke, blood spraying from his mouth, some of the hot droplets hitting Katie as she leaned over him.

An icy terror gripped her and tears began to trickle down her face. She quickly turned Joe's head to one side so he wouldn't choke on the blood, then grabbed his hand with both of hers, as though she could transfer some of her own life force into his body and keep him with her.

"Tell me, Joe," she whimpered. "What can I do?"

Joe cleared his throat.

"It hurts like hell," he murmured. "I'm tired, Katie, so tired."

His eyes closed briefly then opened again, staring directly into hers.

Katie saw the agonized expression in the deep blue and wanted to scream.

"I know you're tired, Joe," she answered hearing her voice tremble, "But stay with me. You have to stay with me, you hear me? Listen to my voice. Focus. The medevac will be here soon and we'll get you to the CTH. You're going to be fine."

Joe shook his head slightly. "Let me go, Katie," he whispered. "It hurts so fucking much. I'm done. There's nothing left."

Katie stared at him horrified, realizing what he was trying to say.

"No!" she shouted at him. "Don't you dare fucking leave me. You can't leave me, Joe. I love you. Damn you, stay with me!"

Joe raised a shaking, bloodied hand and cupped the side of her face.

"Let me go," he repeated more softly then groaned, the sound erupting from his mouth, spiraling up and up into the dusty air until he was almost screaming.

Katie crawled up to kneel beside her husband's head, lifted him by his shoulders, and cradling his upper body in her arms, held him as tightly as she could.

Watching the pitiful scene, Louis Eastman hung his head. He was done. There was nothing of him left. Emotionally and physically exhausted from the scene playing out before him and from the events of the last few days, Louis wanted out—from the Marines and from Afghanistan. He wanted a peaceful life with his wife and children. Seeing his friend and marine buddy lying badly hurt on the ground had brought home just how old and mentally burned out he felt.

He heard movement beside him then the remark, "What the hell?"

Glancing up and to his left, Louis saw Corporal Dan Reed standing beside him, watching his staff sergeant and Katie Anderson in a scene that was representative of a man and woman who were more than a squad leader and a CTM.

Louis sighed, shook his head, and said, "Let it rest, buddy."

He watched anger appear on the young corporal's face, accompanied by a look of confusion and betrayal.

"What the fuck is going on between those two?" Dan Reed asked again.

Feeling a whiplash of anger overtake him, Louis moved in front of the corporal and snapped, "He's not doing so good, and he's her husband. Your fucking personal feelings about this are the least of their problems. Have some decency. Now fuck off and leave them in peace."

Louis watched as enlightenment dawned on Dan Reed's face, then an expression of hurt and finally silent understanding followed. Corporal Reed backed away and stood with hands on hips, head lowered.

Cradling Joe in her arms, oblivious to everyone around them, Katie watched him closely. Sobbing quietly, she rocked him gently.

Joe stared up into her face as though seeing her through a mist. "I love you," he mouthed, and Katie heard the weakness in his voice. "Always."

"Please," Katie begged, shaking her head, the tears now trickling faster down her cheeks. "Don't leave me."

In the ensuing silence, she heard the sound of a helicopter approaching fast and she raised her head.

"It's the medevac, Joe. Hang on."

For an instant she felt hope — hope that the CTT would get there in time to save her husband. Hope was all that she had at that precise moment and she wasn't going to give it up without a fight. However, as she glanced back down at Joe again, she saw that his struggles to breathe were becoming harder and he was gasping for air. There was a look of panic in his eyes as he suddenly hitched in one final breath. It hissed out of him slowly and his chest did not rise again.

Katie froze, saw the life fade out of Joe's unfocused eyes, and shook him violently. Oblivious to everyone around her, she screamed, "No! No!"

Joe did not move or breathe again — and she ran.

Chapter Twenty-Nine

Bending forward on her knees, Katie dug her blood-covered hands into the dust and sand, scooping up a handful and letting it trickle slowly through her sticky fingers. Most of the grains stuck to the dark red, swiftly drying fluid on her skin, each granule of brown sand seeming to hold a fascination for her eyes. It sparkled dully in the harsh rays of the sun, each grain a pinpoint of light flaring in her numb mind.

Cocooned in a silent zone of her own making, Katie felt safe and protected from the harsh reality of her surroundings. She heard none of the sounds around her, could smell neither the gunpowder odor of explosives, pungent clouds of smoke or the coppery essence of blood. All five senses had fled at the slamming shut of her mental shield, as though defeated at the impenetrable barrier.

Katie dropped her hand limply to her lap where it landed on her thigh and where she saw blood saturating the material of her combat trousers.

Where had that come from?

Sheathed in the same dark red, she raised both hands to stare at them closely, trying to sort through her chaotic thoughts for an answer as to whose blood it might be.

The medic approached the woman slowly and carefully so as not to scare her. He had watched her run to this place behind a tent and knew that it had been a frantic attempt to hide. Reaching her side, he crouched down and stared at her. She did not acknowledge his presence and when he looked into her lowered face, he was concerned at the blank, almost catatonic expression that he found displayed there.

"Katie," he said gently.

When she did not respond, he tried again, "Katie, look at me."

Katie began to rock gently backward and forward where she'd knelt.

Lance Corporal Henry Barrow placed a hand on Katie's shoulder, raised his voice slightly, and ordered, "Katie, look at me."

Henry Barrow understood from long experience in a combat zone, that if he allowed Katie's unresponsiveness to continue that she would sink deeper into catatonia — perhaps never to come back from the protective place to where her mind had escaped. Henry squeezed the woman's shoulder.

"Katie, you need to listen to my voice. Come on. Look at me."

For a brief moment, Henry saw her frown then she glanced at him.

He tried to coax her to respond to him further.

"Katie. Come on, love. Come back. It's all right. It's me, Henry."

He felt sympathy surge into his heart. He noticed that the skin of her face had the pallor of cream and an expression of intense pain twisted her pretty features. Within the space of a few seconds, it was as though a shutter had fallen over her face and she was once more staring at him blankly.

Henry sighed. "Katie, if you don't respond I'm going to have to give you a sedative."

Katie could hear the voice—much closer now—and her mind shied away from the pull back to reality that it portrayed—a reality which would force her to confront a memory that she felt might destroy her.

She felt panic well up inside her. The mental shield she had hastily erected was beginning to crumble— slowly but surely. The insistent voice was becoming too compelling in its strength and firmness. Struggling to remain numb and unresponsive but failing, she shuddered inwardly.

There was something wrong with what the man had said—something that I couldn't do—must not do.

A frown marred her bloodstained forehead.

What was it I must not do?

The man crouched beside her, shrugging out of a med pack and unfastening the Velcro, finally captured her attention. A voice in Katie's mind suddenly screamed at her and she physically jerked.

"No!" she whispered, her voice sounding rusty and emotionless to her own ears.

Henry—hearing the low voice—stopped what he was doing and turned to look at her. "What?" he asked. "Who am I, Katie?"

Katie swallowed, struggled to remember, and finally answered, "Henry."

Henry nodded. "That's good, Katie. Now, I'm going to give you a sedative." He went back to the open pack beside him.

Shaking her head vigorously, Katie said loudly, "No. Can't."

Henry turned his attention back to her. "Why not?" he asked.

A sudden onslaught of hideous images destroyed the last vestiges of the mental fog that was protecting her mind and Katie suddenly raised bloodied palms to her face, completely ignoring the red smears that streaked across her cheeks. "Can't," she repeated frantically. "I mustn't."

She looked wildly at her companion and before Lance Corporal Barrow could question her wild denial, she blurted, "I'm pregnant."

Henry Barrow nodded. "Okay. It's all right, Katie. It's okay. How far along are you?" he asked gently.

Katie began whimpering as the nightmarish images in her mind began to become much clearer.

Joe — her husband — shot!

So much blood.

So much devastation to his beautiful body.

He had stopped breathing.

He had died. Her husband was dead!

Finally remembering the events of the last hour, Katie suddenly raised her face to the sky and let out a wail of utter horror and desolation. As she began to topple forward, Henry caught her and completely unprofessionally, folded his arms about her.

"Joe!" Katie screamed piteously, feeling tears roll down her face. "Oh, my God. No!

"Ssssh, Katie, who's Joe?" Henry asked.

Katie felt a grief and pain that was deep and infinite. All she wanted to do was curl up and die and for her agony to stop.

"He's my husband," she screamed. "He's dead."

Epilogue

Katie closed her eyes, lifting her face skyward to bask in the warm rays from the sun. Taking a deep breath, she inhaled the aromas of a warm summer's day, her senses immediately noting the smell of newly-mown grass, a myriad of odors from the riot of flowers in the landscaped flowerbeds and the fragrance of pine needles. She heard the abundant song of birds and the soft soughing of the warm breeze stirring the branches of huge fir trees at the end of the garden. Her body began to relax and she opened her eyes to gaze about her.

The large garden stretched in front of her, the colors bright and pleasing to her. The whole scene brought her a sense of peace and contentment and a small smile played about her lips as she felt the tense muscles in her shoulders and neck loosen.

A sudden wriggling in her stomach interrupted her relaxed mood and a tiny foot thudded against the base of her rib cage, causing a sharp stab of pain as it collided with her internal organs. Wincing, she rested a hand on her abdomen and rubbed it in slow circular motions.

"Ouch, little one," she murmured. "Stop kicking the hell out of your momma."

She moaned softly as a second kick followed the first and her lower back vibrated in sympathy.

"You're not a baby. You're a full grown footballer," she scolded aloud.

She jumped slightly when, from behind, an arm snaked around her once-slim waist and a hand rested atop hers as it lay on her stomach. Katie felt the tickle of her hair against her left ear then warm breath as a familiar voice said softly, "Hey. I didn't know talking to yourself was a symptom of being pregnant. It's supposed to be the first sign of madness, you know."

Immediately recognizing the voice, Katie giggled and snuggled back against the man standing behind her.

"I'm talking to *your* child," she answered, "who I think has just succeeded in breaking one of my ribs."

She felt the arm tighten about her, pulling her backward more firmly and heard the teasing note in his voice when Joe replied, "Oh, so it's *my* child now. It always is when he or she is doing something wrong."

Turning slightly so that she could look at him, Katie's eyes drank in her husband's face.

"Of course," she answered and smiled, reaching up a hand to trail her fingers lightly down his scarred cheek. His face was still pale from the severity of his injury sustained in Afghanistan, the lengthy time in hospital, surgeries and rehabilitation, with much of his tan faded. There was a slight gauntness to his features from weight loss and new lines etched around his eyes and mouth.

Joe watched her and eventually bowed his head and kissed her, gently but deeply. The kiss turned from soft and sensuous to hard and hungry — as always happened between them — and when he drew back, his breathing was slightly rapid and uneven.

Katie heard him utter a small moan. "God damn it! I can't get close to you anymore," he exclaimed.

She smiled regretfully and replied gently, "I know, Joe. We have to be patient though. It's only for a few more days…I hope."

She watched Joe nod, seeing an expression of resignation on his face as he answered, "Yep. But where you're concerned, honey, patience isn't one of my virtues."

Katie — as heavily pregnant as she was — felt a trickle of tingling pleasure run up and down her spine at his words but changed the subject and asked, "So, how did things go?"

Joe rested his chin on top of her head. He was silent for a few moments then answered, "It went good. My lung is healing okay and it looks like there won't be any further surgery. I still need therapy to get my lung capacity back. It will never reach one hundred percent, but the docs say it's looking pretty okay. As for the other stuff? No court martial if I faithfully promise to attend psych counseling once a week for a few months and take my medication."

He fell silent again.

Watching him, Katie noted a pensive look on his face and when she replied, she put as much enthusiasm as possible into her tone.

"That's great. What else?"

"Well, there's to be no more combat for me," Joe replied.

Sadness edged into his voice and a fleeting expression of regret passed over his face. A surge of sympathy welled up inside Katie, and resting her head on his shoulder, she squeezed his hand where it still covered hers on her stomach.

"The docs say that I'm suffering from what they call battle fatigue. A more modern term is post-traumatic stress disorder but I guess we already knew that. More time in a combat zone would probably tip me over the edge and send me somewhere...that I might not be able to come back from. They didn't beat about the bush, just laid it on the line for me."

Katie knew what he was trying to say to her. In a nutshell, the psych doctors were saying that if Joe returned to combat — if he was subjected to any more trauma and the stressors connected with that — his mind would shut down and he might not be able to recover.

"One good thing," he continued, "is that they've given me an instructor's job. I'm going to train men for deployment overseas, so they're still keeping me in the marines."

Katie felt a profound relief that any opportunity for Joe to volunteer for another deployment was out of his hands. A warm glow filled her when she realized that he could still have the rest of his career in the Marines without losing his self-respect and his dignity, and it made her smile.

"That's great, Joe, but how do you feel about that?"

Joe looked down at her. "Relieved," he replied at last. "I can't lie about it, Katie. I don't have to pretend to be brave anymore or to keep doing something that was slowly killing me."

Katie again rested her head on his shoulder, snuggling in against his warm, strong body.

"Oh, Joe," she said, her tone soft. "You've never had to pretend to be brave. Your courage is as natural to you as breathing. Don't ever think otherwise. Your men have always loved and respected you and would follow you anywhere. Just remember, the mind and body can only take so much. You've done your bit and now's the time to…"

Katie suddenly stopped speaking as a strange feeling began in her stomach. Her hand resting there felt abdominal muscles clench and harden and she instantly knew the cause. The pain came seconds later, sweeping like a dagger across her stomach and around to her back. She doubled over slightly and uttered a small moan at the brief intensity of the cramp, then it was gone, leaving her panting slightly.

She felt Joe's body tense against hers and heard a slight note of panic in his voice as he asked abruptly, "What? What's wrong?"

Katie straightened up, for the moment unable to respond to her husband's question. She blew air out through pursed lips, trying to relax her body that was suddenly tense. This was the second pain she had experienced in twenty minutes and she recognized the onset of the contractions of labor.

"It's okay," she eventually replied. "They're not that bad. I'm okay."

She turned to look at Joe, hoping that she had forced enough reassurance into her voice to allay the concern that she had heard in his.

Joe stared at her. "Huh? What are they? What aren't bad?" he asked.

Feeling amusement at the befuddled expression on her husband's face, a small smile tugged at her mouth.

"Labor, Joe," she answered. "You know, it's usually the prelude to giving birth to a baby." She wanted to laugh aloud as she saw a look of shock flit across his face at her words.

"Labor?" he echoed. "You're in labor! We need to get you to hospital."

"No..." Katie began but before she could finish her sentence, Joe interrupted her.

"Come on, honey. Let me help you into the house and we'll get going."

"Joe!" Katie raised her voice a little, attempting to pierce what she thought was the imminent-father-to-be mode into which Joe appeared to have retreated.

He put his arm more firmly around her burgeoning waist and, ignoring her, said, "Lean on me, sweetheart, I can take it."

"Joe!" Katie pulled herself slightly away from him, almost shouting his name aloud. She felt his body tense again at her firm tone and saw an almost comical expression of bemusement cross his face.

"I am not about to give birth here on the patio," she explained, enunciating each word slowly and carefully, as though to a child. "You won't have to deliver our baby imminently. I've had two contractions. There is no danger, and I'm not about to collapse. I will go into the house though, but I'll make it without your help. Walking is good for labor."

"Right. Okay," Joe responded slowly. "You want to go on a patrol to help this labor?"

Katie glared at him. "Ha! Ha! So not funny," she said feeling uncharacteristically irritated. "Give me your hand."

She took Joe's hand as he reached out to her and she began to lead him across the concrete patio toward the open French doors.

Joe quickly followed her — reaching her side — and he watched her every move as though she were about to drop to her knees and deliver their child on the concrete slab.

Once inside the lounge, Joe stopped at the large plush sofa as though waiting for Katie to seat herself. She, however, had other ideas. Restlessness had taken control of her and she wanted to keep walking. Dropping Joe's hand, she continued to move up the length of the lounge and out into the hallway, where she stopped by a small hall table. She ran the tips of her fingers across the rosewood surface and said abstractedly, "This needs dusting."

She turned to see Joe appear in the hallway, his pace almost a run. He had obviously heard her strange statement and his jaw dropped.

"Dusting?" he queried. "Oh. You wanna do some housework now? Shit." Taking a deep breath, his voice shattering the stillness of the house when he suddenly yelled, "Mom! Dad!"

There came the sudden sound of shattering crockery from the direction of the kitchen and Jack came striding out from its depths.

"What?" he almost shouted. "What's the emergency?"

A calmer voice sounded from the top of the stairs and Maggie descended slowly.

"What is the noise about for heaven's sake? I've just got Josie off to sleep." She stopped halfway down the stairs and gazing over the banister railing, glared at her son.

"Katie's gone into labor," Joe exclaimed. "She wants to do the housework."

"Okay. Okay," Jack suddenly stammered. "I'll get my shoes."

Bemused at the almost comical antics of the two men, Katie watched as her father-in-law ran to a door located under the stairs, opened it, obviously realized that it was the door to the cleaning cupboard, opened yet another door next to it, bent over and grabbed blindly for a pair of shoes.

Maggie stared at her son. "And...?" she asked.

Katie had to bite her lip to stop herself from laughing aloud as Joe frowned. "And...what?" he asked.

Shaking her head, Maggie turned to stare at Katie. She raised an eyebrow and murmured calmly, "Ahhh, good," then added, "It would appear that I'm not going to be able to get any coherent answers from these two," causing Katie to laugh again.

Jack joined Joe and said, "Let me get my keys and we'll be off to the hospital."

Maggie continued slowly down the stairs. "No you won't, dear—not dressed like that. You'll embarrass us all."

"Huh?" Jack looked at his wife. "Dressed like what, honey?" he asked.

"Jack, dear, you have different colored shoes on the wrong feet. Please, dress yourself properly."

Maggie reached the foot of the stairs and walked toward Katie, "So, dear?"

Glancing at her mother-in-law, Katie explained, "Joe thinks that the birth is imminent—that I am about to deliver the baby on the floor."

As she finished speaking, she felt the onrush of another contraction. Turning around, she grabbed for the edge of the table, leaning over it. This time the pain was slightly more intense and longer in duration and she groaned slightly, her mind dwindling down to a narrow point of concentration. She felt Maggie's hand come to rest on the small of her back and begin to rub there in slow, circular motions.

Through a fog of pain, she heard Maggie say, "You should be doing this, Joe. It's your place."

"I should?" Joe asked. "It is?"

"Oh, come here, you big ape," Maggie ordered.

Katie felt Maggie remove her hand from her back and a larger palm came to rest between her shoulder blades. It began to pat lightly but vigorously.

The pain beginning to abate, Katie moaned in agitation, "Joe! I am not a baby so I don't need to be burped."

Joe hastily took his hand away from his wife's back. "This is worse than being out in Afghanistan," she heard him mutter.

Katie finally straightened up and sighed.

"Right, everyone. Let us all go and sit in the lounge for a while so we can relax a bit," Maggie suggested calmly. "There's plenty of time yet."

Joe glanced at his father and mouthed "What?" his question causing his father to shrug in confusion.

Putting her arm through Maggie's, Katie and her mother-in-law walked through to the lounge. Once in the room, Maggie sat down in an armchair while Joe and Jack hovered about Katie.

"I need to walk," Katie announced and began to slowly pace the length of the lounge.

Joe hesitated then, deciding he should be close by in case she needed him, followed behind her. Jack, showing himself to be at a loss as to what to do next, followed his son.

"Feel free, dear." Maggie's voice sounded calm in response to Katie's announcement. She picked up a magazine from the neat pile on the rack beneath the coffee table and began to flick through it.

Katie continued her walk up the lounge, her mind totally focused on trying to get her body to relax. As she passed the open French doors and reached the end of the room, she turned and promptly bumped into Joe. Swerving to avoid him, she almost careened into Jack and her irritation quickly began to turn to anger. Biting her lip to stop herself from snapping out a protest, she continued to walk back down the room toward its opposite end. Again—turning—she found her husband teetering in her path with his arms raised slightly as though he was waiting to catch her.

"Joe!" she exclaimed. "I am not incapacitated. I don't need you hovering behind me all the time. If I need you, I'll scream."

"But…" Joe began.

"I think—" stated Jack.

Maggie looked up from her magazine. "Jack! Sofa! Sit!" she commanded firmly.

Jack made his way toward the sofa, the expression on his face like that of a reprimanded puppy dog.

"I should—" Joe started to say again.

"Sit. Down," Katie spat, pointing at the sofa.

His mouth shutting with a snap, Joe silently followed his father to the sofa, both reaching it at the same time and sitting down on the soft cushions, folded their arms.

Jack turned to his son and patted his arm. "We can keep each other company, son. You just stay here with me. Are you feeling okay?"

Joe nodded. "I'm fine thanks, Dad. I'm doing okay."

On hearing the low conversation, Katie glared at both men. She saw both of them cringe and their mouths shut with almost audible snaps.

Silence reigned in the room for a few minutes except for the shuffle of Katie's bare feet on the carpet and the muted crackle of pages as Maggie perused her magazine.

"Hell hath no fury like a woman in labor," Maggie suddenly announced into the quiet and closed the magazine with a flutter of paper. Putting it back in its place, she suddenly stood up. "I think a cup of tea is in order."

Joe glanced at his father, who arched an eyebrow then shook his head. "The whims of women are far beyond my ken," he announced.

At that moment, there came a faint groan from Katie and all eyes turned to see her bending over with hands on knees, eyes closed, panting gently.

Both Jack and Joe half-rose from the sofa, intent on going to Katie's aid when one word whip cracked across the room, causing their heads to turn swiftly. They saw Maggie standing with a raised finger pointing at them both.

"Sit!" she ordered.

Both men froze in their half-risen positions, eyeing the woman with something akin to child-like terror on their faces. Seeing the glint in her eyes, they sat back down again and fidgeted awkwardly. Maggie waited until Katie straightened up from the contraction and watched intently as her daughter-in-law turned a pale face toward her, wiping a wrist across her forehead.

"Who wants tea?" Maggie asked and almost laughed aloud as out of the corner of her eye she saw both of her men raise limp hands as though they were two pupils in a classroom. She turned her full attention back to Katie and asked gently, "Tea, honey?"

Katie nodded and offered the woman a smile. "Just half a cup, strong, thanks. Do you need any help?"

Shaking her head, Maggie turned. "No, Katie. You just keep pacing." She left the room and after a few moments of silence, they all heard the clink of cutlery from the kitchen.

Katie continued her slow, methodical pacing and some minutes later, Maggie returned to the lounge carrying a tray of mugs with a cup for Katie. She set the tray on the coffee table and selecting two mugs, took them across to her husband and son.

Katie was beginning to feel slightly sick and tired. Her back was hurting her and all she wanted to do was to go to Joe and have him comfort her. Her stomach suddenly tightened with another contraction only this time, the pain hit her with the force of a sledgehammer. It ripped across her abdomen and she doubled over, a small cry of pain escaping her as the intensity of it caught her by surprise. She glanced at Joe and as the pain reached its peak she pleaded, "Joe."

Joe's mug of tea went tumbling onto the thick carpet and he was on his feet, moving quickly to his wife and taking her in his arms.

As he held her tightly he murmured, "Good girl. That's it, honey. Ride it out. You're doing good." He felt her body begin to relax against his and glanced at his mother.

"Mom?" he questioned as he saw that she was looking at her watch.

Maggie nodded. "Ten minutes apart, time to go." She glanced at Jack. "Go and get Josie—her bag is beside her cot—and take her to the Jamesons'. Joe, get Katie's bag from beneath the stairs. I'll drive."

"And what's wrong with my driving, my love?" Jack asked frowning.

"You'll probably drive us into a tree," Maggie answered promptly. "Remember the wrong shoes on the wrong feet, Jack? No arguments."

Hanging on to Joe, Katie let him lead her out to the hallway where she slipped her feet into flip-flops then waited as Jack brought down Josie and Joe collected her hospital bag. Maggie retrieved the keys to the car and they went into the garage. Joe helped Katie into the back of the vehicle while Jack took Josie to their next-door neighbors. Eventually, they were all ensconced in the vehicle and leaving the confines of the garage.

Katie snuggled against Joe—his arm around her—resting her head on his shoulder. She felt protected in his arms, even though she was feeling distinctly uncomfortable.

Joe nuzzled her damp hair and when she raised her face to his, he kissed her gently on the forehead.

"You're doing good, Katie," he whispered, "and I love you."

Katie managed a small smile. "I love you too, very much," she returned then her pretty face grimaced. "Another one," she gasped.

Bowing her head, she pressed her face into Joe's combat jacket and her right hand took a fistful of material and almost shredded it with a crushing grip.

She whimpered. Then, as the pain reached its peak, Joe's arm tightened around her and his warm hand gently stroked the bare skin of her arm in soothing, circular motions. As the pain began to subside, leaving her wrung out and exhausted, she felt her body begin to relax and she raised her face once again.

"Ouch," she managed to joke quietly.

"Ouch is right," agreed Joe, brushing her hair away from her forehead.

"Nearly there," Maggie announced, a note of triumph in her voice.

Within a few minutes, the car had pulled into the car park of a military hospital and Katie experienced a sense of relief that shortly — probably within the next few hours — hers and Joe's baby would be born.

* * * *

Five hours later, Katie — exhausted but happy — watched her man hold their newborn son in his arms. She smiled with amusement at the sight of her big, tough, combat-clad husband clutching the small bundle as though it was made of glass, a stunned and awed expression on his face.

Joe looked down at his red-faced son then at his wife. "He's a big one," he announced, and Katie heard a note of pride in his voice.

Resting her head back against the pile of pillows behind her, Katie grimaced. "Nine pounds, one ounce. Tell me about it. It was like giving birth to a bowling ball."

Joe looked back down at the tiny, wide-awake boy and, lifting a finger, touched the baby's hand. The child immediately clasped his father's finger and hung on.

A soft smile spread across Joe's face and Katie wondered how she could feel so perfectly happy and content.

"So, what's his name going to be?" she asked softly. "You should name him. I named Josie."

Joe studied his son's face. "Luke," he replied and glanced at Katie for her agreement.

"That's a lovely name," Katie agreed. "Luke it is."

Joe moved closer to her side and leaning down, said to the newborn, "Go back to your mom, son."

Katie took the warm bundle and let the infant rest against her breast. Joe suddenly bent over her and cupped the side of her face. Looking into her clear, green eyes, he said tenderly, "You gave me my life back, made the struggles all worthwhile. I owe you my life, Katie. I will never let you or our children go again. I love you so very much." His mouth touched hers and Katie realized that she, her husband and their young family were finally together for good.

They had come through war and trauma, both powerful enough to have split them apart. Their love for each other, however, had endured, proving to be the strongest element of their existence together. There was nothing left that could part them except death.

About the Author

Sharon spent eight and a half years in the Women's Royal Air Force. Originally based in London, after she met her husband, Sharon relocated to Scotland to settle in Edinburgh. Already loving the country after having been stationed there during her time in the military, Sharon has never looked back. She lives with her husband and rescue West Highland Terrier, Snowie, (who thinks that she is a Rottweiler in disguise).

In 2014 Sharon started to have visions of writing a contemporary military romance. The ideas started to pile up and there was nothing for it but to get them down on her laptop, regardless of time and place.

Sharon loves to hear from readers. You can find her contact information, website and author biography at http://www.totallybound.com.